POLLUTO
WAGE SLAVE
ORGY

ISSUE 10

T0315784

Dog Horn Publishing

Published by Dog Horn Publishing, England
Dog Horn Publishing
45 Monk Ings, Bristall, Batley WF17 9HU
United Kingdom
doghornpublishing.com

ISBN 978-1-907133-30-5

UK Distribution by Central Books
99 Wallis Road, London, E9 5LN
United Kingdom
orders@centralbooks.com
Phone: +44 (0) 845 458 9911
Fax: +44 (0) 845 458 9912

Non-UK Distribution by Lulu Press, Inc
3101 Hillsborough Street, Raleigh, NC 27607
United States of America
purchaseorder@lulu.com
Phone: +1 919 459 5858
Fax: +1 919 459 5867

Editor-in-Chief: Adam Lowe
General Editor: Victoria Hooper
Acquisitions Editor: Chris Kelso
Creative Director: Michael Dark
Designed by John Eckert

Visit polluto.com or doghorn.com for submission details.

POLLUTO

TABLE OF CONTENTS

EDITOR'S LETTER

We're back, and this time we're looking at your banks and your bodies, selling sex and labour to the highest bidder. Money, power, oppression and control. The themes explored here are all too familiar right now, and the levels of cynicism offered in this issue could wither a rainforest. Flicking through you'll find a lovely mix of voices, some deep and moving, some important, some angry, some sarcastic, and some humorous or fun - told with the *Polluto* author's trademark twinkle.

Turn to page 13 for our 'Editor's Choice' story this issue, 'The Peculiar Salesgirl' by Nicole Cushing. This story perfectly captures the more sinister elements of our theme, showing the disturbing exploitation that a society obsessed with money and status will allow. The narrator herself is deceptively sympathetic until her own prejudices surface. Her reactions and eventual acceptance grow more uncomfortable throughout the story, mirroring our own world in which the atrocious can so easily become normal.

So clutch your credit-chips close and head on over to see what *Polluto* has on offer: a world of malls, stretching endlessly into one another. Systems of oppression, both real and fictional. Corporations of the future, Flooded London, money and privilege, a human life claimed for art. A mathematician feverishly tattooing his formulae onto prisoners of war. Workers on special offer: cheap-labour, clone-labour and corpse-labour. And bear in mind, valued customers, that nothing comes for free!

–Vicky

JUST ANOTHER CITY NIGHT, 2086

REBECCA FRASER

Give it to me," The Pedlar said. He held out an open palm with a creak of leather.

"Please", wheedled Jagger, hating the pathetic whine of his voice. "I gave you one last time."

The Pedlar merely held his hand out.

"It's too much," Jagger said. "The price is too high. Please, be reasonable. I already gave you one. You can't have another. I'll pay you with coin next time. I'll pay you double."

He knew he was babbling, but he couldn't help it. The cruel fingers of withdrawal were squeezing his heart, his windpipe, his soul. Soon, the shaking would start.

The Pedlar said nothing. Waited.

Jagger knew he would do it again. He wanted to cry for what he would do; cry for himself. But the tears wouldn't come. The Sartek had eroded his ducts a long time ago.

The shaking. He could feel it spasm his knees where it always began. Soon it would work its way upwards and he would be rendered helpless; racked with pain as withdrawal possessed his body.

"Act now while you can still use your hands." The Pedlar smiled.

Jagger moaned in horror and defeat. His hands, already trembling violently, groped at his face. His fingers dug and gouged as he secured The Pedlar's payment. He detached his remaining eye from its socket and thrust it blindly in the general direction of The Pedlar.

The Pedlar wrapped the lengths of optical fibre neatly around the leaking orb, taking care not to fuse the ends together. He placed it in the pocket of his leather trench.

The Pedlar threw a packet of pale blue Sartek at the twitching, howling form of Jagger and stalked off into the night.

FACETIME

TOM GREENE

Out of nowhere, Joy's avatar said, "I think the elevator is broken."

The VP of marketing development's avatar stopped talking and turn to face her. "I'm sorry, Joy?"

In real life, Richard frowned at the display. He panned his PoV camera around the virtual conference table to Joy's avatar. There were no elevators in-suite at Advanced Hypothetics - everybody just teleported their avatars around.

"I think the elevator," she said again, the text floating above her avatar's head.

"I'm not sure what you're driving at," the VP said.

"The new vegan gravlax is dry," she said.

Richard muted his transliterator pickup and said "Cody, can we get a recording of this?"

"No problemo," the virtual agent answered.

Two of the avatars at the conference table said, "I think she's having a glitch." The other five avatars, including Richard's, said nothing.

"If you ask me" Joy went on. "Vegan gravlax is broken."

Joy's avatar emoted a *twitch*, then a *looks around the table*.

"Sorry everybody," the floating text said. "Transliterator fail."

"Not at all," the VP's avatar said. "You should have that looked at."

Joy's avatar emoted a *nod,* and the VP went back to what he had been saying about leveraging deliverables.

The meeting went on. Richard said, "Cody, you can stop recording now and please play back the last 45 seconds on screen two?"

On a second display, the scene of Joy's malfunction replayed. When it ended, Richard said, "keep looping it, please." He watched it again. It didn't look like a transliterator glitch to him. It looked like something else entirely.

The meeting ended. Richard beamed his avatar back to its virtual desk and kept the replay running while he worked on his main screen. After about an hour, Cody's voice came out of the speakers.

"Excuse me, Richard, but you programmed me to point out when you appear to be obsessing about her."

"Thank you," Richard said. "Please archive the replay."

The number two screen went blank and Richard got up from his desk. He crossed the main room - really the only room - of his efficiency flat, picking up stray bits of laundry as he went. He dropped the clothes on an easy chair by the kitchenette. He made a cup of that new tea with the superfood antioxidant pellets in it, then carried it back to his desk. He pulled up his coding worksuite on the main screen and went back to debugging.

The project absorbed him until

lunchtime, when he clocked off and thought about the incident with Joy again. It wasn't the first time he'd seen something like it. He punched up the replay and let it run. After eight more loops, Cody's voice came over the speakers.

"Your browsing pattern suggests you're obsessing again, Richard."

"Shut up, Cody."

"You have programmed me to ignore that directive in this situation."

"Just give me a minute. I'm checking something."

"Don't make me display her last email."

"Okay, okay! Kill it."

The screen went blank. Richard glared at it for a while, shuffling his feet under the desk. His eyes wandered down to his hands, resting on the desktop, to the black X's tattooed on the skin between his knuckles and wrists.

"How many days has it been, Cody?"

"I assume you mean sober days?"

"Of course."

"Not counting today, two-thousand, forty-one."

Richard smiled grimly. "Today never counts." He drummed his fingers on the desk, watching the flex of the Xs, tattooed in different sizes and styles. Five Xs, one for each sober year - so far.

"It's all about removing temptation from your environment," he said.

"Yes, Richard."

"I don't think about it; I don't do it. That's the only way I've made it this far."

"Yes, Richard."

He tugged at his ragged blond beard. "Something might tempt me, I just walk away."

"Just as you say, Richard."

He sighed. "Is there any charge left in the car batteries?"

"Of course, Richard. It has been fifty-eight days since you last used it, and the car only requires ten hours to fully charge."

"Two months? Really?"

Cody posted the car use log on the display. Richard went to the cluttered table by the door and dug out his keys.

"I might be late back from lunch. If anybody asks, let 'em know I'll make up the time after hours tonight."

"Yes, Richard."

In a few minutes Richard was tooling down the interstate, the car maneuvering itself between robot trucks to Keith's house.

Keith lived in one of those 1980s yuppie revival subdivisions where the houses looked like stucco and terra cotta, but were actually mostly cellubond. The neighborhood gate opened when Richard's car pulled up, and the car crawled among the flat ranch houses with their sprawling RepliTurf lawns until it got to Keith's. Alerted by his residential systems, Keith already had the door open.

"Richard!" Keith said. "It's been a long time."

Richard ducked in out of the midday heat. Inside, the illusion was complete. Hardwood-textured cellubond floors and popcorn ceilings concealed the cameras, antennas and power broadcasters. The geothermal heat pump was dressed up to sound - and smell - like central A/C.

Keith said, "Couldn't wait to see the new place, eh?"

"I need to talk to you about something important."

"Still not a fan of small talk, eh Rich?"

Richard met his eyes and didn't say anything. Keith shrugged.

"Okay, go on into the office while I get a cup of coffee. Can I get you anything?"

"I can't drink real coffee anymore," Richard said, going where Keith pointed. "Even if I could afford it, it screws up my stomach."

The office was bigger than Richard's whole flat, all done in burgundy and dark woodgrained Maizeolite with Persian carpets that were probably real and a fireplace that wasn't. Keith's decks and screens were racked on a huge desk facing a window the size of a garage door. Outside there was a deck and pool.

Keith came into the office with a mug in his hand. He hadn't changed much in the few years since they'd last met face-to-face. He must have been working out, because he looked a lot like his office avatar. He wore lightweight cotton slacks and a button-down shirt: the casual work-at-home clothes of an executive. Richard wore baggy dispatch shorts and an Advanced Hypothetics company picnic '34 T-shirt.

"You can swim in it," Keith said. "The pool, I mean. It's that new water substitute; kind of like swimming in Jell-O. But without the chemicals like when we were kids."

Richard sat in an overstuffed chair. Keith sat opposite him.

"So what's so important that you couldn't just message or come see me in-suite?"

"It's about Joy"

"Not again. Rich - "

"No, no. Joy's work."

Keith raised his chin. "Really?"

"This morning at a meeting, I think she was running a bot."

Keith sipped from his mug. "You're sure?"

"Yes. She tried to pass it off as a glitch in the transliterator pickup, but the things she was saying were more like broken code loops. Then when she recovered, it was like she had come back to her desk from somewhere else in her house."

Keith set his coffee cup on a coaster on an end table. "I'm glad you brought this to my attention, Richard."

"Don't go all managery on me, Keith."

"Sorry. Have you told anyone else?"

"I came straight here."

"And you're not telling me just because it's Joy?"

Richard flinched. "I would report anybody I thought was using a bot."

"So your feelings towards autonomous simulacra haven't changed?"

"Autonomous simul- what the hell are you talking about?"

"No need to raise your voice, Richard."

"I'm not raising my voice."

"So you disapprove of anyone running a bot? Not just Joy?"

"I can't believe you're even asking me this, Keith. You know the policy."

"I'm not asking about policy, Richard. I'm asking how you feel."

Richard gripped the arms of the chair and spoke in a clipped tone. "We get paid to be at our desks during working hours. If we're not at our desks, what are they paying us for?"

Keith set his coffee down, stood up, and walked to his desk. "I'm glad you came by today with this, Richard. I had been wondering how to approach you."

He nudged the spongepad on his main deck to bring it up from sleep mode. From where he sat Richard could see, on the main screen, Keith's view of the Advanced Hypothetics virtual suite. Keith's avatar sat at a conference table with other avatars. Even though Keith was away from his keyboard, there was no AFK flag over his avatar's head. While Richard watched, the avatar said, "Can we hear more about that, Duncan?" Real-world Keith hadn't said anything. The avatar was running off a bot program, without Keith's intervention.

"I haven't done a full day's work for over three years," Keith said. "Most days I just let it run itself."

"Why are you showing me this?"

Keith came back to his chair, sat down, and picked up his coffee. "Back when I was just a code monkey, you helped me out. Showed me the ropes. I feel like I owe you, now that things have changed."

Richard shook his head. "A lot of things change, but not this."

"And this is about the - " Keith gestured at the tattoos on Richard's hands.

"I wouldn't wear the ink if I didn't live the lifestyle."

"And since when did straight edge start to include a 'no bots' rule?"

"It's cheating."

"Even though you can never make a decent living as a code hacker? Or hadn't you noticed?"

"What about cheapening your life? Betraying a trust?"

"Come on, Rich. You think AH gives a crap about you? Think they would hesitate for a second to outsource you? The jobs where you actually produce things are dead ends. If you want real security, you have to move up to management, be in charge of people, control a budget."

"And spend all day writing memos and sitting in meetings? I'd rather actually do things."

"Exactly my point." Keith leaned forward. "You can take a manager's salary and do things. Anything you want."

"What are you saying?"

Keith got up and went around beside his desk to a big wooden cabinet. He punched buttons on the lock and let the doors fall open. Inside there was a rack of decks with their ribbon cables running up and down. Each deck had a piece of white tape stuck on it, and a name written in black marker: Doug, Andi, Ursula, Jin...

"A bot farm," Richard said. "This is your whole work group?"

"And a few others. How do you think I get my projects passed up the pipeline?

I control the code, what the avatars say in meetings and write memos about. All our reports and minutes are just boilerplate - the code cranks out pages of the stuff - nobody ever reads it anyway. An alarm calls you if anything major goes wrong. I take a standard fifteen percent."

"Is Joy in there?"

Keith shook his head. "She must be using some other contractor. One of those Asian services I think."

"So I suppose there's a space on that rack for me?"

"Only if you accept a promotion. A bot can't do your coding work - or be worth the trouble on your salary."

"You should know me better, Keith."

Keith shrugged. "I figured I owed it to you to ask at least."

Richard crossed his arms. "How do you know I won't tell? I could go over your head to Silverman about this."

"Karen? That stuff she's always saying about her daughter-in-law is straight off the script of one of those bot farms in Mexico." Keith shook his head. "Wake up, Richard. You're on borrowed time anyway. Some kid in Manila can do your job for a tenth of what you cost. You'd be gone already if I didn't keep stepping in."

"You mean if your bot didn't keep stepping in."

"What's the difference?"

Richard stood up, brushed off the front of his shorts. "The fact that you can even ask me that shows how little you understand."

He walked to the door.

"I'll give you a week," Keith called after him. "After that, I'm turning the bean counters loose on you. Think it over."

When Richard got home, he still had some time left on his lunch hour, but he wasn't hungry. He logged in and took his avatar for a walk around the virtual office.

Advanced Hypothetics Associates was set up in a Vista Conquista space: an off-the-rack suite with lots of sweeping galleries, brushed metal textures and long, floor-to-ceiling windows showing a summer coast that you couldn't actually get to. Hundreds of avatars sat at desks, representing work-at-home users scattered around the world. Just one of thousands of global distributed workforce companies that did business in the ManiFold network. People had always thought that when work went online, it would take gadgets - brain implants, VR goggles, whatever. It had all turned out a lot more ordinary: flat displays, keyboards, and text bubbles that made translation between different languages easier.

Richard paused at a conference room window to look in at some avatars having a meeting. He couldn't see the text of their speech from outside, but he was starting to see how a bot programmed with a particular general goal could handle such a meeting. It was mostly routine stuff, easy to parse.

Even some whole workgroups could run on automatic. They could start initiatives, hold meetings, write reports, and come out with recommendations that would be filed away and ignored. It could take months and hundreds - even thousands - of work hours to produce a report that one person could probably cook up in an hour or two.

He went into one of the break rooms and saw Yuriko there. "Hey, Richard," her avatar said. "How's the work on the new tunnel security stuff coming?"

"Fine," Richard said, thinking that a bot would have been able to check his avatar's ID tag when he'd entered a certain radius, could have queried the project database to generate that question. On impulse, he said, "What do you think of the vegan gravlax?"

"Huh? I guess I miss real salmon. Why?"

"No reason," he said, thinking about how easy it would be to parse that answer. He could have written the app himself.

Richard walked around, watching the avatars around him. He started having a vision that everybody in the office was a bot. In the lobby, two AH manager bots traded *shakes hands* gestures with two visiting bots from overseas. Bots stood around the water cooler in the break room, parsing small talk about last night's vids, emoting appropriate *laughs* and *nods.* Bots sat at desks, cycling their *types on keyboard* animations, with occasional *talks on phone* clips for variation. Bots sat around conference tables and spewed boilerplate about 24/7 solutions and maximized efficiencies. Bots walked up and down the corridors. Bots opened and closed doors. Bots paused to look thoughtfully out through the rendered windows. Richard could be the last person actually at work.

And this was just one of thousands of companies that used virtual suites, millions of employees all over the world, moving from one meeting to another, churning out memos and emails and endless forms, collecting paychecks. What work was actually being done? If it could all be done by bots anyway, what was the point of having employees at all?

It couldn't be true. Somebody must be working. It had to be just a few cheaters slipping through undetected on the back of everybody else's work.

But still, he wondered what the cheaters did all day if they weren't working? Waste time watching vids or playing the game servers? Go kayaking? Hang out with friends? Work second jobs? Richard rubbed the tattoos on the back of his left hand. He knew the dark place he'd go if he had unlimited time. He'd been there before.

#

A few days passed. Richard was at his desk when Trent pinged him. Richard beamed to the location Trent had given, the middle of one of the flying causeways near Reverse Fulfillment.

"Thank God you're here," Trent said. "I wasn't sure who else to call. I think she's having a glitch."

Joy's avatar was walking, feet pumping away, into a corridor wall, not going anywhere. She was saying, "Every drop sparkles with shards of dawn."

Richard ran down the corridor. "Joy," he said. "Joy."

She stopped walking, turned to face him. "Oh, Richard."

"Are you okay?"

"I am sooo high," she said. "I think it's eating me."

"You should log off. Before somebody sees."

"It burns, Richard. I think something's wrong."

"Can I call somebody?"

"No, no. No police. I can't get this thing off my back."

"What?"

"Richard, I need you to come over."

"Are you serious?"

"Yes, hurry."

"Okay, log off first."

"Okay, I'm logging. Hurry."

Her avatar glistened and faded, and Richard tapped out his own logoff. Cody started to say something, but Richard grabbed his keys and ran out the door before he could hear it.

He urged the car to go as fast as it would, which wasn't very fast. He tried to remember the last thing he'd said to Joy face-to-face. It had probably been something idiotic about putting things in the refrigerator properly or how the instructions on the tube clearly said to push up from the bottom. He could only remember that she'd left, and later he'd found all her addresses blocked to him.

Joy's place was a freestanding condo in a rejuvenated residential zone. Town houses painted in pastels like an Italian fishing village stretched down the block on both sides. Richard parked on the street and jumped the steps onto her porch. No one answered when he knocked, and the door was locked. The lights on the security cameras glowed, but the lenses weren't tracking him - nobody inside was watching.

He tried the windows on the front porch and one of them (typical of her, he couldn't help thinking) was unlocked. He slid the window up and pushed in past the lace curtains into the living room.

He could see her on the kitchen floor. He moved closer. She was wearing a dingy hospital gown, streaked with green fluid that pooled on the neonoleum where she lay. The canister, a metallic bullet shape on her back, had tubes that ran like spider legs through the gown's open back, into nozzles implanted near her spine. Her head was turned toward him, eyes open, but some of her skin had dissolved away and you could see molars through a hole in her cheek. There was the soft fizzing sound, the familiar fruity smell. It was too late.

He slid down on the kitchen floor with his back to a cupboard. The sun went down outside. The house, not detecting any motion, decided he had left and didn't turn on any lights. In the dark, he watched the red LED on the canister blink, warning that the peptide mix was off. Richard could feel sweat trickling between his shoulder blades, around the two rows of stainless steel nozzles still implanted along his own spine. They'd been too expensive to remove. They were very durable. They would still work if he hooked up.

In the morning, there was nothing left of Joy but bones, and even they were starting to turn to powder. Richard went through the house. It was clear she had been at it for some time. Syringes on the bathroom sink. Pills on the coffee table. Brassworks on the nightstand. Methanol tanks, glass pipes, mini-torches stashed away in cupboards. And the bot server, with a Casting Central logo on it, humming away at her desk, her avatar on the screen arriving at the office for its day's work. He sat in her desk chair, watched the bot go to two meetings and make helpful comments.

He tapped up the bot server's interface on a second display and opened the unsecured source code. It was all there, the things she would do and say in all kinds of situations at the office, a whole proxy identity in code. Richard realized it would be simple for him to pirate the server, rewrite Joy's bot any way he wanted. No one else knew that anything had happened to her. He could keep her at work. He could have her hire him as a subcontractor. He could even make her love him again - at least as far as anyone at the office was concerned.

His eyes fell on the canister still lying on the floor beside the greenish stain where the last bits of powdered bone were evaporating. The house was stocked with everything needed to reset, recalibrate, and refill it. It was the moment he'd been dreading all these years. He could have whatever he wanted.

He reached down and flipped off the blinking LED on the peptide capsule, and then left it there on the floor. It wasn't so terrifying after all.

He sat at Joy's desk while morning sunbeams crept across the floor. He probably hadn't helped his employment prospects by not showing up to work. But he realized he didn't really care. He didn't feel like he needed his tiny controlled life anymore. The thought of going back to his efficiency to bury himself in code again just made him feel sad.

He turned back to Joy's workstation and worked methodically, erasing all traces of himself from the household systems, setting an anonymous tip to the police to fire off an hour from now. Then he switched everything off and went out the front door.

Richard jogged down the steps, got in his car, and told it to drive. "Just go West," he said. He rode away from the rising sun and realized he was really hungry. He'd stop somewhere for breakfast, put in his notice at AH, and think about what to do next. It was time for a change - a new company, a new job, maybe even a new country. Richard wondered what Manila was like this time of year.

THE PECULIAR SALESGIRL

NICOLE CUSHING

Our 'Editor's Choice' Story

One way to avoid the peculiar salesgirl is to never shop at the North Vernon Skin-Mart in the first place. Avoid the store proper. Avoid the entire dingy, crumbling outlet mall if you can. Avoid the walls festooned with unimaginative graffiti scrawled by white trash pseudo-gangstas. Avoid the fractured pavement of the parking lot, overgrown with weeds sprouting in-between the cracks and littered with beer cans and condoms. Avoid, even, the Rustbelt town (just a few miles up I-65) itself. You won't miss much. It's less a town, really, than the fossil of one. Avoid it, and you'll be safe.

When I offer this advice to my old friends from high school, they accuse me of "overkill." In context, it sounds like this: "You snob," they say, rolling their lined, mascaraed, shadowed eyes, "that would be overkill". Sometimes, they remark that I have changed too much since I went away to college in Chicago. They're still "down home" but I'm not, they claim. They cite, as evidence, the big words I use now, my "dykey" short hair, and my newfound toyboyness. They point out the way I shrug the summer 4-H Fair off with indifference, while they see it as an opportunity to flirt with potential beaus.

Sometimes, they scoff at me for other reasons altogether. They accuse me of objecting to Skin-Mart out of some general resistance to fashion and joke that I should join one of the stodgier religious sects – the ones that prohibit women from wearing pants, the ones in which the ladies volunteer for coerced modesty.

"Longskirts", such ladies are called – for obvious reasons. "The trailer park Amish," they're called – for pejorative ones. You can see them in the grocery store, their long hair drawn up in buns, their denim skirts revealing nary a hint of calf, or even ankle. Their dollar-store blouses cover sagging breasts that have suckled too many too long. For you see, no less than five children follow behind the average Longskirt. The youngest of the brood might only be a toddler, but the mother's hair is invariably streaked with gray. Her face, prematurely wrinkled. Her expression, stuck (fossil-like) in the raised-eyebrow grimace of despair.

They drive ancient minivans adorned with bumper stickers announcing that:
IN CASE OF RAPTURE, THIS VEHICLE WILL BE UNOCCUPIED

13

These are the sort of ranks my friends say I should join, just because I object to Skin-Mart in general and harbor a deep distrust about that one, peculiar salesgirl in particular. Their mistake is a natural one. Truth is, the church folks object to Skin-Mart the strongest. They say that Skin-Mart is "of the world" and therefore unwelcome. One would think that their message would find traction, given the region's reputation as a haven for Christian fundamentalism.

But even here, where the Midwest and South meet in a confluence of piety, the numbers of the churchgoing faithful are dwindling. The influence of organized religion wanes when it comes to loggerheads with the promise of new jobs for unskilled labor. It may be true that neither man nor woman can live by *bread* alone, but neither can they live with bread *absent*. I suspect all the locals now employed at Skin-Mart had reservations, at first. But what can they do? McDonald's left town years ago.

I try to assure my friends that I object to Skin-Mart on *humanitarian* grounds, not puritanical ones. "Have you," I ask, "ever read the tags to see just where the skins come from?"

At this, the other girls just sneer. "Julie and her 'skin tags'," they say, giggling. Once, for no less than two weeks, that was my nickname. "Hey Skin Tag," they'd say over the phone, "want to join us at the Pop-a-Top? It's ladies night. You *are* still interested in *men*, ain'tcha?" We're all underage, but the only number that matters to the bouncer at Pop-a-Top is your bra size.

I don't think that the "Skin Tag" joke is funny. I think it's just their way of sublimating their awareness that the skins for sale at Skin-Mart come at the expense of donors who may have been pressured into the arrangement. A cursory glance reveals that the skins come to Southern Indiana by way of some infamous locales. "Made in

Chechnya," one says. "Made In Reno," says another. But my old friends don't know (or care) what goes on in Russian rebellions or Nevadan brothels. They only know that when they wear a skin more fashionable than their own, they feel pretty. Men ask them out. They feel treasured.

The most popular skins are those that come already tanned, tattooed, and pierced. Don't get me wrong, they're exquisite products. Lovely. Soft. Smooth. For all my objections, I'm as guilty of window-shopping at Skin-Mart as the next girl.

"Skin is in," my friends remind me, parroting a recently-aired advertisement. Tempting me into going along with the fashion. It's a hard slogan to argue with, seeing as I'm the only one in our crowd who hasn't given in to getting an F&G (flaying and grafting) even once. Many of the girls I graduated Henryville High with have patronized Skin-Mart more than three times in the past year.

There's a rumor that shopping at Skin-Mart is addictive (after all, some girls have reported "getting off" on the pain of having the old epidermis removed and replaced). But I think the frequent purchases have more to do with the way the skin gets, well, *damaged* sometimes. The domestic violence shelter says wife-beating prosecutions have much declined since Skin-Mart came to town. The evidence of injury disappears too readily, they claim. I suspect they're onto something, because it's not unusual to see a gentleman escort a lady with a black eye or bruised throat into the store, presumably to rid himself and polite society of the evidence of his misdeed.

Distributors furnish Skin-Mart with a wide variety of products from throughout the world. "Black skins" ("Made in Nigeria"). "Brown skins" ("Made in Chiapas, Mexico"). "Yellow skins" ("Made in China"). Perhaps they mistake the outlet mall for a true, vibrant center of commerce that attracts traffic off the interstate, and therefore a more worldly clientele. As it is, foreign skins remain on the racks collecting dust. No one, in this part of the world, wants them. In fact, my friend Mindy swears she saw some of the blacks from down in Jeffersonville drive up one day to get F&Ged into white skins. She tells me this as if it was a point in Skin-Mart's favor. "It's a miracle," Mindy said. "It's not their fault they're black. Everyone *should* have the right to be white, and now they *do*!"

I remain unconvinced that Mindy really saw what she said she saw (and if she did, I'm even less convinced that it was for the best). That's the thing about Skin-Mart, all of us see different things there. Take the peculiar salesgirl, for example. Some of my friends say they've never even heard of her, while others say they're all too familiar with her.

I can tell which of my friends has really seen her (instead of just humoring me and *claiming* they've seen her) by their inability to look me in the eye when they talk about her. Sometimes, there's a quiver in their voice, too. They tell me that if I would only take the proper precautions, knowing just what sort of skin I want *before* going into the store, I would never have to worry about the peculiar salesgirl. The trick, they say, is to get in, make your selection, and then go get F&Ged. Don't dawdle.

If you linger too long, the staff at Skin-Mart will think that you want to buy something special order. Something for those with *peculiar* tastes. That's when they dispatch the *peculiar* salesgirl.

You may, at this point, rightly ask *what* is so damned peculiar about her. The answer is...everything. She is, for one thing, too tall. Well over six feet. Her height is not graceful nor statuesque. It gives her, rather, the appearance of a scarecrow. There is something too soft, almost molten about her skin – as if, perhaps, she started out as a customer of

the store (many times over) and ended up as staff. She is clumsy. Awkward. Hunched over at an angle much more fitting a ninety-two year old than someone of her apparent youth (and yet, still, she towers over me). It's almost as though walking on all fours is her natural posture, and she only maintains a bipedal stance with some effort.

But the most peculiar thing about this particular salesgirl is that she isn't from around here. No one knows her, personally. No one knows her kin, either. There's some suspicion (among those who acknowledge her existence) that she moved here from Skin-Mart's home offices; or, at least, from a larger store.

When the peculiar salesgirl finds you, she takes an interest – a clumsy, too-eager interest, "You, Miss, look like a discerning customer," she says to me each time she sees me, "I reckon I've done seen you here at least a half-dozen times before, but I haven't yet seen you make a purchase."

"Oh," I say (shuddering), "I'm sorry, I can leave if you'd like."

"Oh, no, no," she says. "You're all right, babygirl" There's something about her demeanor that distresses me; the way, perhaps, that she tries to take on the local accent and vernacular. "It just strikes me that you haven't yet found the right product. You might-could be better served by perusing our back room. It's for those with more *sophisticated* tastes."

This is the point in the conversation in which I demur. "No," I say, "that's quite all right. For now, I just want to browse."

She doesn't take rejection easily. I see an emotion (Sadness? Frustration?) creep onto her otherwise-emotionless face. I begin to wonder if she might not work on commission. But that is *her* problem, I tell myself, *not mine*. Most of the times I've had an encounter with the peculiar salesgirl, it ends right there. She leaves, disappointed and I get the Hell out of there. But not today.

Today I start to leave and she scurries – almost *jogging* – to the back room. She comes back with three skins wrapped over her forearm. She is tall enough that they don't drag on the floor.

There's something wrong with them. They look jaundiced. They're dotted by scars, sores, or growths of undetermined origin. There's a liquid seeping from the skins, dampening the peculiar salesgirl's pantsuit. It reminds me of the way my grandmother's bed sore weeped when she was dying of lung cancer. One of the skins looks charred. Another looks as though it boasts an unnatural plethora of appendages.

I have no poker face. I cringe.

"You don't understand," she says. "Skin is in." She points to a duo of far-less-peculiar salesgirls – locals who I remember from Henryville High – hanging a banner printed with that very slogan. It's a slick piece of promotion that bears the pedigree of corporate PR (and, thus, seems odd when juxtaposed against the general atmosphere of rural decay in which the store is suffused). They look like soldiers raising a flag over conquered territory.

In that moment, I reflect on some of the arguments used to counter the criticism Skin-Mart gets when it moves into small towns and displaces mom and pop businesses. "What alternative is there?" the store's boosters sometimes ask. "Who else is going to come into towns like this one and hire unskilled labor?" I look at the two girls hanging the banner. They're missing at least three teeth, between them, but smile anyway. They have wages, two fifteen minute breaks and a half-hour lunch. Their kids' fathers came into town on a tractor trailer and left the same way. No forwarding addresses. No child support or promise of it coming.

Skin-Mart puts food on the table.

Skin-Mart is closed on major holidays. Skin-Mart obeys laws pertaining to the minimum wage. One imagines that the employee lounge at Skin-Mart is adorned with all the announcements the Occupational Safety and Health Administration requires Skin-Mart to post there.

Skin-Mart provides opportunities for moving up in the world. If the girls work hard enough, one of them might (in time) find herself promoted to assistant manager. I contrast this with my suspicions of what their lives would be like without their jobs. Would they have to resort to working at the adult book store in Clarksville (doing, well, *what you know girls have to do there* to make ends meet)?

Despite my wish to support the local economy, I can't quite find it in myself to buy what the peculiar salesgirl is selling. I look at her selections from the back room and shake my head. "No thanks," I say.

Her eyes widen. Her garishly painted lips snarl. I see (for the first time, in any detail) her jagged, too-small, coffee-stained teeth. Her face is flushing and she's clinching her fists. She huffs and the congestion in her throat gurgles. It takes her much coughing to clear it, and when she does she lets out a single high-pitched, raspy word that sounds a little too much like a dog's growl. "Dyyyke...."

An accusation that cuts to the quick. Not the first time I've heard it, but somehow this time it hurts more than ever. It's one thing for my old high school friends to toss around such an epithet when remarking on my change in hairstyle or disinterest in fashion. It's quite another to hear it snarled by a relative stranger like the peculiar salesgirl. For some reason, the accusation takes on additional weight coming from a representative of Skin-Mart. From a representative of a *Corporation*. For some reason, she strikes me as an authority figure who knows what she's talking about.

She takes a deep, wheezing breath, then growls once more. "Mannish dyyykkkkeeeee!"

I scramble to rebut her claim. My heart beats like the hooves of a Kentucky Derby racehorse and I begin to sweat. The racks of skins seem to hover over me like high stalks of corn in late-August. I must convince her she's wrong. I must prove I'm not what she says I am – that I'm every bit as feminine as any other nineteen year old.

I find all of my anti-Skin-Mart principles cast aside in self-defense. "Don't misunderstand me," I say. "I'm a girly-girl, just like all my friends. I just let myself get a little hippie-chick in my first year of college." I stammer. "I-it was just a phase. But don't worry, today's the day that I will get F&Ged. It's just, I think I'll start with something less... well...less *severe*. Do you have any skins that are pre-tanned, with tattoos and piercings?"

Just as swiftly as anger overtook her, it leaves. Her demeanor isn't what I'd call cordial, but it at least retreats from the prior hostility. She looks at me with a condescension she's probably cast toward hundreds of other girls my age. "Our most popular item. I don't handle those jobs. But if you wait until Bobbie Sue is finished hanging that banner, I'm sure she'll be able to assist you." Then off to the back room she goes.

The flaying hurts. The grafting hurts. The only thing I can compare it to is the time I lost most of my right thumbnail. Imagine that, but about ten times more painful, all over your body.

But when I see the excitement on my friends' faces afterward and then hear the approving honk of men in passing cars in the parking lot, I feel (for once) included. More so than I did even up at college in Chicago. In the days after that first F&Ging my friends and I share all kinds of fun. Nights out at Pop-a-Top. Trips to the hair and nail salon.

I consider transferring to Henry County Community College. I could study there with my friends. The only thing that stops me is a large envelope I receive in the mail one hot, hung-over morning in late-July, postmarked Chicago.

It's from the Chicagoland Chamber of Commerce. A letter tells me that Chicago looks forward to seeing me (and all the other college students) again for the fall semester, and encourages me to patronize local businesses. Enclosed with the letter, I find coupons and sales circulars of various degrees of glossiness. One (the glossiest of them all) announces the arrival of a new Skin-Mart opening in late August in a strip mall adjacent to campus. Perhaps there's a new pool of cheap labor available to staff the store, now that the college let go some of its cafeteria and janitorial staff. Or maybe that pool of cheap labor comes from recent graduates who haven't been able to find a job in their field quite yet.

Or maybe the city just isn't as different from the country as it's made out to be.

"Skin is In!" the announcement declares.

I know that the Chicago Skin-Mart will have my patronage. I know, too (somehow) that I will never see the peculiar salesgirl again. Her work with me is done.

THE POPULATION BOOM

STEPHEN OWEN

I parade like a peacock outside the red-brick building. My top hat sparkles in the evening sun, sequins rustling as I usher the people in. "That's the way, sir, step inside and take a seat. Ha! You may *think* you've seen everything, but I can guarantee you have never encountered anything like this!"

An old codger ferrets through his pockets, coins rattling in his gnarled fingers.

"Put your money away!" I say. "This is not the twenty-first century!"

"What's it all about?" He growls and I believe he is genuinely curious. He peers at me over half-moon glasses, toothless mouth a gaping hole in his face. "Why don't I have to pay?"

"This is a non-profit-making function, sir. One of several shows touring the country at the moment – all generously financed by The Computer!" I grin like a salesman who has rehearsed this scenario a hundred times. "Life will never be the same again after tonight and the best bit is it will not cost you a euro-cent!"

"Computers, eh?" The old man scoffs. "Time was, sonny, a computer was what you played games on and sent emails and stuff. Bet you wasn't even born when the internet was around."

He's right, I wasn't.

I dismiss his accusation with a wink and a flashing smile.

The gathering crowd seems largely oblivious to what I am offering. Instead, they mumble amongst themselves, a gravelly babble that could possibly be mistaken for people praying if I wasn't actually catching snippets of their demented gripes.

Some of them grapple at my silken clothing.

Moths around a candle-flame.

Senile grumblings about the price of oxygen and water rationing and does anyone remember when cars were fuelled with petroleum gas?

I hush the nonsense with a wave of my hand and coax them into the building. "That's the way, ladies and gents! First door on the left. Take the weight off your feet, sit back and enjoy the experience. It starts at nineteen-hundred hours." I check my nuclear watch, luminous at all hours. "That's seven o'clock in real English. Less than five minutes."

Number one-hundred rasps a laugh, a noise like leaking air as if he is an inflatable person and his mouth is a faulty valve. My arm descends like an axe behind him.

Cut off point.

"You are the last one, sir."

"But what about my wife?" He looks at the old woman behind my arm, rags for clothes hanging off her scarecrow body. Her sunken eyes stare through me as if I am made of glass. "Can she come in?"

"I'm sorry, but that's not possible." I shake my head, clench my lips in an upside-down smile. "There are only a hundred places available."

"Couldn't you make room for just one more?."

"The Computer is exact with its equations, sir." I spread my arms, jacket shimmering deep orange in the setting sun. "We can't question them."

The old man shrugs, nods thoughtfully.

"Be right back, Anna." He kisses his wife's cheek, squeezes her hand. "Just as soon as I've seen what it's all about."

He shuffles through the arched doorway down the grey corridor. I follow him into the building and close the wooden door behind me.

#

"Attention please!" The red and yellow lights surrounding the stage illuminate and I patrol the platform, footsteps echoing on the floorboards. Hands clasped behind my back, eyes fixed on the crowd.

They sit on blue plastic chairs on an old-fashioned parquet floor. Décor reminiscent of ancient school halls and public libraries. A ten by ten square of bemused reptilian heads gawking up at me. They don't care what they're going to see because they didn't pay. They think they've got nothing to lose.

Wrong.

"The country is full up," I explain. "You can't move anymore. It's like somebody dug up all the graveyards and gave everyone a magic come-back-to-life jab."

An amiable chuckle, half-hearted clapping from the back of the room.

Some goddam dimwit thinks I'm telling a joke.

"If The Computer had controlled things at the start of this millennium, simple logic would have prevailed and we wouldn't be in this mess. Unfortunately, the country was ruled by a government of children obsessed with preserving human life way beyond its natural course."

"Nothing wrong with looking after yourself, young man." A posh-looking lady with a face like a chameleon sits in the second row, earlobes like diamond-studded testicles.

"Madam, this out-dated compulsion for healthy living existed for centuries until The Computer took over. We can't all live forever, it simply isn't feasible."

"So a machine makes the rules now, does it?" The lady's face droops in feigned lament, gains a few sympathetic nods and a pat on the back from her cadaverous-looking counterparts. "And just what is this 'computer' doing to improve overcrowding?"

"The reintroduction of cigarettes and alcohol will eventually restore some sort of natural lifespan and the Fast Food Amendment Law means hot dogs and burgers can be sold legally for the first time in almost a hundred years."

"You can't do nothin about it now, sonny." A shrivelled man of about a hundred-and-thirty-five sits in the front row, glances back at the posh lady. "Lots of people living longer. Evolution, that is."

"But it's not the way it's supposed to be." I stroll across the stage, eyes bulging, teeth clenched, and he shrinks from my lunatic stance. "You remember how successful the ancient Victorians were? They had a life expectancy of about forty years! Damn! Our children are still at school at that age! We live to see almost two centuries on this planet and we're bored out of our tiny minds before the end of the first!"

"What you gettin at?" asks the man.

"We need to do something about it." I raise my voice, an edge of frustration in my tone. "All the smoking and drinking and high-cholesterol junk food in the world won't solve this problem overnight. We need to speed things up. The Computer has decreed a depopulation of at least fifteen million over the next twelve months."

The locks on the windows and doors clunk in unison.

Sounds like a guillotine.

I can hear the gas already.

"And we start tonight!" I raise my hands, a magician poised at the climax of his most powerful illusion. "This place is now air-tight, ladies and gentlemen! Please remain seated for your own safety."

"What's happening?" cries the posh lady. "Are you poisoning us?"

Her very words command a panicked uprising from the audience. Chairs tip. People shout. They are on their feet scurrying around like ants in a nest I just dragged my foot through. Skeletal fists pound the laser-proof glass and anodized doors.

"Everybody, please calm down!" I pace the platform, try to reassure them.

The posh lady falls to her knees, prays to the god that was proven to be non-existent back in 2057. Classic example of the human psyche struggling with the idea of non-continuance.

"How can you just stand there?" The old man separated from his wife staggers through the hysteria, gnarled fingers clasped in fists. "You want to die too?"

I shake my head, step down from the stage and place an arm around his trembling shoulders. Guide him to the windows and point to the darkening world outside.

Peaceful for the first time in living memory.

"Carbon monoxide," I explain. "It'll be safe for us to leave in the morning."

MARTWORLD
ALLEN ASHLEY & DOUGLAS THOMPSON

Michael only grimaced slightly as his supervisor imprinted a new bar code onto his left wrist. At least he had the skin surface to spare. He knew several ex-colleagues who'd got themselves so heavily tattooed with girlfriends' names, animal pictures and dodgy Sanskrit that they struggled to find the room to get coded up for a new assignment. There was even the possibly apocryphal story of Sammy Shifter who had so many mathematical doodles permanently engraved onto his limbs and body that he could set tills and other electronic devices beeping and emptying out their contents merely by walking past them.

Michael only sported a roaring lion on his right shoulder. He'd never seen a lion in real life.

"We're sorry to be losing you, Michael," Mr Shah told him. "But commerce goes on and we all move round the circle. My father reckoned that saying was based on an old Hindu proverb from the days before the companies. Still, he said a lot of stuff like that and he's not with us anymore. Have you got your stuff?"

"Yes, sir."

"Give us a high five and a handshake then and be on your way."

#

In truth, Michael was being relocated to a part of Martworld that was only half a day's walk away from his most recent posting. It would feel like a new world, though. He would be so much closer to the grand indoor sports arena and attending matches would seem less of a tremendous trek. He had a pass for the forthcoming local derby - Sainsbringham versus Waitroford - and that occupied his thoughts as he sat in the second carriage of the internal transporter. The screens in the vehicle offered the usual mix of infomercials as a counterpoint to people's constant jabbering on their walkies. After a while, though, he decided to look out of the window and take in the sights passing by. The concessions in this part offered goods of slightly higher quality with a concomitant price surcharge. Gradually, there was more open or non-commercial space between each counter and these expanses were often filled with plants and flowers in a pleasing array of non-factory colours. He even glimpsed a few sculptures. The fact that they were apparently unguarded and not even roped off suggested that citizens behaved themselves somewhat better around these parts. He smiled at the thought of moving into a much better neighbourhood. He was going up in the world.

At least those segments that he knew about. The education system and his first two sets of parents had never fully satisfied his curiosity about what lay beyond the gigantic shopping mall. Yes, other shopping malls - the deadly rivals due to be vanquished on the football field over the coming weeks. But what about the farms or polytunnels or domes where he believed most of the food was grown? Were there untarnished vistas beyond even those?

It didn't really matter on a day to day or even year to year basis. Keep your head down and your concentration up and the material rewards were multitudinous in this productive world of consumable riches.

His stop. New assignment and new home. Time to alight.

#

"You're a butcher's boy now, Micky!" – Michael's new supervisor beamed, presenting him with a brand new gleaming stripy apron uniform. Nobody called Michael *Micky* ever, and Mr Trevison's forced familiarities seemed as false as his false-teeth smile. But the bad breath was a hundred percent authentic. "Ever wondered where meat really comes from, Micky boy?" *Something that got stuck in your teeth six weeks ago, sir?* –a little voice inside him wanted to answer, but instead he just played dumb, a role he had gotten well used to whilst helping Mr Shah at the shoe repair counter in Central Zone 3a.

Thankfully, Mr Trevison didn't look like he was going to be around much, and left the day-to-day running of the Sector 9d meat counter mostly to Kev and Mariska. Kev was all long black hair and dreadlocks, weird for a white boy, and even weirder for a butcher since his headgear needed to hide all that away for the sake of hygiene. But somehow Kev's dreadlocks, once sighted, left an undying mark on Michael's impression of him. He danced around as he worked, like a mad man, and seemed to speak to himself, but when Michael got up close he discovered to his surprise that a lot of what he said made sense or was at least interesting.

On his second day, Kev dragged

Michael aside and produced the poster again that Mr Trevision had showed him when he first arrived, the stylised photo of real cows and sheep grazing in a real field made of real grass. Kev pointed at the blue roof behind the cows and asked Michael what he thought it was. "Ceiling, roof…?" Michael answered, confused.

"Why blue, though, how blue?" Kev persisted.

"Painted blue by guys on scaffold…?" Michael ventured, scared he was making a fool of himself somehow. Kev laughed like a drain then drew Michael close and whispered. "Listen mate, that's the **Sky** that is. Oxygen and ozone, with clouds, water vapour, cumulostratus. Bet you don't know what any of that means. But I've seen it with my own peepers. Sky is what's above this roof, above everything, out there!"

"How could you have seen it?" Michael answered suspiciously, but Kev just tapped the side of his nose and spun around and resumed his arranging of the duck paté pots and parsley sprigs across the cold cuts display.

He'd thought Mariska was quite plain when he'd first been introduced to her, but now she sought him out in his lunch break and spoke to him up close in a whisper and then he began to notice how lovely her big dark eyes were, and lose track of what she was actually saying. "Be careful of what Kev tells you, don't get too close to him, the central management are monitoring him you know. He's a dope head, he's been busted twice, reconditioned. Used to work at Central Supplies before he was demoted…" Drugs were bad news. Michael's overseer at his adolescent dormitory had given him and his fellow yearlings an intensive vid course about that; the penalties were stiff.

"Central Supplies, really?" Now Michael was impressed, and worried all at once. Next day as Kev was over at the steak display, he started to ask him about what he'd seen there. But Kev said that even he'd never seen a real cow, they were all supplied ready-disinfected from the outside and he was only trained how to cut them up from then on. At this point Mr Trevison glided by in his natty striped hat, and Kev and Michael pretended to be talking about the cardboard Houses-Of-Parliament backing scenery behind the beef display. "Bet you think that's something to do with HP sauce, eh, Mike? But you're well wrong. The parliament was a real building in old London, stood once on this very ground, or somewhere around here at any rate…"

"Bit of local background colour for the new lad, eh, Kevin? Very good, always handy for chit chat with the housewives… they all like a friendly butcher's boy…"

Once Trevison was gone, Kev continued: "Listen, Mike, drop by my pad tonight, I'll tell you more, here take this…" Kev slipped another photo into Michael's pocket and he didn't dare look at it until he'd got home. All the way home on the transporter he found himself craning his neck to gaze up at the white roof far overhead, the cross-braced girders, the occasional cloud of steam and mist accumulating there, released through opaque white vent diffusers. After midnight curfew, dayglow floodlights flicked down a notch further in this sector, a little darker, probably indicating there was less crime to worry about.

Michael's new accommodation was a quite luxurious plywood bungalow in an estate with quiet cul-de-sacs and well-groomed plastic hedges. In Michael's previous house he hadn't been able to stand up in its single room, but here he could walk about in a circle almost twice as wide as his own height and lie out full length when asleep without having to put his feet out the window. When he got it out, the photo was of blue water churned up next to a field, frothy white water, and other animals and birds and a burning light in the sky.

After his micro-meal, Michael opened his door and walked out into the street and strolled to its end to catch a transporter. Next year he might even be able to afford a car he thought, if he kept his nose clean, in which regard meeting Kev might be dangerous. But hell, he needed friends in his new neighbourhood. He quite fancied Mariska the more he thought about it, but she'd hardly go out with him if he had no friends, would she? That would be too weird and sad.

Kev's house, in a similar suburban cul-de-sac to Michael's, was a whole twice the size again. They could both actually sit in chairs and talk to each other and have a little bit of space left between them when the bed was folded away. A third person might even have fitted at a push. But Kev had better use for his spare space. Leaves of a strange plant were hanging everywhere under weird blue lights, something Michael had never seen at any salad counters, and Kev was expert at rolling the leaves up into cigarettes and smoking them. Kev urged Michael to share one with him, then pointed at the crumpled photograph Michael was folding out again on his lap. "Those are waves, Mike, waves at the edge of the sea, on a beach…One day I want to get to see the sea…"

Michael was beginning to feel queasy and Kev's voice suddenly seemed far away and hypnotic, like a Discipline Officer's voice during a neighbourhood crackdown. "Where is the sea, Kev? And where did you get these weird leaves?"

"I've told you, Mike. The answer's the same every time. The outside."

"But we're not allowed to go there. No one is."

"They just want you to think that…" Kev exhaled, narrowing his eyes like an ancient mystic, whatever they were, or a senior stockist of the central committee, "someone must be allowed out to get the meat carcasses and the proper fruit and vedge... and I've been out like I told you, it can be done, it's just dangerous that's all... if you get caught..."

#

The next day, Kev noticed Michael watching Mariska in a quiet moment, as he stood sharpening the steak knives, thinking he was hidden behind the hanging garlic bulbs.

"You've got no chance with her, boyo, you're not in her bracket. She only puts it out for managerial class, time and motion men from the central monitoring bureau. They ask for a quick feel of her gammons and she does them round the back."

"A sex booth?" Michael asked, embarrassed, crestfallen, trying not to show it.

"Nothing so grand, dude; Trevison keeps one of the fridges switched off just for the purpose. He gets a cut, as it were, and we get an extra hundredweight of sausages. Sorted..."

#

This had been the right move for Michael. When he checked his balance, he found that he was, marginally, richer than he had ever been in his life. Just think of all the things he could buy. Things that would be his for a day or even a week, cluttering up his living quarters before having to be returned to Central Services. Useless consumer luxuries the like of which everybody dreamed about. Maybe even Mariska would be impressed.

It was a boom time for the local economy and he capitalised by working extra shifts whenever they were offered. Mr Trevison beamed like a Vitamin D lamp and promised Michael that hard work always brought requisite rewards.

He had little time for the news or the dramas available on his walkie. The plotlines of the latter seemed to mostly revolve around young citizens rebelling by dabbling with drugs, growing their hair, criticising the managers but eventually seeing sense and knuckling down to the daily grind. He would have called the stories clichéd if he had known the word. The tales had always bored him because they seemed so unrealistic. Until he met Kevin.

"I think I've inhaled too much of this weed, man," his colleague confessed. "I think I'm going to have to spend a little time in the communal facilities."

Alone in Kevin's apartment, Michael let his curiosity inspire him to investigate a few burning questions. Such as: what was actually in the cigarettes? And why did the contents feel, smell and look exactly the same as a luxury rug nestled by the sleeping couch? As for the pot plant - touch it, sniff it, roll one of its leaves between your fingers, or try to... it was plastic. I've been smoking the carpet, Michael thought, and any buzz that I've got is just from the shared belief that we were doing something illegal. Fake, more like.

Kevin's face looked whiter than usual when he returned. He should have cleaned his dreadlocks more carefully with the running water. His spirits were not dampened any.

"This is mind-blowing stuff, Micky boy," he continued as if their conversation had merely been paused on the walkie. "Opens the questioning lobes. This world we live in, Mike, haven't you ever wondered?"

"Sure, sometimes."

"And, Mike my friend, haven't you always wanted to... get out? See what else there is?"

"Not really, Kev. I've always believed in that adage 'The chrome always seems brighter in the other shop.' It's late, uh, *man*... I'm going home."

#

Mr Trevison had instituted a new sales pitch and staff were required to wear bright white T-shirts emblazoned with the red legend, "Buy More Meat!" Kevin spent most of the morning nudging Michael and delivering luscious comments about Mariska in her uniform and double entendres on the meaning of the message in her case. In fact, the clothing's logo was subtly different on the inside and the hard slog helped the sweat imprint it craftily by the end of the shift, so that when you exited the shower and glanced at your chest in the standing mirror, the slogan on your body now read, "Sell More Meat!" Just a perk of the job, Michael supposed.

At the end of the week, Michael went to see Mr Trevison to claim his upgrades and bonus credit. The boss had his walkie hooked up to a screen and was watching a recording of events from Kevin's flat.

"Ah, the old placebo effect," Trevison chuckled. "One day that boy will rebel too far and lose all privileges. Whereas you, son, have passed a test with flying colours, whatever that archaic expression means."

"Do you mean Kevin might be put on zero credit, sir?"

"It's happened to others, Michael. No purchasing power, just an extended bout of window shopping before sadly expiring. But that's not your future, so fret not. Actually, I see great things ahead for you. Mariska is the key. She has the ear - and other appendages - of management. She can take you where you want to go, even if you don't know where that is yet."

"I want to stay here for now, Mr T, sir. Show the range of what I can do."

"And you shall, for a while at least. In the meantime, it's black T-shirts all round until that temporary tattoo stops showing through. Can't go telling all our secrets to the customers, can we?"

#

The following week Mariska grabbed Michael from behind just as he was about to go off shift and bundled him into a storage cupboard. His immediate instinctive reflex, learned since early childhood, was to raise his walkie to chest height in defence and salutation. Mariska pressed her own walkie against his, producing a loud beep of information exchanged, tagging him for a sex-booth appointment. Then he expected her to start kissing him, but instead she was whispering urgently into his ear: "Listen up Mikey, Kev's about to get busted, I need to talk to you. Trevison hasn't noticed us yet, we've maybe got half a minute before I have to dash back out of here. You leave a minute or two later, got it?"

"Got what? What's happening?" Kev started to waver nervously until she silenced him.

"You've been spying on him for Trevison, right? He always tries that with the new boys. But this is something bigger. Kev didn't just tell you about all his daft drugs thing, did he? What else did he show you?"

"Just crazy stuff. Pictures of blue roofs and frothy water. The outside, like he thinks he's been there."

"Shit, shit, I knew it!" Mariska drummed her feet and peered anxiously through the slit of light at the door threshold, on the look-out for the ever-twitching stripy hat of Trevison.

"So w-what?" Michael stammered, "it's just a myth, the guy's cracked isn't he?"

"No, no!" Mariska whispered urgently. "Well, yes, but no. He's cracked alright, but the outside is real. I know because it's me that took him there…"

"You've been outsi--"

Mariska put her hands over his lips, then drew back for a second and eyed him penetratingly in the dark. Then she lunged forward and kissed him passionately on the lips. "Listen, whatever happens, say nothing about the outside, say nothing about what I told you. If they take you in then just sit tight until I come to visit you. Trust me, I've got contacts." She put her hand on the doorknob, about to go.

"What about the s…"

"Sex booth? We'll talk there next, if we don't get the chance before… see ya!"

As Michael left the stall five minutes later, he saw a white van, conspicuously unmarked, as only those owned by Central Services could be, drawing up on the corner. Its windows were one way black glass. He shivered and hurried on to the transporter stop.

But he'd only been home ten minutes, just time enough to flush the weird pictures Kevin had given him down the lavatory, when they came for him also. Kev must have implicated him. Surely Trevison would speak up for him, get him released within hours. The Services men wore white plastic overalls like meat inspectors, their faces obscured by white surgical masks. They held him down over his couch, inadvertently thrusting his head through his open living room window as they injected him in the backside with morphine. His vision faded as he found himself looking down into the plastic chrysanthemums in his flowerbed.

#

Michael woke up in a room of blinding yellow light, strapped down on a gurney as blurred men in white coats moved around above him. A huge television screen seemed to be filling one wall, emitting odd whispering voices. "Kevin Watson has been withdrawn from public display permanently, Michael." A calm deep fatherly voice spoke directly into his ear, as if someone was moving around inside his brain. "But we found contamination on him.

Germs. What did your dormitory masters always teach you about germs, Michael?"

"A clean environment is a safe environment, sir. Dirt and germs and careless risks, that's what did for the people before. The Careless Ages, before they founded the covenant of Health and Safety…"

"Good, Michael, good. Very knowledgeable. But too much knowledge can distress the mind, like an untidy cupboard where no one can find anything, where quality goods might go out of date without proper regulatory measures."

"Yes sir."

"Kevin Watson has brought in germs from somewhere, contamination. Do you think he might have contaminated you, Michael?"

"No, no, sir!" Michael tried to sit up in alarm, but his restraints bit harder than ever.

"Did Kevin ever mention the outside to you, Michael? Did he say that he might have been there?"

"He talked all sorts of crazy stuff like that, but I never believed him, ever."

"Did he ever give or show you anything that he said was from the outside, Michael? Think carefully before answering now."

#

When Michael next woke up he was in an ordinary hospital ward, or so it appeared, with about fifteen or so other patients. A friendly-looking young doctor was accessing Michael's walkie with a little stylus, where it lay by his bedside, switched to intravenous, its wires trailing under the covers to monitor points on his wrists and temples.

"When did you last have sex, Michael? You appear unusually behind on your intercourse credit chart. Do you have someone we could call in for you, to help you recuperate? You've had a nasty shock, a close scrape. The full decontamination procedure, you're almost a new-start, biologically, now isn't that nice?"

"Ma—Marisk…" Michael found himself trying to say, but his throat was incredibly dry after whatever they had done to him.

The doctor looked at him blankly then consulted his walkie again, flicking through thumbnail pictures. "Mariska Kovac… Would that be her? Perfect, we'll signal her in and she can help you out for us…"

#

The hospital Sex-Booths weren't quite as cool as the street varieties. Less up-to-date range of music and video and a reduced selection of lighting and aroma effects. Even the porn was a bit clinical, as befitted the setting. Nonetheless, unlike all Michael's previous loveless experiences, he found he was enormously excited, pulse rate racing, as Mariska and he dropped their clothes into the vacuum shoots to be cleaned and warmed up while they performed together, ready for them again on completion. In the red flickering half-light, to a funk-jazz soundtrack with numerous video couplings taking place on the walls around them with theatrically over-done sighs and moanings, Michael found himself confronting Mariska's beautiful breasts, round as honeydew melons from the exotic fruit counter. Across them were emblazoned the pleasingly wobbling but cryptic words TAEM EROM LLES… He looked again, as Mariska turned the music up, a trick of the light, the phrase seemed to be saying something else now… team… lies. Mariska directed a quick blast of liquid from a wall nozzle against his erection, turning the temperature down to freezing, instantly bringing him to his wincing senses. "Forget

that stuff for now, big boy. We can talk here for another four minutes with the music up before we have to pay for more and the monitors start wondering if we're impotent or on drugs. I've brought you a map, look…"

From between her swinging breasts, Mariska unhooked a tiny silver casket on a chain necklace from which she produced a rolled-up scroll of white paper like an old-fashioned till receipt. "It's a map, Michael… the same way I took Kev. You have to try it, to escape. I've seen it, the blue sky, it's real…"

Michael was appalled, even as his erection began to reassert itself in the face of all this unnecessary information and complication. "But why? I'm quite happy! I just want to keep my nose clean…" he inched closer to her.

"And get your cock dirty…? For all of three minutes before the antiseptic sprinkler phase decontaminates and sterilises us, eh? Michael, you're so green. Don't you get it? Kev is you and me in another five years. Worn out, brain cells blasted by boredom. The Company chew and spit out all of us. Who do you think Kev had to betray, how many hundreds, for Trevison, to get what little promotion he got? Then his conscience got to him, the memories, the guilt. It's all his reconditionings that wasted his brain, not his imaginary drugs. The outside is our only chance. Memorise this map, then we'll destroy it now together. You make your way tomorrow, start out at first light, end of curfew, in disguise, steal some clothes from a bargain bin or something, wear a hood, don't look at the security cameras. I'll cover for you at work for as much of the morning as I can, claim I thought I saw you clock in, say you were in the cold store or the toilets. Get to the outside and wait for me. I'll follow you in a few weeks, I promise. Just wait where it says on the map, then when you hear the big door creaking, run for the light…"

The completion clock was ticking

out its countdown now, the overhead nozzles priming for spermicide spray, vaginal irrigation wands emerging from the warm stainless steel walls. "But how will you find me out there... if there is *a there?*" Michael gibbered desperately, "Haven't we even time for a quick blow job?"

Save your strength! Mariska just had time to mime, and blow him a kiss... before the floor split into contrary conveyor belts, the showers started pelting down, and the short methodical sequence of returning them to sanitized everyday life began.

#

Michael had been encouraged to wear his team's colours for the match tonight so that the whole of his end would look resplendent in the orange and dark blue favours of Sainsbringham. He'd donned his replica shirt below his white apron and had been extra careful not to further decorate it with any blood splashes. He'd been almost rushed off his feet today, holding the fort alone owing to Kevin having been "reallocated" and, equally worryingly, the enigmatic Mariska absent without apparent reason. However, Mr Trevison had been bright and breezy all day, particularly about Mariska's activities away from the butcher's slab.

"Oh, she's just off with her not so secret company supervisor boyfriend. No sex booths for them, sonny - they get themselves a luxury hotel suite."

Michael loved his football but tonight he was finding it unusually difficult to keep his focus on the game. Although the away team Waitroford were playing in their traditional white kit with green piping, they had lately adopted a whole new swathe of product logos which tended to blur stupidly from this distance into composite, compound colours and even on the big screen monitors it was not always easy to tell the two teams

apart. Still, he had a good seat and a small range of buttons on the left armrest allowed him to call for any delicacy or sustenance he wanted, letting the match serve as mobile, mildly exciting wallpaper. He fiddled with the device and a small option screen popped up. The selection was so tempting. The first time he ever went to this stadium, he had left with bag after bag of short-term souvenirs and varieties of Sainsbringham kit that desiccated after only six washes. Everything's there to be bought, he mused; nothing is ever for keeps.

A sudden burst of urgent, demanding action on the Astroturf pitch. 2-1 to the briefly rampant home team. He cheered the winning goal enthusiastically enough, high-fiving his fellow fans as the whistle went for full time. He knew that the crowd would be kettled upon exit and was prepared to tolerate it with good grace, watching instant replays of key match action on his walkie while he waited.

Then his screen went awry. He poked at the device, held it close to his face, even sniffed it for corroded batteries or the like. There was a sudden feral roar from the guys around him and people were starting to surge forward. It reminded him a little of that "seaside wave" that Kevin had described and Michael had no real option other than to rush along with it. Several vendors and their pitches got knocked over in the melee and Michael was glad that he had not lumbered himself with any purchases tonight; it was all he could do to keep his feet.

The mindset of the crowd; the mentality of the mob. A rabid rumour started to spread through the throng that the mythical Sammy Shifter was somewhere in the vicinity and had caused the local electronic systems to go haywire. Some folks were already indulging in a free-for-all - looting, fighting, and generally gushing about the area like liquid released from a shaken lemonade bottle.

Michael realised that this was his chance. If he was ever to make it to The Outside here was the moment to do so. But did he want to? He was not entirely sure. He doubted that Mariska would be there. He even went so far as to doubt that the fabled place - this legendary paradise lost - actually existed. Beyond the shop-floors, thoroughfares, and dormitories must lie simply hundreds of grow-domes and the like, that's all. Might be fun to visit, might look and smell pretty pleasant… but that was hardly heaven.

Still, in present time, he decided that he wanted to get out of this many-headed, increasingly unruly mob. The counter barriers were down as were the exit corrals and, probably, the CCTV too. Veer left, then left again, then central and now right. Keep going, don't stop.

He wasn't sure exactly where he was anymore and he couldn't read Mariska's micro-map without the zoom function of his currently malfunctioning walkie. But there were vehicles moving freely just ahead, maybe just outside the affected zone. One was a recycler - resplendent in knowing green and with an open back. Sprinting like a winger racing for the byline, Michael caught it up and jumped in.

Soon wishing that he hadn't. Within, he landed upon a liqueous, gelatinous, unstable surface that threatened to disintegrate beneath his weight at any moment and plunge him into something unimaginably worse. And the smell! He fought back the gag reflex and tried to cover his mouth and nostrils with his already slightly ragged shirtsleeve against the overwhelming stench of rotting food. It was hard to tell in this putrid dimness but he suspected he might have secreted himself inside the carcass of a cow.

He put up with the stench and the bumping and the sense of never quite being balanced and stable until he could take no more. Judging that he was at the very least

well away from the football riot, he clambered out as the vehicle finally stopped.

Just fifty yards from the incinerator.

A close call, to be sure but a lucky break, also. This building was at the edge of the occupied areas and therefore -

"Hey! What are you doing, pal?"

Just celebrating a famous Sainsbringham victory in my stained shirt, he thought sardonically; but his legs were quicker than his wit and he began to run, zigzagging, heading on instinct for an exit.

Or entrance.

#

At the end of the avenue he could see thirty-foot high doors, creaking open, blinding light flooding in, a lorry of fresh vegetables emerging from the haze. An uncannily cool breeze brushed his face. To the left of the road stood the incinerator building, its chimney reaching up to penetrate the roof. On the right, echoing sounds emerged from a huge run-down warehouse. Michael remembered Mariska's map, and ducked inside, hiding himself behind some derelict machinery. The guy pursuing him had got a friend with him now, the two of them came in and hovered uncertainly at the entrance. *Breaker's yard*, Mariska had written. The sparks and mist and general untidy confusion seemed as alienating and unfamiliar to his pursuers as they were to Michael. Nothing seemed labelled or branded. A completely non-sanitised environment. Quite a daunting prospect. While his pursuers retreated for reinforcement, Michael made his way through the warehouse, keeping his head down, running and crawling between obstacles. At the centre of the space, men with masks and torches were dismantling fridges and display cabinets.

Michael knew what he was looking for. Somewhere about halfway along the huge rear wall, there was a particularly old pile of scrap with something like a wrecked transporter in the middle of it. He registered faintly that it resembled something he had seen in the old Houses Of Parliament display behind the meat counter. *Routemaster RML 2619* a curious embossed logo on its side said, then *159 : STREATHAM STATION* above its peeling red paint and twisted metal bones.

He slipped round behind the vintage vehicle, and there it was, concealed by a dense cover of dirty plastic curtains. Michael pulled the slippery material back and got the same blast of cool rich air in his face again. He breathed deep and began to feel dizzy, remembering Kev's mythical drug stash. He heard voices behind him, and flinched. He had to go forward now. But into what? Mariska had said it was a door, but this ragged hole looked more like a light, a yellow fire. Intoxicated, foolhardy in the rushing air, he lowered his head and pushed forward.

Outside, if that was what it was, Michael thought he'd gone blind at first, and fell to his knees, whimpering, coughing, then remembering those behind him, stretched out his hands in front of himself desperately and felt his way, crawling slowly on all-fours.

Some time after he had begun to accept the inexplicable blindness as a magical curse from the supreme store manager, Michael found his sight gradually returning. He rubbed his eyes, and stumbled to his feet...

Above him were what Kev had called clouds. They seemed incredibly far up, but they were thick and grey, no blue sky. Maybe Kev had never really been out after all. Maybe Michael been duped into being the first, but surely Mariska hadn't been lying to him? There was a path of sorts beneath his feet, brown dirt between areas of grass and tall untidy plants not unlike Kev's weed. Somebody had been here before alright. He turned around to look at where he'd come from, but found he had to keep walking for another half hour before

he could get far away enough to actually see it all. He began to understand it. Martworld, his home, his world... was a white dome of gargantuan proportions, its vast muscular steel stanchions vanishing into the earth like the flexing legs of a terrifying spider. But it appeared inert, sterile, lifeless from out here, whilst behind him and all around him now there were... new sounds and sights, activity, but none of it human. He walked on in astonished curiosity.

He walked along hedgerows and borders, along the banks of streams, under trees, among long unruly grasses, between enormous fields of crops, cows, sheep, pigs. He saw white figures moving and thought they were human at first, ducked for cover, then heard one coming near, making strange humming noises. They were robots, dozens of them, completely oblivious to his presence, methodically watering plants and handing out feed. He heard birdsong, and saw species he had never seen before outside cages in the pet stalls. As new to him as he to they apparently, some of the smaller ones even landed on his hands and shoulders.

The land was flat to the horizon on all sides, and Michael thought he could see another white dome, perhaps as large as Martworld, in the far distance. He kept walking until the light went dim, then slept, shivering and uncomfortable, under a tree amid the swishing of grasses. The wind rushed over him as he slept, and a strange pale silver light rose up above him during the night, shining through the clouds. When he next woke up, he was more astonished still. Kev hadn't lied. The grey clouds had gone while he slept, and now a vast blue dome stretched over his head in every direction. A blinding yellow light, that Kev had called the sun, was warming his skin now, and he found himself laughing hysterically where he sat on the ground, then inexplicably crying, tears streaming down his face.

#

On the third day of walking he began to see something unexpected in the sky above him. A very large platform of white metal girders like those that had formed the roof of Martworld, was floating up there, miles above him, with people and machines moving about over it, construction workers. To Michael's alarm, some kind of white vehicle fired its engines and came hurtling down from the structure towards him. Instinctively he tried to run, but the machine landed in a clearing in front of him and the pilots stepped out and shouted to him "Hey kid, why you running, we mean you no harm! We don't work for your bosses! Chill out, we're friends!"

He ducked behind a bush and peered back at them, and finally on a strange impulse that he began to realise must be hunger, stood up, and walked towards the strangers. Their uniforms were different colours from any he'd seen before, and they seemed interested in his.

"Hey, you're from Martworld, right? No sweat, you've nothing to fear from us. We're from Skymall, see, under construction…" –The taller of the two smiled broadly and turned to gesture up towards the hovering colossus behind them.

The smaller one looked at Michael closely then frowned, "Kid, you look starving. You want to come with us? I'm Stan and this is Jared by the way. We've got burgers and chips up there. Pizza and fizzy drinks. You look like you could do with a pick-me-up alright…"

From the sky truck, as they called it, Stan and Jared showed Michael what Martworld looked like from the air, and then further up, other distant domes that they called Tesclondon and Asdaborough to the north and east, only one of dozens they said, all over the country, all over the world.

Skymall would be finished in another eighteen months they said proudly, as they led Michael across its miraculously floating substructure, over which ducting and floorboards were being rapidly laid, the constant sound of welding and bolting, the shouts of crane operators and labourers filling the air. Enormous arcing beams like the ribs of a monster's stomach were being slowly erected overhead.

"Why will people want to live in the air?" Michael asked Jared, pigging out on his third ice cream tub as he walked with them, killing the last vestiges of his hunger.

"Oh it won't being staying here, matey. Don't they tell their people anything inside Martworld? This place is headed for the stars. Mars first, then Europa, eventually Alpha Centauri maybe…"

"But what about all that green space down there? –The left over bits between the domes?"

Jared and Stan looked at each other then laughed heartily. Stan slapped Michael on the back. "Oh boy, you're green, aren't you? They never taught you history either. Land's too valuable on earth to let anything as messy as people all over it. They trashed it when they could. Now they don't get the chance anymore. Apart from you today I suppose, but you're out-numbered by everything, you're safely insignificant."

Green they called him? Michael remembered Mariska calling him this, and seeing the doubt in his eyes, Stan asked: "Hey, when you going back to Martworld anyway, you want a lift?"

Michael shook his head. "I'm never going back. They'd discontinue me if they found out I'd escaped. I'm out for good now…"

The two men looked at him in surprise. "Brave boy…" Jared finally said, and Stan whistled. "What you going to eat? Want me to tell you what some of those crops are down there? You ever used a fishing rod?"

Michael blushed and shook his head, looking at his feet, then the green world between his feet, giddyingly far below him.

"Oh boy, you better start learning. We'll take you back down now. But hey, sure you don't want to work for us?"

#

Michael didn't have much luck at first fishing with the stick and string Stan and Jared gave him, but the apples and carrots he took from under the noses of the robots tasted fresher than any he had ever tasted before.

Even so, he was finding it hard to adjust to a life not spent wholly surrounded by other people. He'd flirted with radical ideas of being alone but this new feeling, one he supposed must actually be loneliness, was new and disconcerting. Where were the faces, the places? Where were the stalls and the walls?

On the seventh day after his escape he finally made his way to something rather special that he'd seen from above: the open sea and a long sandy beach where waves rolled in just like Kev had described them, but a hundred times stranger and better. All his senses were intoxicated and overwhelmed. He even tried to drink the water at first until he found the salt made him thirstier and more than a little queasy. He sat down on the rocks at the headland and took his walkie out. He knew it was dangerous and foolhardy but there was a weird and unfamiliar feeling inside him now. Sort of like the hunger or thirst, but different. An aching that he decided was probably loneliness. He called Mariska. If Martworld traced him he'd be a goner, but how else could Mariska know where he was and that he'd got out? The line went down after a minute, no connection, battery dead.

Would she ever come to find him? Tear herself away from the prime meat of the chief inspector?

Two days later, he sat on the same spot watching the sun go down in a sky of pink and golden twisting clouds. He was cooking the first fish he had ever caught, on a bonfire on the rocks, when he heard footsteps behind him. His heart lurched. Jared and Stan, perhaps; a crack division of the Martworld police; or maybe, just maybe…

THE SALVATION AGREEMENT

MIKE RUSSELL

At first I thought it was a train I could hear in the distance: the quickening huff, shrill echoing whistle, clatter of pistons beating out their clackety. It used to be that I would run outside whenever one went past, shouting: Train coming, Pa - look at her go.

But this time I was older and I soon knew it wasn't a train because the noise wasn't right. There was no rhythm to it, just a sound like wind, not steam, a shrieking gale growing louder. Coming closer. Rattling the cups and plates on our kitchen shelves. It had been two years or so since I'd run outside to see a train go by. Now a different noise drew me, Ma too, into the bright sunlight.

A droidman had landed his grey patrol ship a few hundred yards from our farmhouse. The horses were going crazy in the corral, the chickens scattering in panic, and I suddenly wished that Pa would come back, along with my brother, from their long ride to town. It took a while for the dust and grass to settle. We had to shield our eyes as the downdraft from the droidman's jets raged. Everything hushed: the horses, the hens, and the flitter of windblow. We waited. I wondered what a droidman was doing out here. Did he want something...from us?

After a brief silence the ramp of the beetle-shaped patroller went down and the droidman, in a black skin-suit, bareheaded and blond-haired, like they all were, emerged. Ma squeezed my shoulders. "You...you don't have anything, do you?" she whispered. "A machine, a talker, anything?"

"No," I hissed back. I had an old physics book I could barely make sense of, but surely the droidman wouldn't be interested in that. He looked at us for a few seconds, recording our presence. Then he walked under the front of his ship, craning his neck to inspect something. He pulled a wire from his suit, reached up and connected it to the hull, opened a wrist panel on his suit to check a read-out. After a few moments he disconnected the wire and opened a hatch on the underside of the patroller. He pulled out a tool from his thigh panel and a ladder telescoped to the ground from above his head. He climbed up, the tool gripped in his mouth.

We watched. I could feel how nervous Ma was as she fretted next to me. The minutes passed and he showed no sign of coming down the ladder. All we could see were his legs, from the knee down, as he worked inside, fixing whatever was wrong.

"His ship must be broken," I said.

Occasionally I saw a droidman patrol

in the distance, heading towards town. They seldom bothered with single houses, unless there was anything obviously illegal like a working car or electricity; they could detect those from miles away. Nothing more advanced than the steam train or the telegraph - that was what the agreement said, although it was signed many years before I was born.

The droidman didn't look like he was going anywhere soon so Ma wanted to go back inside to finish her cooking. She started to pull me with her, but I protested. I struggled. This was too interesting, too unusual, to miss by hiding inside the house. She let me go with a warning.

"OK, but do not move from that spot," she hissed, jabbing every word. "You can watch, but don't go any closer. Understand?"

I promised to obey her, wondering why she was getting so angry with me. She hurried away, casting fearful glances over her shoulder as she went. Within a minute of Ma disappearing back inside, I started to edge nearer the patrol craft. I could hear the squeak of his boots on the metal rungs of the ladder, a high-pitched whine that sounded like a drill. Then there was a flash from inside the hatch, and a bang, a puff of white smoke, and the droidman's legs bent, his black-boots slipping down a rung, two rungs. I saw his hand on the ladder as he steadied himself. I ran forward, curious. He descended slowly, seemed to sway as he stood, his head giving funny little jerks. He stretched his black-clad arms out, flexed his bare hands, opening his mouth wide as if to scream. But no sound came out.

"Are you OK?"

After a few seconds he looked at me, flexing and bending his left arm at weird angles.

"Motor function...impaired," he said. "Current overload has reduced operational capacity to 96.4 per cent."

"That sounds good."

"Good," he repeated, still working his left arm. "That is...not good."

Staring straight at me, he seemed to remember something. He stretched out his right hand, balled his fist, and his forearm panel opened from its bump, his scanner extending with a whirr. He waited, and so did I. Something was expected of me.

"Your existence code," he said, with an edge of annoyance in his voice.

"Oh," I said, rolling up my sleeve. "I forgot. I haven't been done for ages."

He scanned me, but I could see him look over at the house. Droidmen had all sorts of built in scanners, and zoom cameras in their eyes, so I'd heard. He read my results in his arm panel.

"Aidan Hercher. 12 years old. Son of Thomas and Amy. You have a brother, Carl, 18 years old. Tell me, Aiden, why do you live so far from the nearest town?"

I shrugged, embarrassed, and then annoyed I was embarrassed in front of a droidman.

"I don't know. We like it here."

"I see. Is the entire family unit present in this property?"

I nodded. I hadn't seen a droidman this close before, not so close that I could reach out and touch him. It made me nervous.

"Is your ship not working? Can it still fly?"

There seemed to be other more interesting things for the droidman to study, like the house and the barn, the corral and the chicken-coop. He crunched away over the dry ground without answering my questions.

"Section 5 clause 4 of the Salvation Agreement states that agreement enforcers are empowered to inspect any human property at any time."

He strode towards the barn, stopping to look at the house every few steps, with me hurrying along behind him. There was nothing in the barn for him to see except straw and tools and the sick calf we were nursing. It came and stuck its wet snout through the wooden slats of the pen, expecting more milk. The droidman looked at the calf, and it gave a watery high-pitched bleat at the prospect of being fed.

I stood and watched, amazed, as the droidman extended his arms and let his fingertips, each on the end of a thin wire, go exploring, like tentacles sniffing and searching the barn. I had seen droidmen do this before, but not up close. I figured we didn't have anything to worry about, unless Pa had some old devices hidden where I couldn't find them.

From the droidman's left hand, one of his extendable fingertips just plopped limply to the floor, where it twitched and sort of hopped along the concrete, trying to follow the others. The flash must have damaged it.

"Motor function impaired," I said, before I could stop myself. I grinned.

The droidman turned to me for a second, then looked straight ahead, his head moving slightly as he sensed through his nine tips, seeing what they saw. By now they were at least 20 feet long, three from his right hand darting up into the hayloft, where they rustled among the dry stalks. The ones on the ground floor tapped on surfaces and inspected stains. His fingertips could pick up electronic signals, detect plastic and other fossil fuel-based materials. Contraband. The stuff we weren't supposed to have any more.

There was nothing except a can of linseed oil, so I followed him to the house. I shouted for Ma but couldn't find her. A big pot bubbled furiously on top of the woodstove. I moved it to a cooler position and its lid stopped rattling.

"She was here just a minute ago," I said, puzzled. "She was making dinner."

The droidman did the same in the house as he did in the barn. When he'd finished with the ground floor, he went to the stairs, started to climb, his fingertips yards ahead of him, apart from the middle finger of his left hand, the broken one.

On the last step up to the landing he stopped. A few seconds later I saw two of his fingers withdraw from my bedroom, their wires wrapped around a book, my physics text from under my bed. His fingertips all withdrew into their fingers and he held the book, flicked through it. I wondered if he could absorb all the knowledge in it just by speed-reading.

"Item prohibited," he stated. "Salvation Agreement section 2 clause 1. Practical knowledge of atomic fission." He turned to me, the book in his hand. "This item will be retained by Agreement Enforcer 91-AF."

Horses were coming, galloping fast, thudding to a whinnying stop near the front porch. There were shouts. It was Pa and Carl, and I could hear Ma's voice as well. Where had she been? The droidman jerked his head, listening.

The door flew open and set the brass weights inside the old wallclock jangling. Although the door had just missed him, the droidman didn't flinch.

"Aidan Hercher's father, Thomas, and brother, Carl. Your existence codes, please."

"We got nothing, we done nothing," said Pa, coldly, standing in the doorway with the daylight at his back. Beneath his dust coat I could see his pistol was in his hand, pointed at the floor but ready to come up. Behind him, out on the porch, my brother clutched his shotgun, tensed, twitchy. They'd been away nearly a week and they needed a shave and a bath and some good food. Pa caught sight of my book; the droidman had it clutched to his chest like my teacher does when she's holding a book. With less certainty, Pa said: "There's nothing against the agreement in this house."

The droidman looked from one to the other.

"Existence codes, please," he repeated, his tone unchanged.

They waited. I stood close to Pa. When he put his hand on my shoulder I could smell his sweat, and the horse he'd been riding for six days.

My brother started to speak. "We ain't..." But Pa holstered his gun and pulled up the sleeve of his coat with a sigh, unbuttoning the cuff of his shirt.

"Here," he said roughly, bearing his forearm. "Then you can leave us in peace."

Reluctantly, my brother did the same, obeying Pa but none too happy about it.

"The female," said the droidman when he'd finished Carl. "I must scan her existence code."

Pa stiffened. "There ain't no female here. She... she had to leave." He paused. "Her friend is dying and..."

I looked up at Pa, his eyes fierce and dark but scared with it. "He knows," I said. "He saw Ma. And he heard her outside with you."

Pa pushed me away in the direction of the kitchen and stepped into the hallway, raising his pistol and pointing it at the droidman's chest. Carl held his shotgun at waist level, aimed at the same target.

The droidman spoke calmly. "It is unlikely you will overpower me or cause me serious damage. In the event that you do, the emergency recall beacon in my ship will activate. This automatically attracts four other patrol vessels, one of which will be a gunship."

My brother raised his shotgun, clicked the safety off.

"We are designed to withstand such a weapon."

Carl moved closer. The muzzle of the shotgun's double barrel was now barely three inches from the droidman's face. He looked

down the barrels the same way he looked at everything else, like it was nothing at all.

"Discharging your weapon will activate my full combat mode and engage the relevant procedure for resolving this scenario. My extensors will engird you and a charge of approximately 30,000 volts will incapacitate. And the other ships will come. Under the terms of the Salvation Agreement, disabling an agreement enforcer is punishable by death of the perpetrator and all his or her accomplices."

There was a movement in the living room, and I saw her.

"No," said Ma, in tears. She must have crept in the back door. "It's OK." She was sobbing, shaking her head as she tried to compose herself. "I'll do it. Let's get it over with"

Pa started to get angry with her. "Amy, no."

But she shook her head sadly.

"It's too dangerous, Tom. It shouldn't have happened anyway." She pulled up the sleeve of her jumper.

"This isn't fair, it isn't right," growled Pa as the droidman scanned Ma's arm. "What you're doing to us. Killing us, keeping us... like sheep, to be tagged and controlled." He put his face close to the droidman's, his spit flying. "But what do you care about any of that, you're just a machine, a policeman without a mind of your own. You're not alive - you're just a thing, like a rock or a lump of horseshit. No, less than that, at least shit is good for the ground. What are you good for?"

The droidman paid no attention to what Pa said. All he was interested in was Ma's scan results. Once he'd read them, he looked at her.

"Item prohibited. Salvation Agreement section 2 clause 3. No more than two offspring per pair bond. A global carrying capacity maximum of 1.2 billion of the dominant primate is required for homeostasis. This in vivo foetus of approximately nine weeks duration must be cancelled."

They'd come from the constellation Orion to save us from the radiation and all our other pollution, because we were one of the 16 pure worlds. They created the droidmen to make sure we kept to our side of the bargain. Then they left. Pa had been told all that by his Pa, and had accepted it, once. But I could see he didn't care about the reasons anymore. All he felt was hate, and I wanted to feel the same.

Pa took a deep breath and, with as much force as he could muster, spat right into the droidman's expressionless face. The saliva slid onto his shiny black bodysuit, plopped onto the carpet. Unconcerned, the droidman injected Ma with something.

"Mrs Hercher must attend the nearest sterilisation centre within 14 days or there will be a penalty. Goodbye."

Picking my physics book up off the table, the droidman considered it, and me. He riffled all the book's pages. Then did it again, stopping about a third of the way from the end. Quickly and easily, he ripped the book down the spine, kept one part, and held the remainder out towards me. Without thinking, part of me wanted to take it, but then I remembered what he just done to Ma.

I stared at him, ignoring the offer, until he took the book back. For the first time I saw emotion on his face. It was confusion. He turned smartly and left.

Ma clutched her abdomen and let out a gasp. She went limp and Pa caught her in his arms. My brother, incensed, aimed the shotgun at the droidman's back.

"Carl," Pa shouted, carrying Ma through to the living room. "They'll come for us all, you understand? Swallow it boy, just swallow it and help me."

But just as Pa finished speaking, Carl pulled the trigger. Not far from the droidman,

the ground jumped into life as the shotgun charge threw up dirt and small stones. The droidman, now about 40 yards away from the house, stopped.

Within a blink he'd turned, stretched out his right arm, and two fingertip extensors flew through the open door, whipping the shotgun out of Carl's hands. A second later the droidman held it in his hands. My brother whimpered. Just like I would break a twig, the droidman snapped the shotgun in two, shattering the linchpin. He dropped the pieces, turned, and strode away to his patroller.

Silently, I cursed myself for going anywhere near the patrol craft. If only I'd come inside with Ma...

I knew what I had to do. I ran into the kitchen, grabbed a stool, and reached up to the top of cupboard. I found what I knew to be up there: our copy of the 200-page-long Salvation Agreement, signed by long dead leaders and covered in dust. In the town, the agreement was like a bible to some people: what we'd done to the planet and how we deserved to live like this. Although it was over 40 years old it was printed on some kind of indestructible paper so it would always be new. I took our copy and ran after the droidman.

When I caught up with him he was walking up the patrol craft's ramp. As I reached the bottom, I threw the book after him.

"You can take this one too, you fuckin bastard."

The copy of the agreement landed right at his feet. He picked it up and stood looking down the ramp at me. My heart was thumping and I didn't really know what to do next. Maybe he'd electrocute me or break me in two before I could do anything else.

"Item Mandatory," he said. "Section 3 clause 5. Households not in possession of a copy of the Salvation Agreement face a penalty the nature of which is to be determined by the attending enforcer."

He weighed me up, considered a response. Then he threw the thick document back down next to me, and it landed with a puff of dust. Before I had time to respond, the ramp withdrew and the door to the patroller slid shut.

I picked up our copy of the agreement. With all my strength tried to tear a page out. But despite my straining effort, it refused to rip, and I fought the tears of hot rage pooling as I wrestled with the book.

A whine sounded within the guts of the droidman's craft, building in intensity. I could see him seated in the cockpit, the bastard, working the controls.

The down-jets started and I had to back away, covering my face in the crook of my arm. As the ship rose I was nearly blown off my feet by the blast of warm air and dust. The patroller reached a couple of hundred feet then shot off over the valley and into the blue, a speck turning left over the far hills, probably heading back to the old air force base where they had their area command.

On the dry ground, the pages of the agreement fluttered in the breeze. The horses quietened in the corral.

A train huffed in the distance, its whistle echoing through the valley. It was a sound that used to summon me. Now all I could hear was my mother wailing and my father shouting. I picked up the broken shotgun and our copy of the agreement and went inside, full of hate.

THE MEN WHO VALUE EVERYTHING IN MONEY

JAMES EVERINGTON

They will come for you during office hours, but remember: all hours are office hours to them.

They seem like men in grey suits, until you look too closely - their skin is almost as grey as their suits and their eyes almost as grey as their skin. Their lips are thin and their faces perfectly symmetrical.

And they are constantly counting off numbers on the long fingers of their grey hands.

You won't know how they got into your house, but they have, and they stand over you with their fingers tapping at each other, counting. Like idiot sign-language. There will typically be two or three of them and despite not being identical you won't be able to tell the difference between them. Their eyes are calculating.

Literally, they are calculating how much you are worth.

Not the value of your house, nor of your bank account or chattels - but you. The sum total of your life.

But your emotions, your inner beliefs and triumphs don't come into it, for they are the men who value things only in money, and they will not be swayed in this despite anything you might say.

Their long grey fingers will tick off the pounds and pence of your soul.

And then they stop counting. And they will tell you.

And you can't argue with the result, for who can argue with arithmetic?

You might be worth something, in which case you are left alone and the grey men leave.

Or you might be worth too little, in which case you are left alone, too. But only to value and revalue your own life, in an attempt to prove them wrong. The fingers of your own hands will start tapping against each other...

But it is too painful to value your own being in pounds and pence, and sooner or later you realise: much better to join the ranks of those who value other people's.

THE SYSTEM
CLAUDIA SEREA

These poems are part of the series titled *The System* inspired by Claudia Serea's father's experience as a political prisoner in Communist Romania. They speak out against repression systems everywhere. The chapbook *The System* is forthcoming from Cold Hub Press, New Zealand.

THE INFORMANT

Some see toads
jump
from the tip
of my tongue.

I see money
and back doors
open
for my family's
escape.

I see
faces,
white as flour,
in the window
at night.

I brush them off
and go back
to sleep.

THE THIRD WITNESS

I only did
what I was told.

With my mouth,
I shoveled,
dug a hole,

and buried a man,
alive.

How was I
supposed to know

the other man

carried death
in his pockets?

THE JUDGE

I'm not
interested
in truth,

only in
the law.

When one
life
is ruined,
it's a tragedy.

When millions
of lives
are ruined,

it's
history.

THE COURTROOM CLERK

In the end,
all that remains
is paper,

carbon-
copied
minutes,

years
gathered
in a file.

No one will know
whose fingers
typed
those lives away,

only the hands
that signed
and stamped them.

THE COURTROOM AUDIENCE

We're being led,
led into darkness
by a few

a few hands.

This way,
this way.

Clap all at once,
at once.

Put on these masks.

And these.

Wear these hoop
hula-hoop

earrings

and rings

made of bones,
clean-picked bones.

THE BLANKET

I can't protect you from nightmares,
or from the hands that grab you in the dark
and push you back
into the beating room.

Forgive me.

I'm so thin,
worn to threads by the bodies
I covered before you,

I can't even protect you
from the cold.

But I can offer you my checkered field
where you can move the armies
made of bread,

molded with saliva
and hardened
into soldiers,
horses, bishops, towers,
and queens.

At last, this battle is yours to win.

THE PIECE OF GLASS

You guard me with your life.

You spit on me
and smear me
with shavings of soap,

and sprinkle lime dust
from the walls

until I have a new,
smooth skin.

Now I've become a surface
for poems

and equations
with multiple unknowns.

Today's lesson is French,
taught in whispers.

Write down the words
with a sharp twig
and repeat them.

No one can wipe them
off your mind:

Je suis,
tu es,
il est.

I am.
You are.
He is.

We are.

THE PRISON CLERK

1.

Sign here,
on the dotted line.

Here's your belt,
your keys, your shoes.

You're free to walk.

You're free to close the gate
on nightmares.

2.

Let them visit
only at night.

The outside world
will fold around you,

and unfold women,
flowers, clouds.

You're free to look
and marvel at their faces.

Don't they know?

3.

Do not look back.

Don't tell anyone
what happens here—

who'd believe you anyway?

4.

Go on.

Here's the list
of things to do.

You're free to sing
the pre-approved songs,

to work,
even to whistle.

THE INFORMANT

I follow a man
who walks,
works,
sleeps
like any
other man.

I follow him
in his dreams
on steep streets.

Today, he buys pears
and eats them
with abandon.

His past is a closed door.

I tempt him
to open it.

He offers me
a pear.

AT NIGHT, THE TRUCKS

KURT NEWTON

Albee awoke as he always awoke, dropped on the doorstep of morning like a bundled newborn.

A dreamless sleep is a seamless sleep, and a seamless sleep is a restful sleep leaving nothing to contend with the matters of the day ahead.

It was a perfect philosophy for a perfect world and Albee never questioned it. He was happy living the life he knew, for there was nothing to show any different.

He stood and stretched, fully rested. He went to the refrigerator and poured a glass of orange juice.

Morning light streamed in through the windows of his living quarters, providing a soft glow to the eggshell white and beige décor. In fact, there were two such windows. The clear horizontal strips, positioned near the ceiling, allowed exterior light in while maximizing interior living space. There was also a smaller window at eye-level in the middle of the apartment's front door, which wasn't really a window at all but a wide-angle lens that allowed Albee to view visitors before deciding whether to invite them in or not.

A private life is a lively life, and a lively life is a satisfied life with nothing to distract one from the recreational pleasures at hand.

Another quote from the Handbook On Living A Happy Life; a book that didn't exist, but if it did, the city of Norum, the city in which Albee lived, surely would have invented it.

Albee showered and shaved. He stood before the mirror and counted to ten, then wiped his face clean of the depilatory he had lathered on. He checked for spots missed. Satisfied, he dressed in his usual casual knitwear and left for work.

The city of Norum consisted of row upon row of one- and two-story buildings. There were shops and markets and an abundance of living quarters. The cobblestone streets provided a pleasant, airy separation between rows. There was nothing too tall or too short, too narrow or too wide. There were pale yellows and soft blues; smooth surfaces and crisp lines. Nothing to ruin the overall aesthetic. It was clean. Spotless, in fact. Norum was a beautiful city. A perfect city. It was the only city its citizens had ever known.

Albee walked the quarter mile to the nearest tube entrance, greeting neighbors and strangers alike with a smile. He descended the stairs into the underground station. The station smelled of warm pastry and hot coffee, flowers and fresh fruit. With his stomach growling, he waited in line and hopped on the next car that came along.

Norum's underground was just as beautiful as its surface. The translucent cars floated on magnetic rails that moved quietly through well-lit tunnels. Depictions of the city's perfect streets and sky graced the tunnel walls. It was very much like riding above ground. But that wasn't allowed. Preservation was key to Norum's beauty.

Albee worked in the North Quarter at the Norum Institute for the Development of Society, or NIDS, a twenty-story office building submerged eighteen stories below the surface. He held a position as an ergo-architect designing living space for Norum's future generations. Albee had wanted to be an ergoarchitect for as long as he could remember. In fact, there were days he got the very distinct impression that he had been nothing else.

The tube car swept into the NIDS seventeenth floor platform, which was one floor beneath the surface. Albee joined the rest of the morning's arrivals as they spilled out into the main lobby. Before stepping into one of the ten available clear-view lifts, he grabbed a copy of the daily newspaper off the stack by the lift door. "Seven, please!" The indicator for his level lit up. He nodded to his fellow passengers, tucked the paper under his arm, and waited for the door to close. The lift descended.

Well-lit, realistic depictions of various office interiors floated by. The dioramas were designed to immerse the NIDS employee in an environment conducive to the daily tasks ahead.

A focused employee is a motivated employee, and a motivated employee knows exactly what is expected of them, and then some.

Level Seven. Albee stepped out.

"Good morning, Gala."

"Good morning, Albee."

"Good morning, Rav."

"Good morning, Albee."

There was not much else to say. In Norum, the weather never changed. Health was hardly an issue. There were simply good mornings and really good mornings. A really good morning was the day after a really good evening or in anticipation of a potentially really good evening. And a really good evening usually followed a really good day. Overall,

things were quite good.

On Albee's desk sat the breakfast he had ordered the night before, delivered just moments before his arrival. Two eggs, easy over, two soybeef links, two slices of toast -- all still pleasantly warm; and a glass of chilled orange juice, just the way he liked it. As he ate, he reviewed the proposed changes to the East Quarter's large Public Recreational Gym, or PRG. He had a mid-morning appointment onsite with redevelopers to discuss the changes. When the time came for the meeting, he took Rav with him as a second set of eyes.

#

The East Quarter of Norum looked pretty much the same as the North Quarter, only farther east. Although some sections of the North Quarter were farther east than some sections of the East Quarter, and some sections of the East Quarter were farther north than some sections of the North Quarter, and the same could be said for the South and West quarters of the city. Norum was a circular city, each quarter shaped like the wedge of a pie. Also, much like a pie, the city was also slightly crowned in the middle. The city was so large, however, that the bend of its streets was hardly noticeable. Only as one approached the city's center, where the government buildings appeared taller than the rest, was the curve of Norum's underlying geography apparent. As such, the very nature of the city's design made it virtually impossible to get lost, a design proposed by the very first ergoarchitects, an occupational lineage to which Albee proudly belonged.

The Public Recreational Gym was a large complex that spread beneath several city streets. Its two-story surface pavilion provided a quiet sunny location to read a book, sit with a cold drink, relax and enjoy the moment, or to conduct a business meeting. It was here that Albee and Rav met the two re-developers, Brandt and Sethe. They spread their plans on one of the many circular tables that also, with the press of a button, doubled as a 3-D imager.

"Smoother surfaces mean fewer lines, and fewer lines mean --"

"The illusion of empty space," said Albee.

Rav and the two redevelopers looked at Albee. Brandt looked to his partner for understanding. "Illusion?"

"Yes," said Albee. "We are creating illusions to induce calm, to reduce stress, to direct the collective mind toward the space's overall intent. In this instance, a spectator-friendly sports stadium."

"We don't consider 'illusion' as part of the equation," said Brandt.

"Our plans are for the betterment of the overall experience," said Sethe.

"The term 'illusion' is too closely partnered with the term 'dream,' and, as you know, we gave up dreaming long ago."

"Because it fostered jealousy and hatred."

"And an overall dissatisfaction with our working reality."

Brandt and Sethe talked as if speaking from the same mind.

Albee didn't know what to say. He felt embarrassed. He had stepped into a territory of thought that was socially forbidden.

"Of course, you're right," said Albee. "It was a poor choice of words. Fewer lines mean fewer points of interest, and fewer points of interest mean less detail to consider."

The two redevelopers nodded. "So you approve then?"

"Without reservation."

They shook hands and parted company.

#

In the station lobby, Albee excused himself to go to the restroom. He needed a moment to collect his thoughts, and once collected, rearrange them until they were once again properly aligned. He couldn't explain it but, like a subtle design flaw in an otherwise perfectly realized concept, something felt...off. As he stood in one of the privacy stalls, a person walked in and stood in the stall next to his, even though there were several other, more distant, more private, empty stalls to choose from.

"I overheard your conversation," a voice said.

Albee had never experienced anyone talking to him while standing in a privacy stall. The concept of a privacy stall was fully understood by everyone. It was private! Albee at first refused to respond.

"There's something in the water." The voice was low and its timber rumbled the floor beneath Albee's feet.

"Excuse me, what did you say?"

Silence. For a moment, Albee had the distinct impression that he was still alone.

"There are chemicals in the water that keep us from dreaming."

Albee was close to finishing up. "Wait, who are you? I need to talk to you?" There was a panic in Albee's chest he had never felt before. When he stepped away from his stall, the next stall was empty. The urinal flushed automatically, drowning out the sound of footsteps leaving the restroom. Albee rushed out into the station lobby --

-- into the lunchtime crowd. Rav leaned against an information kiosk. He straightened up. "Is there a problem?"

Albee glanced around the station hoping to catch a glimpse of a man who matched the voice he had heard, but nothing appeared out of the ordinary.

"No, no problem. I'm just not myself today."

Rav looked at him strangely.

"Would you like to stop for something to eat?" Albee offered. He needed to move on and forget what had just happened.

Rav grinned. "I pick, you pay?"

Albee nodded.

They boarded the next car that floated in from the South heading North.

#

At lunch, while Rav talked about relative dimensions as applied to perfecting the ultimate interior landscape, Albee stared at the tall glass of water sitting before him. Tall glasses of water sat on every table in the restaurant. People drank and sipped and absent-mindedly ran their fingers down the glasses. Albee wondered just how much water he drank on a given day, in coffee and in juices, in dehydrated soups. As Rav continued to talk, Albee silently reprimanded himself for once again skirting the territory of forbidden thought.

Forbidden thoughts are hidden thoughts, and hidden thoughts are hiding for a reason.

Lunch ended, and though he was thirsty, Albee decided not to drink.

#

The rest of the afternoon was relatively uneventful.

When Albee arrived home, he ate a small meal of asparagus tips, potatoes, and toast. He didn't boil the potatoes, using the autosteamer instead. He tried to read. *The Partiality to Spatiality: The Ultimate Guide to Ergodesign.* Another in a series of texts published by Norum University Press. But as darkness fell he could no longer keep his eyes open. At last, he climbed into bed and turned off the light.

At some point during the night a rumble crept down into his sleep, a rumble very much like the rumble he felt in the restroom earlier that day, only louder. It shook the dead landscape inside his head, and with a jumpstart of his heart, his eyes flashed open and he stared into the dark.

Could this be a dream? he thought, his heart racing.

But how would he know? The dark he now stared into looked the same as the dark he saw when he first slipped into bed and closed his eyes.

Maybe I'm dreaming I'm awake? he posed.

But the probability of even posing that question somehow proved the question untrue.

And while he was posing and positing, the rumble of his thoughts pulled him back down under the cover of unconsciousness, and he didn't wake again until his usual morning wake up time, the rumble forgotten.

He climbed out of bed, shuffled into the kitchen, and pulled a glass from the cupboard, but when he opened the refrigerator for his usual morning orange juice, he hesitated. Something skittered and danced in his stomach. He placed the empty glass back onto the cupboard shelf.

That's odd, he thought, moving on to the next morning duty.

He stepped into the shower. But when he reached for the faucets, his hand trembled.

The touch of water on the skin means something horrible might get in.

His fingers retreated. The showerhead appeared as if it were about to spew something unimaginable. He decided to skip his daily shower. He dressed instead and left for work.

A busy mind is a fruitful mind, and a fruitful mind means no time wasted on dead-ended endeavors.

But unlike every other day, when Albee stepped out onto the clean cobblestones

POLLUTO

of the city street and he looked up into the perfect sky, the sky appeared not quite as perfect as he recalled. The great expanse of blue now appeared awash in subtle shades of lighter blue and darker blue, a nearly imperceptible patchwork of overlapping spots and splotches.

Albee gazed at the buildings up and down the street. Their usual soft, soothing shapes and colors now resembled cardboard cutouts, like one of the miniature 3-D models on his office desk only scaled to size and repeated over and over in a crude semblance of reality. It wasn't until he saw the same aspect reflected in the murals painted on the tube tunnel walls that he began to question his perception of these things. Was the city's beauty fading? Or was he seeing the city with a critical eye for the first time in his life?

When he arrived at the office he asked Gala.

"Gala, did you notice anything different about the sky today?"

Gala's clear blue eyes gazed up at him. "It was beautiful," she said. "Why do you ask?"

Albee eyed the glass of water that sat on her desk. In fact, Gala always had a tall glass of water sitting within arm's reach. She reached for it just then and drank several gulps.

"Of course, Gala, you're right. The sky is beautiful. Everything is beautiful. How can it not be?" Albee spun a pirouette, his arms flung wide.

Gala watched him, the expression on her face condensing into one of genuine concern. "Is there a problem?"

"No, no problem. But don't you think it strange that nobody in all of Norum asks 'Is there anything wrong'?" Albee continued to spin. "Don't you see, Gala? A problem implies there is a solution. The word 'wrong' implies something is not right. Like the sky this morning. Like that glass of wa-

ter you are unable to detach yourself from. Problem? Oh, no...no problem at all. But something is...indeed...quite...WRONG!"

Albee stopped spinning and clung to the reception desk. The room continued to spin. He quickly staggered off to his office before Gala could see the look on his face. He didn't know what the look looked like but if it looked the way it felt then he was sure it was something he didn't want anyone else to see.

He sat at his desk while the room slowly ground to a halt.

He stared at the PRG designs in front of him.

He checked his schedule.

He quickly gathered the designs and stuffed them into his briefcase and left. He passed Rav on his way to the station. "I'll be back," he called over his shoulder, not sure if he would be or not.

#

The tube car floated toward the East Quarter. Albee stared at the mock cityscape as it passed by, as if witnessing it for the first time. He now noticed the imperfections: an off-angle rooftop here, a misaligned stretch of cobblestone there. Just how old the paintings were was a mystery. It was rumored the paintings were there before the city was even built and the builders simply copied what they saw underground.

Several passengers eyed Albee from across the aisle. Papers jutted from the briefcase he held. Albee caught a glimpse of his reflection in the window glass and saw that his hair was uncombed, his face smudged with dirt. He ran his fingers across his chin and realized he hadn't shaved.

#

At the East Quarter's Public Recreational

Gym, Albee rode the lift up to the pavilion and sat at the table where the meeting was held the day before. He waited. He didn't know exactly what he was waiting for. He hoped it would come to him, whatever it was.

People came and went. The daylight brightened then dimmed again. At one point, Albee walked over to the tall glass windows that looked out toward the eastern edge of the city. The Wasteland loomed like the edge of the world. The Wasteland could be seen from any second story window. It wrapped itself around Norum like a vast black apron as far as the eye could see.

Albee grew very thirsty. His head pounded. A sickening nausea crept down from his head into his stomach. As the afternoon waned, he decided he needed to go home. As he stood on the PRG station platform waiting to board a westbound car, a voice called to him.

"Excuse me, sir, you dropped this."

Albee turned and was met by a disheveled-looking man. The man's eyes were underscored with dark circles and his face was unshaven. The man handed him a sheet of paper that had apparently fallen from Albee's briefcase.

"Thank you," said Albee, trying to decide whether he should be repulsed or not. He stuffed the sheet in with the rest of the papers and boarded the car. The man did not get on. In fact, as the car pulled away, Albee looked for the man but the man appeared to have vanished from the station platform as completely as an unpleasant smell disappeared into a ventilation duct.

Under the tunnel's version of Norum's bright blue sky Albee pulled out the sheet of paper the man had given him. Instead of a design sketch, there were three short handwritten sentences.

Eat bananas. Their skin is thick. The water doesn't penetrate.

Albee quickly folded the note and stuffed it back into the briefcase before anyone on the car could see.

Random thoughts are speechless thoughts, and speechless thoughts are better left unspoken.

#

Three messages awaited Albee when he arrived home. "Play messages," he commanded. The sculptured messaging device sitting on the entry table glowed with a soft blue light. The first message was from Gala. The second was from Rav. The third was from a Doctor Restig at the Office of Medical Practioners, or OOMP. The first two calls warned him about the third call. Albee set aside the bag of bananas he had purchased on his way home. "Respond. Doctor Restig." After two beeps, a deep emotive voice came through the sculpture's tiny speaker.

"Hello, Albee, this is Doctor Restig. How are we feeling today?"

"Good." Tiny blips registered Albee's response.

"That's great to hear. The reason I'm calling is we received a report about your recent behavior."

"A report?" More blips.

"Yes. The report states that your words and actions have been inconsistent with expected societal norms. Is this true?"

Inconsistent with expected societal norms? Someone on the tube car must have reported him. Or perhaps it was Brandt and Sethe from the other day. Or Gala...

"Should I repeat the question?" the voice that was Dr. Restig said.

"No," said Albee. "I just don't know how to answer the question."

The blips sounded like tiny bubbles surfacing in a thick fluid. Albee wondered if that was how the brain worked: thoughts bubbling up and breaking the surface, waiting their turn to be expressed. What happened when too many bubbles went unexpressed?

"The report states you left work and did not return?"

"Yes, I had a headache and needed to go home," said Albee.

"Have you been sleeping well?

"Yes, I'm sleeping fine. A restful sleep is a blissful sleep." Albee didn't know why he needed to lie.

"That's great to hear, Albee. Eating well?"

"Good food, good drink. Oh, boy, let's eat."

There was a pause, followed by more blips.

"Bowel movements?"

"Clean as a whistle."

There came a series of rapid blips and a couple of beeps, followed by what sounded like a burp.

"I'm scheduling an appointment for you for tomorrow. Call me first thing in the morning and we'll set up a time. Sleep well, Albee."

#

Albee didn't sleep well that night. In fact, he didn't sleep at all. He lay in bed, staring into the dark, waiting for sleep to come to him. But his mind raced. Thoughts filled his head. He could almost hear them inside his skull bubbling to the surface with tiny pops.

Amid the pops, he heard a rumble, and the sound of it triggered a memory from the night before when he thought he had been dreaming.

What makes you think this isn't also a dream?

Albee considered this.

Maybe you've fallen asleep without even knowing it? After all, when do we really know when we fall off to sleep? And isn't it odd that we use the term "fall," as if sleep

were a thing like a black pool or an empty void we fall into when our consciousness leaves us? Where do we go?

If Albee had to guess he would have guessed he was now dreaming due to the rambling nature of his thoughts.

But isn't that what dreams are, after all, disjointed bits of the real and the imagined combined to form an interesting yet ultimately meaningless shadow play?

But that wouldn't explain the rumble he continued to feel and hear. The noise traveled through the floor, through the legs of his bed, into the bed's firm mattress, into his muscles and bones. The rumble grew louder and deeper with each moment he spent wondering, his thoughts bubbling. There was only one way to prove which was true. Get up, he told himself. Get up out of bed and see what it is! And he did just that.

He sat up in the dark.

It was as if a sheer black hood had been pulled from his face. The darkness of sleep was replaced by the darkness of his bedroom. The air coated him with a dangerous, naked frisson. He reached for his robe.

He opted not to turn on a light, navigating instead through his living quarters using only his memory and his sense of touch, careful not to stub his toe in the process. He followed the rumbling sound to the front door. There, the look-out lens gleamed like a watery eye. He put his own eye to it and peered out.

The cobblestone street and the long row of apartments and shops standing tightly and neatly on the opposite side were bathed in darkness. All except for a shopkeeper's light here and there casting thumbnails of yellow. Albee saw nothing out of the ordinary, until something bright began to glow at the end of the street.

Albee strained to see what it was. The glow grew brighter, and even when what produced the light came into view Albee could not believe what he saw.

A truck. A very large truck. Its squat body, constructed of oddly-shaped plates like pieces of a puzzle welded haphazardly together, filled the street from sidewalk to sidewalk. It came rolling up the cobblestones, its single white spot like a cyclopean eye sweeping from one side of the street to the other. And, perhaps most disturbing of all, there was a man running in front of the truck, desperately trying to escape its slow, impending pursuit.

Albee watched as the man zigged and then zagged. At one point, the man stumbled to the cobbles and crawled on all fours before scrambling to his feet again. Albee watched as if in a dream, partly removed due to the protective nature of the look-out lens, as the man homed in on his apartment as if possessed with the ability to sense being watched, and collapsed on Albee's doorstep with a heavy thump.

The truck continued to roll, the rumble now shaking the entire building. A knock came at the base of Albee's door just then, and a voice that sounded eerily familiar shouted, "Wake up!"

Albee reached for the knob on the door -- he wanted to show the man he was awake, that this wasn't some horrible dream they both shared -- but his muscles seized, preventing him from turning the knob.

If this isn't a dream then what is it?

Before Albee could decide, the truck's spotlight swept across the cobblestones and pinned the running man to the doorstep with its beam. Light entered the look-out lens, momentarily blinding Albee. But the light was suddenly blocked when the man on his doorstep stood. Albee once again peered into the lens. When he did, the man turned to face him. The man stared at Albee and Albee stared at him, their eyes only inches apart. "Run!" the man screamed before scrambling out of sight, the truck rumbling after.

Albee strained to watch him go. He noticed the man's clothing was torn and soiled. His hair was knotted and curled, his face embedded with grime, but in that moment of light Albee recognized him as the man from the station platform at the East Quarter's city gym, the same man who had whispered to him in the bathroom stall and warned him about the city's water.

#

Albee sat in his robe in the dark with his back against the apartment door for quite some time. Like clockwork, every half hour a truck rolled by, sweeping the streets, making sure they were clean and empty. Albee wondered just how many trucks there were circling the city at night.

An unventured life is a sheltered life, and a sheltered life is a life not worth living.

With enough night left till morning, Albee created a backpack using a pillowcase, two belts and a length of shoelace, and stuffed it with clothing and enough food for two days, and very little water. No one knew what lay beyond the walls of Norum in the territory known only as the Wasteland. Perhaps it was a place, like death, once entered, one could not return from. Albee was willing to take that chance.

After the next truck passed, Albee stepped out onto the cobblestone street and, as instructed, ran.

As an ergoarchitect he knew the city's design well. He knew where the emergency entry points to the city's underground were located. He knew where the city's power generator was housed. He also knew that where the quarters of the city met there was a narrow section of outer wall that didn't meet. The two walls ran past each other, allowing for the expansion and contraction of the city as it breathed over time. The west-north expansion section was not far from his apartment.

He ran past shops and markets and living quarters, past the unlit tube entrance, weaving his way toward the city's outer rim. He listened for rumbles in the night, hiding whenever he heard an errant sound, his heart hammering in his chest. When at last he reached the spot where the west and north quarters met, cleverly masked at the back end of an alley between two shops, he took a moment to catch his breath. In the scant light, he inspected the overlap. To his dismay the gap was no wider than his fist, clearly not wide enough for him to squeeze through. In fact, the air at the other end of the gap was so black, he had to wonder if he was peering into nothing but an empty void. But this became the least of his concerns as there came a sudden rumbling beneath his feet.

The rumble quickly gathered in volume and a spotlight pinned him to the alley's back wall. A truck the same dimensions as all the other trucks he had seen blocked the alley's entrance some forty feet away. The alley was too narrow for the truck to enter, and Albee was too afraid to move. Albee thought they were at an impasse, until a panel opened in the truck's front plate, and a tongue-like appendage shot toward him.

Albee flattened his body against the alley's sidewall. The tongue missed him by inches, hitting the bricks with a sticky wet slap. The tongue then recoiled in preparation for another try, but Albee decided it was best not to wait around.

Using the alley's walls as leverage, his feet on one side, his hands on the other, Albee climbed the space between the two buildings. When he reached the top, the truck's tongue shot toward him again, this time hitting him in the chest. Instead of reeling him in, however, the blow knocked him over the lip of the wall. For a moment, empty air was all that surrounded him before the ground met him hard and knocked the breath from his lungs.

A numbing quiet descended as Albee lay face down in the dark. The smell of dirt entered his nostrils. He lifted his head. The city wall loomed above him, its rim glowing softly with city light. He heard the truck's muffled rumble fade as it continued on its nightly sweep.

Albee sat up. He inspected his body for injuries and found none. Slowly, he got to his feet and readjusted his backpack. He gazed up at the wall again and something tugged in his chest. There was only one option for him now. He turned away from the city and began walking.

#

Eventually morning arrived to the city; however, the sky directly over Albee remained dark. Albee, now miles away, witnessed the full beauty of Norum as it rose like an island oasis amid the endless black sea of the Wasteland. Above the ringed tiers of buildings a circular sky glowed. The artificial light limned the top of the city's outer wall. It was a beautiful city. It was the only city its citizens had ever known. But it was far from perfect.

There had to be something beyond the Wasteland, something beyond the dark.

With the city at his back acting as his compass, Albee continued on with the hope of finding that something. Or perhaps of something finding him.

DU BOIS BEFORE ACCRA
AHIMSA TIMOTEO BODHRÁN

Talented Tibetan Tenth. Traveler. Who in your family doesn't have a degree?

The places you feel comfortable in are the places my family built and cleaned.
You have not worked before, are unfamiliar with what it means to have a job.

Your family didn't want to spoil your education.

My hands known floors, dishes, pots and pans, the cleaning of kennels, stretch
of garbage latex against skin, lick me with that, wooden splinters of mops, badge
of security, smell of dogshit and urine, bleach.

Perhaps you will see homelands I have never known.
Perhaps you will receive passport stamps from them in languages I cannot read.

ROUGH
AHIMSA TIMOTEO BODHRÁN

we sniff salts to move us back into consciousness.
give me the recipe for ammonium carbonate.
too rough, you said, in my hands,
even in bed too eager, left you sore where you didn't want to be.
this baby born without lotion.
yours was a high class mixing.
mine, ghettos y barrios, people who'd never flown in a plane,
only knew this land. yours, a diplomat's diaspora.
tus padres: modelos. your six languages? lose count, stumble with my few.
i trade you mango-wet kisses by the projects.
roaches scatter.
you see the world laid out wide before you.
i see stones in the path, am checked for weapons at the gate.
you float on through, emptied oysters at your lips,
pearls and abalone around your neck.
my soon-to-be-revoked passport.
you are always arriving, and i always waiting for departure.
comment on my way of eating,
my inarticulate manner of speech.
you shift red to my blue at this station, Doppler effect.
hurtle life. i am surprised our trains do not collide.

ON THE RECYCLING DAY:
A RECURSIVE POEM
CHANGMING YUAN

One neighbor took out a blue box
Full of cat skulls and dog legs
Rather than glass or plastic bottles

Another carries out a yellow bag
Containing human bones, mostly children's
Instead of magazines or paper products

A third pushed out a green bin
Filled with failed evils and devils
Where there should be leaves and twigs

Behind every house in a neighboring back alley
The garbage truck is placing a big time bomb

EPILOGUE: A PARALLEL POEM
CHANGMING YUAN

Just as both God and Devil are man's incarnation, so are Heaven and Hell both man's construction.

1

From the front yard of a melodious morning
From the busy road of a sweet Saturday
From the moist corner of a heavy march

From the back lane of pale winter
We have come, here and now, all gathering
In big crowds gathering in big crowds
Gathering in ever-bigger crowds gathering
For the boat to cross the wide wild waters
Before the fairy ferry is fated to fall
Under our feet too heavy with earthy mud

You may well hate Charon
But you cannot help feeling envious:
That business of carrying the diseased
Across the River Styx is ever so prosperous
The only monopoly in the entire universe
That has a market share
Larger than the market itself
Daydreaming, on this side
Of the river, how you might wish
To be an entrepreneur like him
A success American dreamer

Flying between sea and sky
Between day and night
Amid heavenly or oceanic blue
I lost all my references
To any timed space
Or a localized time
Except the non-stop snorting
Of a stranger neighbor

Then, beyond the snorts rising here
And more looming there
I see tigers, lions, leopards
And other kinds of hunger-throated predators
Darting out of every passenger's heart
Running amuck around us
As if released from a huge cage
As if in a dreamland

CHOPPY STICKY CHOPSTICKS
CHANGMING YUAN

Yes, yes, yeah, we are simply too barbaric
To enjoy the delicacy of raw snails or oysters
With steel forks and knives

But we are certainly civilized enough to chop
To stick cats, dogs, snakes, frogs
Ants, rats, pupae, anything that moves
With more than one leg, and we love
To eat pig ears, cow tongues, goat penises
Shark fins, sparrow nests, chicken hearts
Duck feet, and all other living corpses inside out
With our mouths open from ear to ear
Chewing plants as noisily as we like
Sucking noodles and soup like pigs
Yeah, we are what we eat, how we eat
When, where and why we eat

What I want to say, pal, is this simple fact:
Chopping and sticking makes our fingers more adept
Just as chopsticks make us fitter to survive and succeed
More important, they have turned us from carnivores to herbivores
Though we are still more primitive than you fork users and knife wavers

PROGRAMMING
CHANGMING YUAN

With a single mouse click
The programmer vanishes
Into the plasma waves
Of the screen, with another key-hit

The computer flies away
Into the depth of the cyberspace
Like the legendary yellow crane

I was the one sitting there
In the coffin-like attic, trying
To program the destinies of
Both man and god

MORNING MISTS

CHANGMING YUAN

Unable to endure the constant burning in hell
The suffering souls finally find their ways
Out of the topsoil, trying
To rise together
With the summer sun

Yet they are dispersed
By its very first rays
Into the darkest moment of last night
Where the ghosts of the newly dead, the invisible
Linger on, staring at one another
No one knows how many of them
Were still holding their authentic
Human shapes, how many of them
Became deformed, agonizing
Between pools of stinking blood
And piles of rotten flesh

CLEAN UP
DAVE MIGMAN

S633/98 b Team A 06.15am (L.T)

WORKCAM:

Door hatch (hydraulic biomech portal serial no.575757577533000) opened, the party entered (all types - mode 33657), and progressed through the bolt lock area (pause rate; *slacking*), sealing the doors behind them. They then proceeded towards Sector 779xb (lit by diffuse tactical lighting systems see sub notes factory policy, lighting effects). Following main route 12.

The pipes trailing the corridor looked like ancient earth armour, banded into one continuous appendage, a strange serpent gleaming coldly in the frosty light.

Party changed into their standard issue protective gowning as supplied by Galglo Corp TM when they entered the bolt-lock (in adherence to Co. Policy, Health and Safety in Workplace Manual, section 17 article 456).

They moved slowly up the tunnel, indistinguishable from one another in their white suits, save Pritt who had four Fezzbacks tracking by his side. Two of the others carried large, lumpy apparatus in their hands, fusion burners, their tapering ends fitted with funnel-like translucent filters.

It is noted that two men (Faldrain and Hock) were not carrying their burners in accordance to safety procedure SAW 78001 - 'Proper Usage Of Cleaning Equipment' Section six, paragraph sixteen 'Handling Tools'. This being duly noted their files will be sent for further assessment. (Suggest they will have to revisit the safety bureau again).

The crew reached the first intersection of the tunnel. Alliston called out 'Left!' and they all filed in his wake. This corridor was their undertaking for the next day. Dusting down all exposed pipes, cables and fittings. Then, using tiny void pods to suck up dust particles. Anomalies were to be reported and test samples collected before incineration.

The cam hovered above them as each man dispersed along the corridor to carry out his appropriated task. Responding to a new series of instructions from head office the pod, no bigger than a fingernail, swivelled suddenly. Soundlessly it floated down the corridor, gaining velocity once it exited from the lock gate. This tunnel was wide enough to handle the transports and trolleys that took raw materials to the Core Gate, seven kilometres further down. Only empty trolleys returned from the core and it was with them that the cambot flew. Gathering more velocity as complex machinations flickered through miniscule circuitry - a secret dialogue only itself and its controller knew about.

POLLUTO

S633/98 b team A 09.45 (L.T)

GRETSEL:

One time I thought, 'this is it.' I remember finishing SchoolCorp and thinking 'I'm set now. I have nothing to worry about. The company will look after me' and if I was productive I would get a fatherly pat on the back. Those days are gone. I must have been a fool to believe all that. To think the company would protect me. That it cared. Those days are gone.

The haze cuts us off from our past. We eat here, sleep here, work here, shit here, piss here, breathe, talk, think, make friends and enemies here. It's a blur. My life, thirty-six years of the same motions with only Trayia to break the monotony of working life. Twenty two years in the house of haze... twenty two years cleaning these systems... I never really thought of it like that!

I remember the first time I sat with Trayia. By the huge windows of the central lobby, back on the Spiral. The cosmos was a scatter of diamonds on a board of cadmium black. I held her hand and neither of us spoke. There were no brash stories for the boys the next day. No boasting because I could not raise a lie when my heart felt so full. When I held her hand that day it was as if I had awoken from a slumber. I fell in love. Real love. Glorious love. Not the limpid lie they sell us on the holo-discs. I wanted her like no other. I wanted to love her and show her - ME! I fell into sweetness and bliss. Every day the last few hours of work would drag monotonously, my mind clouded with her image, the memory of her touch...

"Gretsel, quit dreaming! This is a workplace, not a retirement home. Come on put some elbow into it!"

Alliston!

Picture. Picture... nope. No good. That swine has gone and destroyed any chance of sweet memory. Homage to grace. Duster in my hands. This circus act, the performance of twenty-two years.

Arm aches. Smooth duster along pipes, down the back, warm, unyielding, fixed to the fabric of this hulk. Pile of junk. Still it amazes me how the dust gets in here, not much, in fact I hardly see any, but its there, that's what they tell us. Maybe it comes off our gowns. Now that's a depressing thought. Cleaning up after ourselves. Harrowing. Twenty two years.

Alliston answers to Miscous. Misshapen, miserable Miscous. Some woman, that's for sure. At least she hardly comes visit. Her sole purpose is to chastise the crews, she brings such tidings as: 'we've been reviewing the cam again and we believe there is much room for improvement.' Words like 'efficiency', 'job optimism' and 'productive satisfaction' roll off her swollen tongue like fat flies. She has a talent, that's for sure; the great skill of wearing a fake smile whilst she disciplines our sorry hides.

But I've saved. I've worked my back into a permanent stoop, all these years, saving. Hardly go out. Stay clean. Years of planning, years of biding my time. We'll make it Trayia, we'll make it you and I.

S633/98 b Team A 09.54 (L.T)

GOOSH:

The void pod whispers, sups up motes of dust like snow. Like the picture of snow in the holo-box. WerBitz, great device, look at the way it sups it all up. Leaves a sparkling trail, gleaming metal pipes. Like highways. Like pictures of old highways. Vruum, up it goes. Little motes. Good suction, great action, so light, much better than those crappy Redlars. Too bloody heavy those things. This one though, shiny, tough, unbreakable case, incinerates the dust in there, crackles it all up.

More there, I see ya, I see ya, can't escape old Goosh. Dust Master General, that's me. I sup it all up-up-pup-pup. Every little bit. Not like some of the others. No pride some of them. No care, dedication, attention to detail, job optimism. You must clean behind every pipe, even the wire casing, these are the arteries that lead to the heart of the factory. Even when you can't see it the dust is there! Make it clean-clean-clean.

S633/98 b Team A 12.15 (L.T)

HOCK:

I'm starving. I was hungry at ten. That sonofabitch would only let us have a brief rest. 'Put your tools down' as if he was doing us a big favour 'we won't get to main canteen for today.' Which translates as number five canteen. Yesterday's stale offerings. Oh well fifteen minutes to go.

Check out old Gretsel. What's he like? Waddling around like that! He's all right though, he is, not like this fool working with me. Faldrain. What a freak. Weird bastard gets right on my main nerve. Why doesn't he speak to me? He never has anything to say. He's worked with us two months now and hardly a word. Maybe he thinks he's above us. Doesn't even join in with break-time banter. Freak. He just sits with one of those old-fashioned book cards... *reading - what is the point of reading*? Where's the pleasure in that? It's not as though he's an old codger like Gretsel either, he's in his early twenties!

Reading! I tried to talk to him about Ad-news or Clep Sip 9 (surely everyone watches those shows?) but he just grunted at me, didn't even lift his eyes from the card.

Gretsel's all right though. Sound old bloke. Pritt and Est are all right as well, though Est can be a pain sometimes. Alliston's just a slimy bastard.

There's more of that gunge. Well, I'll just burn you away my friend. Oops! Forgot to sample that one. Oh well, Alliston never saw a thing.

"There's more of that slime there Faldrain."

You weirdo.

"I know, I saw it before. Get it next."

Scary fruitcake bastard.

"Yeah you do that."

"Hey Hock!"

Who the... oh Goosh.

"What are you after Goosh?"

"You keep missing patches of Temp. I can't help but notice because when you miss it my job is near impossible."

"So?"

"I have to follow after you Hock. Temp is impossible to move with the pod and it gets the dusters all sticky and clogs up the scrapers. If you were more observant you wouldn't leave so much on the pipes."

"What? You saying I can't do my job?"

"I wouldn't go so far as to say that; maybe you lack a little enthusiasm."

"You've got a nerve you little prick. Why don't you tackle Faldrain, he's working here too?"

"Yes but he's working the left wall, you're on the right, his is clean, yours isn't."

"What's going on down here? Is it lunchtime? No, you've still five minutes left!"

Alliston! Goosh and his big mouth. What's this got to do with Alliston anyway? Who does he think he is? TO HELL WITH THIS!

"Are you my boss?"

"Pardon?"

That knocked the self righteous smile from his face.

"I asked if you are my boss? Do you hold a rank of seniority over me? No, you're just the self-designated team leader so shut your mouth or I swear I'll knock you into next week!"

I'm not joking. THEY'LL BE SCRAPING HIM OFf THE WALLS!

"Wha…? That's it Hock. I'm submitting a report to Miscous tonight. She'll suspend you for that!"

"Why you little…"

"Whoa! Break it up. Hock calm yourself. It's not worth it. Come on! Stand down!"

Gretsel holding me back; Christ he's some grip, squeezing my arm. Back down. Swallow pride. He's right. Calm down.

Think I've messed up there. Suspension.

"In fact I'm going straight to the office. You'll be out by tomorrow; no one talks to me in that manner. Addressing me like that!"

"Shut up Alliston"

"What…?"

Gretsel stepping forward, pushing me back, hand on my shoulder, Est. Shaking his head, can't see his face.

"I said that as politely as I can manage, so just drop it Alliston."

"He threatened me with violence, you all heard. That's not tolerable behaviour in the workplace."

"I'll come round to your Underside apartment and beat you to a pulp!"

"Can it Hock! You don't do yourself any favours!"

Gretsel frowning at me.

"Listen Alliston, you don't have many allies here, you know it."

All eyes on Goosh. I'm sure he just shrank. Cringing little worm.

"What about it Goosh? Did you see anything? Well, I'm sure by the end of the day Goosh will have seen nothing like the rest of us."

"But the cam…"

"Your little spying friend rushed off some time ago; you've no back up Alliston. We didn't see anything and by five o'clock neither will your little pet Goosh."

Ha! that got him. Gretsel you're some guy. You might be an ugly old sod but I could almost kiss your sunken old cheeks. Goosh's face, there's a holo-freeze! Check him out. Go on, scurry away, like the rat you really are!

"Time for lunch then!" Est laughing. Always laughing. Jackal laughter.

S633/98 b Team A 12.29 (L.T)

FALDRAIN:

Tension graven in faces. Alliston's defeat. Gretsel's fiery glare. Hock squaring up, like a great chunk of clothed meat. Beneath the breather I think Alliston's lips are quivering. It's all in the eyes. In these suits you mark a man down through his eyes. The confrontation has taken events somewhere, bottled emotions have been released; conflict, things get done. I must remember that.

Our eyes, our height and shape define us here. Seven holy angels. Seven in white. A sacred number. The number of God. The colour of purity. Cleanliness. Once you peel off the layers we are unkempt and foul as any other, we wash, we scrub our hands till they are pink and the nails white. Our hair is kept short and trim. Facial hair is a no-no. Clean uniforms everyday, shower blast every morning, every night, sonic blast every week; but despite this our minds are filthy. Each of them has it's own disease. No one here is really pure. We are no angels, though looking at us you might be deceived.

Getting up now. Tools down. Check safety is on. Lunchtime. Corridor, warm air, pipes interlocking across the gentle arch of ceiling. Five minutes to canteen. Gate lock, hissing doors, slight delay between double screens. Stripping out of our gowns, the dark blue uniforms beneath. Into the corridor, gentle flow of regulated air. Sweat at base of spine cooling, it will feel like ice by the time we reach the canteen. No one speaking. Everyone lost in their own thoughts. Hock smiling. Gretsel's big old face down-turned ponderously. Alliston's furious.

I still don't know what they make here. What do they make? This place reminds me of corridor on Massel 6. Though that was wider and filled with jets of steam. Reminds me of hiding from the staff, Christoph and Malgy. Down in the ducts and the stairs I found the basement. The smell of age from the wooden crates I opened. Wood! Inside a package of aluminium foil, the treasure, the beautiful, most wonderful things I ever found - books. Hard bound, hard copy. How crisp each page, how refreshingly solid and real. The words stark and inviting. I spent long hours in a shell of silence, secrecy and oneness. Those pages have taught me many things.

S633/98 b Team A 13.04 (L.T)

GRETSEL:

…Trayia… so tired… tired of this sluggish pace… this tasteless mush that drips from these infernal machines… tired of the stupidity of these people… tired. Your eyes. Focus.

S633/98 b Team A   13.04 (L.T)

HOCK:

Mmm. not bad. Tasted worse. What did it say? Fried squid and cream potatoes. What's squid?

"Hey Gretsel, what's a squid?"

"Erm, sorry, what did you say?"

"What's squid? It says 'fried squid' but I don't know what a squid is. Tastes good though."

"It's some Earth thing isn't it?"

"It was a marine beast."

Wow! It speaks! "Mar-What?"

"It lived in the water. It was a kind of long, slimy creature and it had several tentacles sprouting from its face."

"You've just put me off it." He's gone all red. Freak. Has though, put me right off. "Slime, I clean that crap off tunnel walls, I'm not going to eat it!"

"I've heard they still breed them on Taurus."

"Well, there's not much left on Earth any longer."

"Course there is!"

"Whoa! Calm down boy." The freak will be giving lectures soon.

"What do you mean son?"

"Well.. it… you won't hear this on channel news, you won't find it in the links, but the Earth got so bad, so rotten that…"

"Faldrain, I'm not in the mood for lectures." Freak bugs me, talking so much.

S633/98 b Team A   13.07 (L.T)

GRETSEL:

"Shut it Mouth! Go on son, ignore him."

Poor kid's the colour of my soda pop. Sweating.

"Well the truth is that they said the earth was dying. It was overcrowded. There were too many people and so they built the hulks and shipped people out. It took many years of course; they did it in stages, faster and faster as technology moved on. This is how the colonies were established. Every one was told the Earth was dying, that it could no longer support them…"

"You understand anything this kid's saying?"

"I told you to shut your flapping trap!" What a pain Hock can be.

"It was polluted, but given time and the profits the companies acquired it was repaired.

That's where the leaders live now."

"The who?"

"The leaders, the company lords and their families. The elite. They live in paradise. It's beautiful down there."

"How do you know this kid?"

"I read about it in a book. It even seen holos."

Book? A real book? That's old history stuff.

"Books are very old son. You might see them in a museum; they're antiques."

"I saw them when I was younger, back on Massel 6. I…"

That's it, he's clammed up! He'll just stare at his plate, sit in a corner, read one of his digi books.

Paradise? What's he on about? Must be made up. Story like that. In fact he probably read a fictional book, thought it was real.

Poor kid. What is Massel 6, rings a bell?

Overcrowding… the companies?

S633/98 b Team A   13.11 (L.T)

HOCK:

What's his problem? Snapping at me like that and listening to that fruitcake. Asshole! He's up and down all day. One minute he's on my side, the next he tells me to shut it. What's eating him anyway? Been like this for a while now. Must be his wife giving him grief. He should keep her in line. Mine opens her mouth and I tell her close it or I will. She can leave. She's got her job, so it wouldn't be like I'd be leaving her stranded. Though Susan's all right. She's great in bed. She don't talk too much neither, which suits me fine. Couldn't stand one of them gossipy women. I bet Gretsel's wife is an old battle axe with a mouth on her like the garbage hatch of region 77, never closed and full of trash.

Can't eat that mush now, freak put me right off it. I ain't eating slime food, no way.

S633/98 b Team A   13.05 (L.T)

PRITT:

Where the…? WHERE THE HELL?

Wait… Hissing… Pipes… Steam?

What time is it? Christ on a stick! Five past. Those bastards have gone and left me - they forgot old Pritt

"Hear me you little swines. It's your fault. I thought you had the scent you little shits."

Thought they'd got a whiff of Glavvie. The peculiar scent of those little monsters. Smells like sweaty bodies and fish flavouring. Straining the leash. I went ages up the tunnel but no joy.

Is this the right tunnel? Yeah, sure it is. There's the stuff up ahead. Hock's burner. Straight on down to the lock gate. I'll make the canteen soon enough. Alliston. That sonofabitch. He should have come and found me. Could have bleeped me. Not fair I've missed...

Clang!

What was that?

Clang!

What the...? Down that auxiliary tunnel. Fezzbacks are freaking.

"Is it a Glavvie boy?"

What is he up to?

"Get from behind my legs, you idiot! You..."

"Hey who's down there?"

Got the creeps. Neck's crawling. What is this? I feel cold. Hot. I

"Hey who?"

CLANG

CLANG

CLANG

CLANG

Oh my god...

S633/98 b Team A   13.10 (L.T)

ALLISTON:

Pathetic, the lot of them. Save Goosh. I'll recommend him for the workload bonus. None of the rest though. And Gretsel will get the biggest shock of his life because I will report him. He can't bully me. Thinks he knows it all that one. Thinks that knowledge of the job comes with age, but look at where he is. He's been here for over twenty years. What a fool! How could he possibly be content with that? Forget it. Breathe deeply. Doctor Rembrace said breathe deeply when I feel the tension. Gretsel. He's talking to Faldrain about me I'll bet. Gretsel, you'll be off the payroll tomorrow. Why wasn't the cam there? Where did it go? Bad timing. Doesn't often go like that. Must be a reason. Control? Wonder what's up?

Breathe deeply. Aaaah.

Bloody hell! Where's Pritt? And Est? Don't tell me we've lost them? We've bloody lost them! They'll be hell to pay, Ohmygodohmygod.

Deep breath.

I'll have to contact control. No, I'll wait. Still forty minutes, they're probably on their way. What are they playing at? The idiots.

Breathe deeply.

S633/98 b Team A   13.13 (L.T)

GRETSEL:

Christ! He went pale. Wonder what spooked him. He's gone to the Comlink. Wonder what…

Ah! Est and Pritt. Well I imagine Pritt is chasing Glavvies; there's nothing new there. But Est… not like him to be late. If he's lost then he could be in trouble. Company never lets anyone but Alliston have a holo-map so they might have to send out search parties. Remember Glaston, was it Glaston? Yeah, sure, Glaston, he got lost, out-take. It was strange that, he must have stumbled into one of the extractors, minced him up real fine it did. So I heard anyway. Faldrain appeared in his place the next day.

S633/98 b Team A   13.17 (L.T)

ALLISTON:

WHAT THE!!!!!

S633/98 b Team A   13.17 (L.T)

PRITT:

Door opening, faces turning. Mouths open. Out of breath. Flustered.

"What in Hell's name do you think you're …"

"Quick, everybody come, it's Est!"

"What is it Pritt? Est? what's the matter?" Gretsel asking me anxiously.

"Now Pritt, this really isn't on. You know running like that is strictly forbidden in any part of the …"

"Oh shut up!"

"Pardon!"

"Shut it Alliston, just listen to the man will you?" Gretsel. Speak to him.

"I heard this noise. Then I saw him. Est. He was smashing up pipes and raging like a wild thing. I don't know what's up with him. He's gone crazy."

It was Est. His visor was steamed up, I heard him shouting. But his mic was out. His visor cracked. He was furious. And my Fezzbacks, shuddering like it was cold. And it was. The temperature hot, cold.

"My god. My god." Alliston's going to cry.

"We better go" says Gretsel. "The cambot is not around so we might have a chance to stop him. I want everybody to come with me."

"Gretsel, we left all our tools down there. Those burners can cause a bit of damage on full whack."

"Est was in an auxiliary tunnel nearby."

"Right let's go. Alliston, are you coming or are you going straight to control? Don't forget that you never reported them missing. Which, if I'm not mistaken, is a blatant disregard for protocol 168!

"All right. I know. I'm coming. Okay!"

That's told him. Good old Gretsel. What a man. That prat's quivering like a jelly. I can feel a smile breaking across my face. Part delight, part fear, and excitement. Must catch my breath.

S633/98 b Team A   13.30 (L.T)

FALDRAIN

Passing below the ribbed roof. Running. All of us running. If anyone spots us we're in for it. But it's quiet here now. Lunchtime. The cargo trollies whizz by, secured to different levels of automated trajectories. Gretsel's fast. Hock puffing and panting and cursing. Alliston flustered and white. Pritt, nervous but grinning. Groosh, looks scared.

"Gown up if you want, I don't have the time. I'm opening the seal, any of you guys want to change then do so. Up to yourselves." Gretsel pants.

"You can't go in there like that!" Alliston, screaming, hysterical.

Hissssss.

"I just did."

I'm with Gretsel.

"Faldrian are you insane!"

Hock pushing him out the way, stepping in behind me, a little shove. Doesn't like me I know. I don't like him. Pritt's in as well with his Fezzbacks straining on the leash. It's opening.

Hissss.

Faces at the little window. Steaming up the plasti-plex.

Smells like the tunnel. Smells clean.

"Don't worry,; this is intake. There's nothing in the air 'cept the dust of our gowns and our cleaning equipment. Come on."

Big warm hand on my shoulder. Gretsel's out of breath.

Funny he usually looks so harmless, but now his face is serious, brow furrowed, commanding.

"Let's go."

S633/98 b Team A   13.35 (L.T)

HOCK:

Gretsel's inside. Bloody idiot. Get caught doing that and you're out.

WHAT? And Faldrain following him like a shadow. Making me look like a chicken. TO HELL WITH THAT!

S633/98 b Team A   13.35 (L.T)

ALLISTON:

NONONONONONONONONONONONONONONO. No. They can't do that!
    Hock too! And Pritt darting after them. Bastards! I'm for it now. Breathe deeply. Assess
the situation. Right.
    "Gown up Goosh."

S633/98 b Team A   13.44 (L.T)

GRETSEL:

The burners, twisted and useless, the scubbers's plastiplex casing cracked, buckets and void
pods scattered around the corridor. What a mess.
    "Est?"
    "EST!" Hock's loud enough all right. He should have heard that.
    Silence.
    Where is he? "Where can he be?"
    What, wait, a noise. A distant clang. Muffled.
    "Up there."
    "What's that?" Hock. Up ahead, the passage is coated in shining crystals, like a growth
of mould.
    Ice. Like the giant freezers we used to clean in West Wing.
    "Hock, be careful, that's ice. It's slippery."
    "Ice? What's ice?" He's never seen ice; not many have.
    "It's what happens to moisture when it falls below zero degrees." Faldrain informs him.
    Crunching beneath our feet, fractured pipe up ahead. Got to be careful. It's cold right
here.
    Clang.
    There it is again. Keep moving. "Come on Hock!" Blocking my way with his big ugly
frame.
    "Oh Christ."
    What? "What? What is it?" Move damn you.
    "Est, now c'mon man, put that down, there's a good man."
    Hock darting forward, shouting.
    The lights just went out.

S633/98 b Team A 13.51 (L.T)

HOCK:

Gretsel keeps trying to shove past me. I want to get Est. If he's gone mental then Gretsel's hardly going to stop him. That ice is strange. I don't like it. Too bright, too bloody cold. And that freak, what is he, an encyclopaedia?

"Whoa!"

Est. Crouched, back towards us. What's he doing there? Hunched up like that. He's burned the floor away, reaching inside.

"Oh Christ. C'mon Est, put that down man."

The lights! Where's the goddamned lights?

"Est, you mad bastard what are you playing at?"

"Ah!"

S633/98 b Team A 13.50 (L.T)

AAAARRRRRGGGGGGHHHHHHHHHHOOOOOOWWWWWWWWWWWA
AAAARRRRRGGGGAAAAAAAARRRRRRRRRRHHHHHHHH
 Cleanflashlandsdesertsunspillingdriven into eachother suniseyeofgodnessmadnessclea-nallthehulkNarrrRROOOOOOOOOOOOOOOOO
 Back, pullswitch darknowbetter feelshapemanmustgetbyAAAAAARRRRRRRROO
OOOOOOOOOOOOOGGGGGAAAAAARRRRRRRRRRRRHHHHHHHHHHHHH-
HHHHHH

S633/98 b Team A   13.53 (L.T)

ALLISTON:

Noises up ahead, shouts! What the... I hate the dark!

"Goosh?" Can't even see him. Can't see anything!

"Yes Mr Alliston."

"I think we should go back; I'll hold on to you Goosh?"

"Yes Mr Alliston sir."

Phut phut phut.

What is that noise? someone running...

UUUMMPHHH!!

"Arrrkk!"

Something hit me. A person, must have been Est, shoved by me violently. Sure I heard him growling. The lights are back on. The others. Gretsel, Hock, Faldrain, Pritt, running this way. Gretsel looking at me. Hock smirking.

"Well, I guess he escaped."

"Yeah, but where to? Did he open the lock gate?"

Elbow sore as I pick myself up. My gown. I could be contaminated. We'll have to get checked, all of us. That's it, we're finished here. What a disaster!

"I think we should inform control." Gretsel must be insane. But he's right. There's nothing else we can do.

"Where's Goosh?"

"I heard him cry out, but I was pushed. I couldn't see."

"There he is, I see his feet. He's bleeding."

Goosh's thin legs. I'm moving out into the corridor to see him better. Blood around his head. Closer. A halo of crimson. He's so still. Unmoving. His head. I think I'm going to be sick.

S633/98 b Team A   14.00 (L.T)

FALDRAIN:

In one of the old books, there are pictures. Flat pictures of flowers. A type of vegetation that grew on Earth. Goosh's face reminds me of one of the pictures, a flower called a rose. I've never seen a dead man before. Alliston puking in the corridor. Gretsel's face as white as the tunnel walls. Hock staring, like me, transfixed.

What shall we do? Est has gone crazy. He could still be around.

Why did he go berserk?

"S633/98 b Team A" The cambot has returned. Now we're for it.

Alliston just fainted.

"S633/98 b Team A. Team member Est has been contaminated. You also are in danger. Report to the airlock immediately and await further instructions. These directives come directly from Controller Kald. Move there immediately and wait further orders."

"What about Est?" Gretsel. Angry now. "What do you mean contaminated. What about the body?"

"Do not touch the body. You may risk infection. I have been instructed to search the tunnels for Est.

No one has entered the airlock, so he must have disappeared into the auxiliary tunnels.

"Tag him, so they can send out the flush squad?" They'll kill him. No doubt about it. He's cost the factory a fortune. They'll have to shut down for a day or so to deal with the mess.

"How did he get infected?"

"Gretsel, I suggest to learn not to care. My report suggests that careless working procedures caused this mess."

Bot swinging in the air, zipping down the corridor. Gone.

Gretsel looking at me. Shaking his head. Turning and walking down the corridor.

"But Gretsel… you heard what it said."

S633/98 b Team A   14.12   (L.T)

GRETSEL:

No, there's something else. I feel it. Est's gone crazy… but why?

"HEY GRETSEL! Airlock's this way!" Fuck you Alliston.

"GRETSEL! Hey, where do you think you're going Hock? Stay there Faldrain. Right, that's it, you're all on report… I'm going straight to the top. You'll be out by tomorrow."

A shout, up ahead. Voices… it's the bot… and Est.

"Hear that?"

"Yeah. It's Est."

"What do we do?"

"Take a look." But be careful.

There! I see Est now. He's shouting at the bot. He looks crazy enough; maybe he is contaminated… but with what?

"Est, you hear me?"

Nope he's gone. What's he saying? I can't make it out.

"S633/98 b Team A return to the airlock immediately. A Flush squad will arrive imminently. You do not want to be here when they arrive."

Suddenly Est whips around. He doesn't look so mad. Just scared.

"Gretsel… they're going to kill me… they're gonna wipe me out… but I saw it…"

"Just calm yourself Est. What is it man?"

"Because of them." Pointing at the bot? Or beyond it, down the passage?

"What, Est? What?" Shouts Hock impatiently.

"Hey, maybe we should go back Gretsel."

"Come, come and see."

He's running down the tunnel. Oh, what the hell!

S633/98 b Team A   14.22

HOCK:

"Gretsel!" Where's that lunatic off to? We're for it now. Well, I'm through for sure. Nothing to lose. Fuck Alliston, fuck the Bot, fuck the company… it's Est and he's part of the old team.

Poor Gretsel; he's really out of shape, never visits the gym like I do. He's fast but sweating. The Freak is behind me, I can hear him breathing.

"Est where are you going?"

"S633/98 b Team A! Return immediately. Flush team 644RT have entered the airlock. We cannot be held responsible for any actions resulting in injury or loss of life."

Parasite! They're going to kill us too.

Where are we? Never been here before. This isn't our section. Doesn't this belong to another squad? Section door is open. Different squad cleans here… different… hey wait a minute… this is the core!

"What the fu…"

No. this isn't right. That can't be!

They had entered a long vault filled with plasti-glass spheres. Inside each one there stood a perfectly formed human. Each one blinking but uncomprehending. Their eyes were fixed on some distant point. They floated in clear liquid. Tubes and wires and probes drooped from every orifice. And every single one looked like Alliston.

Gretsel glared from face to face, mouth hanging open. "See! See this shit! And that's not all!" Shouted Est. He beckoned them into yet another huge chamber. Row upon row of giant test tubes lined the factory floor. They moved along conveyer belts.

"See that… there's a full team over here. Look!" Est jumped up onto the conveyer.

"Gretsel, meet Gretsel. Hock hey here's Hock… and you Faldrain… yeah, you're not so different… there's loads of you too. And as for Goosh…"

"What is this?" Gretsel just stared.

"Bravo! So now you have found exactly what you shouldn't."

The voice issued from the tiny camera that hovered near them. Each shocked face tuned towards the tiny robot as it spoke. The voice was no longer the reedy voice of the little device. A human addressed them.

"This is Controller Kald. We are in a bit of a mess here, aren't we? Some fool left the core gates open."

"What's going on here? Why have you cloned us?" Gretsel demanded.

The little bot sighed. "I believe you have the right to know. You see, decades ago a cheap labour force was needed; the colonies were not producing enough workers and alternatives had to be sought. Cloning from young proved too costly and time consuming, so an older practice was redeveloped. A practice previously banned on old Earth, which meant nada in deep space. Cloning from a group of selected specimens, each proficient in several fields; the clones were grown as adults. The system was augmented with selection of acceleration drugs and protein bases. Each clone matures quickly until reaching the age of the original sample. In other words, you are not as old as you think. Once clones were assembled, memories were downloaded from various databanks."

Gretsel blinked at the camera.

"Trayia?"

"She doesn't exist Gretsel, she never did, only as a figment of your imagination, as some one else's dream."

"I see her every evening!"

"No, you don't. You see gentlemen, it's all lies. Every night, when you finish, we simply switch you off and the rest is like a dream. You don't even leave the factory. We gas you in the changing rooms then pack you in a box until you've rested. Simple, and very cost effective."

"But I'm from Massel 6…" Faldrain looked shocked.

"Where you once found a secret room, filled with ancient books, and you would spend hours down there reading. Yes, nice touch, but totally false."

The men stared at each other. None knew what to say, save Gretsel, who stood there quivering, tears flowing down his face.

"No, it's not right, she must be real. I love her… I sing poetry in my head every day in her honour. We're going to save up, going to escape from here… she's the only thing that keeps me going, through this monotony, through 22 years… she must be… she has to be!" He wept.

"I'm sorry. We gave you dreams to get you through the monotony of your time. If you go to

sector 576 you'll find another Gretsel who also pines for his Trayia. You'll never meet him but he sleeps in the same factory as you, shares the same plug-in reality system that simulates your life outside work. Sorry, you are not people; you are commodities, you are our tools."

A hatch slid open behind the men. Several figures waited. They wore dark uniforms and helmets.

"This is the flush squad, gentlemen. I advise you to go with them. We'll take you for a nice little sleep and tomorrow you'll be right as rain and ready for work."

"SHE'S REAL!" Gretsel flared in defiance. "REAL!"

"Then go along with the Flush squad and you'll see her again very soon." Kald said.

Hock stared at the ground and stumbled back along the corridor. Faldrain followed, still stunned and pale.

Gretsel's fists clenched. Unclenched. They rose before him as the flush squad moved towards them.

S633/98 b Team A   15.05 (L.T)

GRETSEL:

She's real she's real she's real she's real…

HOW MUCH FOR A GOOD TIME IN THIS TOWN?
J. J. STEINFELD

I tried all morning
and half of the afternoon
to write a funny poem
about overconsumption
and rampant materialism
wanting to confront
both greed and rapaciousness
and couldn't even after two beers
and going to the fridge for a third
maybe this evening
when I look at my new flat-panel TV
smallish but serviceable
and dream misshapenly about one
three or four times larger
you know, the absurd difference
between Lilliput and Brobdingnag.

Tomorrow I will attempt
to write about the lavishness
and excess of nothingness
as an art form
and giving up the world
but first I'll return my beer bottles
and get my deposit back

THE OLDEST PROFESSION REVISITED

J. J. STEINFELD

You want a sexy, everything included date?
I'm from the beyond, Mr. Horny Soul,
and I'll stroke every sensitive organ
and orifice and synapse you have
or can imagine, believe me,
a seductive otherworldly voice offers
enticing reminiscent salacious words
monotonous as broken yet beautiful watches.

Beyond what? the horny man wonders
measurements of confusion, disorientation,
and immeasurable distances from certainty
beyond the beyond.

He imagines a bright-eyed cheery-voiced ghost
with eternal sexual experience
love shaped as a tape measure
clutched in difficult to describe fingers.

Then the transaction is made
the currency and souls exchanged
one remains prosperous
the other shortchanged.

SHIVERING, UNNOTICED

J. J. STEINFELD

First appeared in *An Affection for Precipices* (2006)

The tragedy, is it in the knowing or the not knowing,
in an argumentative deity or a fully supplied theology?
These are my thoughts and simple incarceration
as I sit on the ground, shivering, unnoticed,
near the site of a long-past undoing
my thoughts bracketed by the emptiness
of what is left out of the newspapers,
history books, and gravestone inscriptions.
Were they young?
Were they vain or frivolous?
Were they believers in sensefulness?
Were they dreaming of an embraceable world
and accomplishments to be that had to make you smile
and tell a neighbour of the extraordinary youths
down the street, the shimmer of expectation in their eyes
in love, young, too young,
but others had gone to war this young
and returned or not returned
documented with almost Biblical tenacity.
Then it occurred, swift as God's miscalculation,
at least with the lava flows
they might find a vanished family
a hundred years later
a textbook entry or a tail-end news report
now all that remains is my sense of sadness
of waves of sorrow and unfairness
like the most predictable tides
but this loss
this utter disappearance
is your fiction
as no one sees you or turns at your thoughts
but someone to be born in a generation or two
might think of you
in the most profound terms
as they sit on the ground, shivering, unnoticed.

THE DOERS
CHRISTOS CALLOW JR.

1.

"Today's my first killing spree, right? Oooh, so excited! Will there be lots of blood? Will there be, you know, ACTION?"

The man in the white suit kept chewing his croissant and didn't reply before it had disappeared inside his beard. The other, a skeleton-thin late teenager in formal black costume and huge yellow sunglasses, had put his hand in his pocket and was holding something proudly. His teeth chattering. His eyes behind the ridiculous glasses so wide open they would pop at any time, bounce on the glass, and fall back into their holes.

"Get in there" said the man in white, interrupting his thoughts.

Trembling, and trembling more for trying not to show it, with his hand still in the pocket, the man with the yellow glasses entered the crowded cinema. The movie was about to start, so he was on time.

"My first kill… oh, first killing spree…" he murmured joyfully as he walked among the unsuspecting crowd. His bearded partner had stayed behind in the vehicle, waiting for him to finish the job.

In the room, people were still trying to find a seat. Someone's frog had followed him inside and they were chasing each other all around the place. An obese family had brought their dinner with them, while a nudist was walking up and down fully dressed to protest against the stereotypical presentation of the lead female character in last week's movie.

Many of the people in the audience were dressed in Halloween costumes, some of which were related to the movie, but most of them not. The man with the yellow glasses finally found a place to sit next to a sixteen year old lad who was wearing a shirt with the letters "fuck the world" on it.

Finally, the man took the hand out of his pocket, bringing it near the kid's face. He was holding a remote control. He pressed a button, then quickly put the remote back in the pocket. Then, as if he had felt the sudden need to invade the toilet or to answer a call of significant importance, he left his seat and ran from the room as fast as he could.

He almost fell in the dirty river outside, but managed to hold his balance and jump to his partner's vehicle, which took off immediately. Once inside the winged transparent sphere of the Raincopter, his trembling, and all the music of agony inside his head, slowly but steadily faded out.

"If they ask, you'll say you ran away to escape from the murderer" said the bearded man when the cinema building was a good way behind.

"My first killing spree, Papa…" murmured the man with the glasses, while trying to imagine what must be happening back there. He had been informed the boy was part of a gang and went everywhere armed, as many people did anyway, and hoped he had created a good amount of chaos. "My first killing spree…"

The bearded man didn't reply. When, minutes later, the man with the glasses abruptly released a burst of orgasmic laughter, he told him to shut up.

"But Papa…"

In his mind, he heard the screams and recalled all these faces… In his imagination, he painted them all in blood…

2.

The man with the yellow glasses and the black suit was John Du, 24, the latest personal assistant to secret agent Papa Nick, more commonly known as "The Doer" or "the man who does things".

As an agent, Papa was only active in times of great crisis when his services were needed the most, as only he had that special talent required to *do* things. Not to do them well, necessarily – just to do them.

"You know, Johnny, to be a Doer, following orders is never enough. You need to improvise also. Watch this."

He stopped the vehicle and opened its only door-window to talk to an old man who was crossing the river on his toad.

"Excuse me, sir, but will you promise me you won't take it personaly?"

"Take what personaly?"

"That" said Papa Nick, taking his ray gun out and pointing it at the poor old man. The gun went pew-pew and the old man went "ow", or he would have gone "ow" but he had already turned to liquid and liquids don't usually go "ow".

"What the hell was that?" said John when they were off the ground again.

"Wait, I'm not done yet." Papa activated the computer screen, which was itself part of the vehicle. He needn't press a button; most of the inner side of the Raincopter consisted of a series of touch screens.

"Old man gone missing" he reported to the computer. "Possibly dead. Last seen driving a Frogse in central river of Flooded Lon."

The screen now showed a Frogse, also known as "the horse of the lake", a particular kind of mutated frog that could easily be trained to become a means of transport, and was preferred by the poor population who couldn't afford a boat or an air balloon. After the great flood, when Lon was conveniently renamed Flooded Lon – though it still remained the kingdom's capital – these Frogses could be found all over the place. Even so, the old man's Frogse would find a new owner in no time.

"I still don't get it. I mean, I get why we organized the killing sprees. I get why we organized all those accidents, murders, rapes… But to actually do it, to actually shoot the man yourself, with your own weapon…"

No sound came out of the big black beard. Johnny continued.

"Of course, you might say, killing someone with a gun feels the same as making someone else kill someone with a gun. Still…" Johnny looked into Papa's indifferent eyes. "Still, murder is murder whichever way you commit it. Through an object, say, a gun, or through another person, say, someone you control. I mean, you yourself don't feel like the murderer… Do you?"

Papa changed the subject.

"What's the next thing on the list?"

Johnny examined the various lists that appeared on the screen. He knew his wife was in there somewhere, but would rather deal with that later. He kept reading.

"Well, there hasn't been a rape on Cannibal Street for almost three months… I guess their hunger is more powerful than their lust. And there hasn't been a terrorist attack on the palace since... ever. That's because terrorists are programmed never to attack the palace. What about a threat, though? Tell them terrorists have planted a bomb in...? I don't know, somewhere, anywhere, just mention terrorists!"

Papa sighed.

"Don't underestimate yourself, boy. We don't do threats. We do the action."

He said "we", John thought. He means we're both Doers now. This is my reward for "doing" that killing spree. Now I'm a Doer too.

They were now crossing Absurd Street where the Palace stood. The river passing in front of the Palace was always flooded with blood, real blood, from all those countries Her Majesty, the Mother Archetype, had invaded in her long career as warlord. Recently, though, she had been on vacation, postponing her invasions in order to organise the Games. Normally such warmongers were banned from joining this multi-national celebration of Peace, but the Games had been devalued to mere spectacle to keep the enslaved population entertained.

"It's almost three o clock. Can I...?" said John to Papa.

Papa stopped the vehicle.

"You can't be serious."

"Please, Papa! I need to!"

With a grin on his face, and the disappointment of finding that his newest assistant wasn't any cleverer than the last, Papa opened the door-window of the Raincopter, and a hand extended forming the Queen Ant Salute. A soft voice was heard singing in front of the palace, joining millions of others chanting simultaneously all over the kingdom.

"God save our noble Mom,
'cause some people are noble
and some are not!
Equality's bad!
O Lord of Hell arise,

scatter her enemies,
and make them FALL!
God, there's much hatred
such fascist hatred
in this song!"

John Du, with a big smile on his face, feeling useful and intelligent, proud that he was part of the kingdom, but mostly proud that he was proud, sat back next to Papa, relieved he had done his duty as a citizen of the empire and was now ready to continue his day of doing things.

"What's the matter?" he complained to Papa. "Every day at three o' clock we must all salute the Great Mother. Because it is three o' clock only if the Great Mother wants it to be. We learned that at school. Didn't you? Don't tell me you don't enjoy singing the national anthem, at least for the sexual pleasure of it, the pleasure of feeling important as part of the empire, as servant to Her Majesty, the Mother Archetype... Or don't you love your Mother?"

"Are you done?" said Papa, frustrated, lifting his hand for a moment as if to slap him, but then slowly scratching his bald head instead. "Let's get back to work then. We have a thousand things to do before the opening ceremony tonight."

While flying across the river-streets of Flooded Lon, they saw an unhealthy amount of people on their way to the Stadium. Thousands were on Frogses but most of them were swimming all the way, through the radiated water and the blood of a thousand nations. Looking down at the masses of untitled people, the Lords, a.k.a "Superior People With Titles", were heading in the same direction in their air balloons.

3.

"Ok, now that you are officially an agent in her Mother's service, I can reveal to you that you have been lied to about pretty much everything since you were a child. You have been told, for example, that in order to exist, you must constantly *do* things. You must work hard to exhaust your body, and then you must have fun in order to keep your body exhausted. You must never have energy left to think. You must never have the time to think. You are a Homo Chronoborus, a Time-Wasting Man. Think of this. What do you do when nothing's happening? When you're not kept busy?"

"I don't know" said John. "I guess, I just… think about things. The body rests and the mind thinks."

"See? That's why people must be busy. But now there's a crisis and it's hard to keep them distracted. That's why the Great Mother is hosting the Games, and our job as Doers is to make sure people forget about the crisis in the meantime. It's a very delicate situation, which is why we have been summoned. Now, we'll need at least a couple of murders this week; one could be a hate crime against a minority person, say, in public view, the other… I don't know, that would take some planning. Don't forget about improvising."

"What about the ceremony itself?"

"No, we cannot attend that. It's an excellent opportunity to do things while the rest of the world will be watching the opening ceremony. I'm thinking of the good old accident technique… What about a nice explosion?"

"But I want to go… I want to see the Mother Archetype…"

"Grow up. You're a propaganda agent now, you can't be fooled by the very propaganda you are responsible for. Or can you? No, really, you have to grow up, Johnny Du."

4.

The whole world was watching the ceremony while John Du was working. He had spotted the interesting case of a family of slaves, bound with flags of the empire instead of leashes, barking the thousand names of the Mother Archetype from their floating home on Colony Street.

These slaves were only one of many families the Empire had received as payment for the loans their poor country had taken from the Great Mother, after the Mother herself had ruined that country through cultural warfare. Finishing them off would make Papa proud.

"Give me details" demanded Papa when he heard of John's achievement. He always wanted details. John told him he had used the remote control on a nearby gang of Frogse-riders who, under his control, cannibalized the entire family.

"Now that's what I call improvising," said Papa. "I'm thinking of promoting you to my permanent assistant, after all."

What happened to the last one?"

"I killed him."

They had a coffee in one of the air-cafes above the city. It was late at night and they could hear and see the herd in the city below, cheering for one crowd-pleasing spectacle after the other. Thousands of years after the days of the arenas and the public floggings, and nothing had really changed.

"What are we doing tomorrow?" asked John.

"Tomorrow we kill your wife" said Papa, very simply. "You will choose the way, of course."

John paused and looked outside indifferently. It was raining as usual. Their Raincopter was recharging. In the background, the naked children of the dying culture of childhood were floating around on wide-opened umbrellas, chained to the air balloons of their parents. Occasionally, some would be sacrificed to the Mother Archetype, since all children belonged to her anyway.

"Drowning" said John finally. "If she must die, let her die from lack of breath. I don't want her face ruined; I don't want her death to change her appearance. If it must be, let her drown."

"You know it's part of the process. Unless of course you don't want to be promoted."

"I want to live" said John. "I know it's either this or my death. If it must be, let it be her death. I'm in. We'll do it your way."

"You're smarter than originally thought" said Papa. "I'm happy for you."

5.

John's apartment was in the underwater part of Flooded Lon. Most of the remaining middle-class lived here, afraid of the wild city above them. Fewer gangsters and less organized crime. This is where the random people lived.

There were posters all over the city, and waterproof ones too on the submarine buses and the sunken ruins. "Random people will kill you. People without a past. Be forever wary of the random people."

The posters were designed by the same organizations for which Papa Nick had been working his whole life. He knew of the technique. He must have explained it to John a thousand times.

"People don't just turn into murderers. People can't make big decisions anyway. They don't have free will. They have microchips. We have the remote controls. We find one of the random people. We press a button. And here's our serial killer. Or our terrorist. Thanks to us, there is news on TV every single day. Thanks to us, the Doers, things happen. The

things we want to happen, all the time. We make them happen."

It was early in the morning when the Raincopter's sphere dove underwater, and the Doers were outside John's place in no time. Behind the glass window-walls, John saw his young wife, Angela, almost an adult, reading a pre-apocalyptic romance in her bath robe, her unending dark hair wet, almost covering her face.

"What is she doing?" said Papa.

"She's not doing anything, just reading."

"I know, it's crazy. But your kind is becoming extinct, you know. Normally, people are either poor servants or rich masters. Neither can read. You underwater people are getting rarer every day."

"Yeah, I know" murmured John. "It's crazy."

John used a more common remote control to open the main gate, and then, when the Raincopter entered through, the gate closed and the corridor emptied of water. John stood, sceptical, by the door that led to his apartment.

"Are you ready to do this?" said Papa.

John knocked on the door. Angela took some time to open it, but was very polite when she did, and kissed John passionately as if she hadn't seen him in ages.

"Hello, Mr. Nick" she said to Papa.

"Oh, you've been expecting me? That's very sweet" said Papa. "But let's be brief, shall we, because John and I don't have much time. We got – how should I put it – things to do."

"Please take a seat" said the woman as if she hadn't heard him. "I'll be back with you boys in a minute."

Papa sat on the sofa and John perched on an armchair opposite him. He was trembling. Not like he was trembling when he entered that cinema. Now he was trembling with fear.

"Why is it taking you so long?" Papa asked while the woman was away in the bathroom. "If you want to say goodbye first, just do it. We don't have time to waste. It's just a push of a button and she will do whatever you want her to do."

"You're right" said John. "I'm sorry."

On the wall-TV screen behind them were images from yesterday's opening ceremony. The Mother Archetype was trying to look cool. Her slaves were proud that she looked cool. The Lords were pleased that the slaves were pleased, because that meant they wouldn't start a revolution anytime soon.

"There's no point in saying goodbye" said John finally, after taking a heavy breath he would never have released if he could. "Get in here, Angela."

She did. She stood in front of him. Obviously didn't like his tone but he was too nervous lately and his partner was there – more like a boss – which obviously made him even more nervous and abrupt.

"Sweetie" said John. "I wish I didn't have to do this to you but… you know the society we live in is cruel. Sacrifices have to be made and I really have to do something I would rather not in order to get this promotion… But I don't have a choice, because…"

"Get it over with " said Papa.

"I won't say goodbye" said John, and pressed the button on his special Doer remote control, the one that would instantly turn Angela into a puppet with only one thought in its mind: suicide by drowning. Then, as if a sleepwalker, Angela walked to the front door, closing it behind her on the way to her watery grave.

Papa was pleased. His advanced Master Doer's version of the remote revealed on its tiny computer screen that the command of suicide had indeed been given, and that meant John was eligible for the job

of permanent agent. He would be promoted immediately. There was only one criteria: to be ruthless. The killing spree was nothing compared to looking into the eyes of the woman he loved, the woman he once chose to live his life with, and order her execution.

It is amazing what people can do for a king or a queen. There was no doubt that for the Mother Archetype, John was prepared to do anything. He was more than a slave-citizen. He was a person who would sing the anthem without shame, who would wish the Great Mother "long to reign over him" with pride, as if being ruled aroused him sexually, mentally, or otherwise.

"I am proud of you, son" said Papa Nick, putting his hand on John's arm.

And now they had to go *do* more things, the things that Doers do, the things that kept people busy so they can't think, the things that kept people distracted from the real problems in times of crisis, and separated them into smaller groups that could do little on their own, that had little in common with the rest.

Papa opened the door to the world outside and was met with an unpleasant surprise. He did not see his favourite Raincopter where he had parked it, right outside John's apartment door. Instead, he saw her, the woman who had been ordered to die – and his computer had confirmed the order – but was still very much alive. She was doing nothing but standing. And smiling.

Papa pointed his own remote at her. He pressed the button. Nothing happened. He wished for her to strangle herself that very instant. She didn't. He then wished for her to eat herself. He kept pressing the button. No response. No ACTION.

"I had her microchip removed" said John coldly. "Don't ask me how, we both lost a lot of blood. Oh, I had mine removed as well, obviously. There is a group of revolutionary surgeons; they all live underwater so you people can't spot them. Well, let's not waste any more time. There's no point in saying goodbyes, right?"

Papa was sweating all over. Angela was keeping a safe distance. She was now aiming at Papa with his ray gun – Papa's own ray gun which she had taken from the vehicle – the vehicle that itself was nowhere to be found.

"Our friends have taken care of it" said Angela to Papa. "If it's your vehicle you're thinking about, I mean. They want to study its technology. We're tired of moving around on Frogses, you know? There're a lot of places a Frogse can't go, such as the Floating Lon above ground."

"But…" said Papa finally, to John. "But you were loyal to the Great Mother. You couldn't be a thinking man, you were singing the bloody irrational anthem! And you killed people, you destroyed the lives of people!"

"I have never really used that remote" said John. "Well, not until now. As for all those horrible things, the killing sprees, the order I gave to that gang – which was my gang, by the way – all that was just theatre. I wanted to get you down here, into the underwater part of the city where the thinking people live, in my own place where I can destroy you without any witnesses or cameras. And without any difficulty, too. By the way, pointing that remote control at me, it's getting really annoying. Why don't you put it down?"

"Why don't you put yours down?" said Papa.

"Because mine works. Yours doesn't."

Papa wanted to shout, but the voice coming out of his beard was suddenly too weak. He had never felt so insecure.

"It does work" he protested. "It is the Master Doer version, the most advanced technology on the planet, designed by her Majesty's top scientist-servants and loyal secret agents."

"Sorry, Papa" said John. "It might work on the Mother's citizen-slaves but it doesn't work on thinking people. My apologies, but, you know, following orders is never enough. One also needs to improvise. Watch me."

That was the moment John Du pressed the button. Papa was about to reply, but his mouth magically snapped shut and his mind was suddenly elsewhere. He tried to think, but was too busy getting himself killed by hitting his head repeatedly against the glass wall. The impenetrable glass wall.

Angela did not want to stay and watch, and returned quietly to the house. John waited until his ex-partner was dead, then kindly took the Master Version remote control from his pocket. The most powerful weapon in the universe was now in a revolutionary's hands. The last Doer on the planet was dead. The time of the Doers was over.

The time of the Thinkers had come.

POEM FOR H. R. PUFNSTUF

JACOB EDWARDS

First appeared in the *Toucan's* poems of the week.

Piffle the puffle, sniffles and snuffles
spiffy as Jiffy the magic mush truffle hog
Pittance the puffin, mittens and muffins
smitten with Kitten-cat's good riddance duffle coat
Piffle and Pittance go down to the sewer
Piffle spits spittle and Pittance skips school with her
Brown all around them, the hot bed of sludge
calls to hot-headed Piff, "Give that puffin a nudge."
"You've found him, now drown him in warm chocolate fudge!"
so Piff, she does push, but the puff, he won't budge
Pittance the puffin, once bitten, twice nothin'
twitters through gritted beak, "Don't you try snuffin' me!"
Piffle the puffle, catch whiff the kerfuffle
miffed by his drift, she goes off in a huffle

ASSHOLE FACTORY

MARK MELLON

First appeared in *Like Frozen Statues of Flesh*

O'Hare reached the plant fifteen minutes before Shift. FastTrakt management had assigned parking. Other employees, no matter how senior, scrambled for spaces in the plant's crumbling asphalt lot. O'Hare headed for the back where it was relatively easy to find space to park the van.

"*Ain't no fool, maintaining my cool,*" the antique rock'n'roll blared.

He parked by a ten-foot chain-link fence topped by concertina barbwire. Train tracks and rows of shabby, two-story duplexes lay past the fence, a blue-collar view rendered even more stark by pitiless halogen streetlamps that denied even night's fleeting cover. O'Hare combed back graying hair and looked though the smoke filmed windshield at a lamp someone left on in a room. He killed the stereo and shut off the van. *Maintain your cool.* That had been his mantra for weeks, to keep from losing his temper.

He got out and suited up. Other employees, halfway into their gear, stopped to wave hello. Employees bought their own hazmat and put it on and off in the parking lot, rain or shine. That or wear the cumber-some gear to work, drawing questioning stares at every intersection. Fast Trakt didn't have locker rooms.[1] There was more than enough time to hazmat and key in before Shift started, but why delay the inevitable? Others did kill time. In his SUV, Colaciello fired up his hash pipe. Hvartic shamelessly knocked back vodka in plain sight. O'Hare thought nothing of it. People got through Shift as best they could. O'Hare had a Xanax and two quarts of Irish stout ready at Shift's end, at home with Maggie and the boys.

Once hazmatted, workers made their way to the employees' entrance. O'Hare and the others were coated in a sickly red glow by a massive neon sign's light. The five-story, glowing scarlet letters towered near Exit 13 of the Jersey Turnpike: "FastTrakt, America's Alimentarist Since 1942." Despite eight years there, the sign still irritated O'Hare as it had generations of FastTrakt employees before, that and the mocking constantly flashing, cartoon image of Reddy Colon, a jolly large intestine.

He walked through automatic double doors and was verbally assaulted by Shift Su-

---

1 "We provide wages, no more. Our relationship with our employees ends there." A. O. Speculum, FastTrakt's founder. Mr. Speculum began FastTrakt in 1942, at the height of World War II, making drill sergeants for the Army and Marines by himself in the back yard of his house in Ashley Heights, NJ, equipped only with a tub of raw rubber and a pile of cow manure.

pervisor A. Culissimo. A six-foot colon, Culissimo squalled at O'Hare from the sphincter that hung between his bent, stick legs.

"So you get in, O'Hare," he said, "just six minutes before you're late."

"I believe that's five minutes early anywhere else," O'Hare said.

"Shut up," Culissimo said. Eyes that topped the long, sinuous, flapping intestine regarded O'Hare evilly.

"Don't think FastTrakt can't do without you, O'Hare. Remember, I'm a full colon, not a semi. That means I can fire as I please. And demote as well, Shift Foreman. Got it, O'Hare?"

The colon Grouchoesquely wiggled cartoon eyebrows for further emphasis.

"Got it, boss," O'Hare said.

"Go to work," Culissimo farted.

O'Hare held his badge to a plaz reader that ID'd him, autologged time of arrival, and opened another set of automatic doors.

He entered the plant. Day-Shifts walked past, finished for now. Some waved so long. Some said hello. Others jocularly gave the finger. Each one's hazmat was caked in filth. O'Hare's counterpart Tony Culotta stopped to talk.

"Buck. How's it going? Culissimo give his standard ass-chewing for coming on time?"

"I got off easy," O'Hare said. "Guys that are late, he splutters shit on their hazmats."

Culotta laughed. "Maggie and the kids OK?"

"Not bad. Try getting married yourself, you good-looking goombah. How's the plant running?"

Culotta drew conspiratorially close and said, "Watch Number Five. She's hot, no let-up for two weeks."

"Why the sudden demand for angry, old white men?" O'Hare said.

"You never know with FastTrakt,"

Culotta said. "Long as we got skins, management wants 'em filled, no delays. Just keep Number Five greased. Keep Sadsacki alert."

"OK, Tony, but if we run her too long, she'll blow."

"That's not your problem," Culotta said. "Yours is to keep production up through your Shift. Another thing."

"What?" O'Hare said.

"You said you needed help. So here's a new guy to break in. He seems willing enough. Stu?"

"Yes, Mr. Culotta?"

He was a tall, muscular man, blond, crew cut, with inset, pale blue eyes, in an orange kemtex-coat coverall, rubber boots, and a hard hat.

"Tony's fine," Culotta said. "This is Buck O'Hare, your supervisor. Buck, this is Stu Karpinski."

"Congratulations on being one of the few in North Jersey these days with an honest, paying job," O'Hare said. "That is, if you can take it. Polish, right?"

"Yes, from Warsaw and I speak English fine," Karpinski said. "You show me how to work here, yes?"

"More like survive, if you're lucky," O'Hare replied. "You've got a fair start on hazmat, but you need a synthresp. Lend him yours, Culotta."

"Aw, Buck," Culotta said.

"Foremen should set an example," O'Hare said. "I'll bring it by your place after Shift."

Culotta said, "Whatever. Here you go, Buck. I'll see you around. I got a date with a hot shower and a mattress."

"'Synthresp?'" Karpinski asked. "This is what?"

O'Hare handed the Pole a black plaz rectangle.

"Hang that from your neck by the lanyard," he explained. "Let's start with skins. This way, kid."

Karpinski followed O'Hare. Intimidatingly large, the plant was a complex, open, multi-floored structure. Convoluted metal and plastic pipes of all sizes stretched and bent in every direction, hooked up to arcane machinery.

"Why'd you take the job, Karpinski?" O'Hare asked.

Karpinski said, "The pay. Fifteen dollars an hour. I have wife with two babies. What is this to you, O'Hare?"

"Oh, nothing. It's just I sometimes hope somebody will work here whose life doesn't sound like a fucking Bruce Springsteen song. That's all."

"I don't know what this means," Karpinski said.

"Forget it, kid," O'Hare replied. "Just my rotten sense of humor."

They walked through an enormous warehouse filled with row upon row of enormous, hundred foot tall, black plastic tanks. The horrible reek even made a strong, young man like Karpinski wilt. O'Hare took Culotta's synthresp and slipped it over Karpinski's face. The Pole took a few breaths and said, voice distorted by the vocox,

"Thank you, O'Hare."

"No problem, Karpinski. Better get your own synthresp at Home Depot after Shift."

"Thank you again, O'Hare. What is that smell?"

O'Hare smiled. "Roses and fine wine. It's FastTrakt's principal ingredient, what makes the system go. FastTrakt may claim a thousand products, but basically, when you get right down to it, everything is ninety-five percent dog shit. This is where it's kept. FastTrakt doesn't miss a trick. The methane runs the turbines that power the plant. You know Jersey gave us a 'Clean Green' award last year?"

From the warehouse, they entered another sizable structure, low and flat-roofed. An open end received a fleet of tractor-trailers, involved in a slow, continuous, elaborate ballet. A truck would back in with a full load while another pulled out, loading done, ready to carry FastTrakt products to the ends of the earth.

"More trucks than FedEx, UPS, and the US Post Office put together," O'Hare said.

Robotic forklifts loaded and unloaded the trucks. They scooped up large yellow, plastic tubs covered with bright red Korean ideograms and set them down at the building's opposite end. Workers pried off the vacuum-sealed lids. They carefully extracted large, slimy, gray sheaths from the tubs.

"Come on, Stu, time you strung some skins, just to get the feel. This is so delicate, FastTrakt still needs humans for it."

O'Hare and Karpinski walked to the skin tubs.

"Hiya, Martha," O'Hare said. "Glad to see you back."

"Hi, boss," Martha Smend said, cheerful despite a lingering cold. "No choice with only two sick days a year. Plus I love twelve hours straight work."

Five-foot two tops, a hundred pounds max, sole support of two kids, Martha stood there, nose red and dripping snot, hanging tough, refusing to crap out.

"Me too, Martha," O'Hare said. "Keep hanging. Show Stu here how to string skins."

"OK, boss," Martha said. "Listen, kid, first, don't tear any. Tear 'em before you string 'em, it comes out your paycheck. Got it?"

"Yes, got it," Karpinski said.

Martha stuck a rubber-gloved hand into a tub. With obstetric delicacy, she took a skin between her thumb and forefinger and slowly extracted a slimy skin.

"Like delivering a baby, that's how you think about it, kid," she said.

With practiced ease, she ran her fingers down the skin's central seam to a fleshy eyehole.

"Hook 'em from the bottom. After all, we're making assholes."

She laughed only to violently sneeze, a snot explosion Martha covered as best she could with a red bandana. She deftly inserted a hook into the eyehole and tugged on an attached thread. The skin flitted away, another vaguely humanoid form on an endless conveyor belt into a gaping, square, black void.

"Another condom on a string," Martha said. "You try, kid."

Karpinski grimaced, but nonetheless set about yanking a skin from a tub. O'Hare watched the Pole go about it. Carefully, but not to the point of immobility, he tediously tugged at a greasy skin until it slipped free. Karpinski found the eyehole, put a hook through it, and gave the thread a yank. He was obviously repulsed, but also plainly hell bent on sticking it out. O'Hare set to hooking skins himself. For a time they worked in silence, bent upon their task. Skins flitted past like gray ghosts of long forgotten, unlamented souls.

"This one has no hole," Stu said.

"Put it in the blue recycle tub there," Martha said.

"Kid, you're all right," O'Hare said. "Martha, take a break. Get a Sudafed from my stash. Drink some Gatorade too, but be back in five."

"Thanks, Buck," Martha said.

O'Hare said, "OK. Kid, now that you've seen how we start, we'll go to Number Five."

They exited into an endless, fluorescently-lit corridor.

"This place, it is so confusing," Karpinski said.

"Yeah. You never get used to it either," O'Hare said. "I got a map you can have, but it don't make much difference."

They saw the number "5" in gold letters. An awful reek emitted from the arch below the number, rotting dog shit accented and strengthened by an indecipherable mélange of other disgusting, exotic stenches. They donned synthresps. Inside the cavernous chamber below the arch, skins ascended and descended, a thin, plaz line attached to each one's feedhole. The skins were in various stages of plumpitude as the noxious mixture swelled and filled potbellies, withered legs, and angry, furrowed brows. Stubby fingers grew long and clawlike and toenails turned thick and yellow with age.

"Climb to the control panel," O'Hare shouted over the industrial din.

They climbed a vertical, aluminum ladder to a metal superstructure that gave a panoramic view of Number Five. A man monitored a control panel.

"How's it going, Sadsacki?" O'Hare said.

Old as O'Hare, but a lot sourer about it, Sadsacki squinted and said, "Only half an hour since Shift started and she's already ready to blow. Look at them gauges, Foreman. How long you think she can hold? I warned 'em twice already."

Every gauge was near redline or past it.

"You know there's nothing I can do," he said to Sadsacki.

"Each gauge monitors what's fed into the skins," O'Hare explained to Karpinski while Sadsacki fumed.

"They're color coded. Brown for you know what. Then your trace elements, gray for granite, red for tabasco sauce, and yellow for cat piss and vinegar. The computer automatically adjusts ingredients for regional differences."

A small army of wretched, crabbed old men grew before their eyes.

"Ever wonder where they all go, Sadsacki?" O'Hare said.

"No," Sadsacki said. "Maybe a lot of lawns got kids on 'em that need chasing off. I really don't give a shit, O'Hare. What I worry about is this whole ball of wax in flames around my ears."

"Tell you what, Karpinski and me will grease wires. That should help things run smoother."

"Grease what you like," Sadsacki said. "Won't make shit worth of difference."

O'Hare sighed. "Come on, Karpinski."

They climbed down the ladder. O'Hare picked up a grease gun and handed one to Karpinski.

"Lube the wires heavy."

They walked around the chamber, squirting purulent, yellow-white lube on the intricate network of thin steel cables that conveyed hooked assholes in various stages of completion around the chamber. The wires led to several bays. Each was equipped with a cryopress. O'Hare stopped Karpinski by a bay.

"Watch this," he said. "This is the tricky part."

A finished product approached, skin maggot white, sparse, few hairs arranged in an elaborate comb over. Rheumy, muddled brown eyes came to life, dentures rattled, and a voice creaked,

"This country doesn't need any more mouths to feed-"

At the very second he sparked to life, the cryopress slapped shut on the coot with a rush of hyper-refrigerated air. Cyrocooled to 20 K, twin plaz leaves enveloped him at six hundreds pounds of pressure per square inch. Frozen sealed like a salmon slab, mouth open in mid-rant, the asshole slapped to the floor and slid through a chute for transport. Another old fart came down the wire and sprang to life, spouting halitosis-scented racist filth, only to be frozen in turn.

"Just think, kid," O'Hare said. "It never ends. Come on, let's grease some wires."

He turned his back. Catastrophe hit. The cryopress's ordinary smooth swoosh became an awful screech of malfunctioning machinery.

"There ought to be a goddamn law," a coot raved, voice unquelled by plaz.

Another asshole plowed into the still standing, unsealed one. Fragile at this early stage, they merged, an awful slopping together of dogshit and other vile ingredients. A two headed, multiple-arm flapping monster garbled nonsense as another new asshole headed its way, slammed into the twofold blob, and made it three.

Red warning lights went off. A siren howled.

"I told you so, O'Hare," Sadsacki screamed over the racket.

O'Hare ran to manually shut off Number Five. Lines of assholes juddered to a halt.

"Goddamn young punk. Fucking get you."

An awful beast crept toward O'Hare. Three giant, multi-faced, fused condoms filled with turds, leaking acid that burnt the concrete floor, scrawny arms extended in a strangling grasp. O'Hare stood frozen, caught like a bird in a snake's gaze.

Karpinski charged the triple asshole, armed with a fire axe. The big Pole split the middle head wide open. Dogshit spattered everywhere. He brought the axe down again, the pointed end this time, and ripped another querulous old face into shredded latex.

Dogshit flew like muddy rain. O'Hare almost choked to death despite his synthresp.

The multi-asshole lay dead, hacked into mung by the brave Pole's axe. Karpinski stood over him, shoulders hunched, heaving for breath, hazmat soaked in shit and gray skin shreds.

Culissimo charged in screaming.

"What's going on here? Why'd

production stop? Tell me what happened, O'Hare, but keep in mind you're responsible, whatever it is."

"Cryopress Six locked," O'Hare said. "I shut Number Five down. There was a merge before I did. Things looked bad, but this new kid, Karpinski, hacked that multi-asshole to pieces like a drunk lumberjack going after an outhouse shitpile. He literally saved my bacon, Mr. Culissimo."

"What do I care?" Culissimo said. "I warned you. You're just a shift worker now for holding up production. Sadsacki's foreman now, at least until he fucks up. And as for you, Kapronsky or whatever your name is, you're fired. Draw one day's wages from the cashier and leave the plant immediately. Sadsacki!"

"Yes, Mr. Culissimo," Sadsacki called down.

"You and O'Hare get Number Five up, this fucking instant."

"Yes, sir, Mr. Culissimo," Sadsacki said, grin shit-eater wide.

Culissimo stomped out. Tears shamelessly streamed from Karpinski's eyes, drawing tracks on his filth-streaked face.

"Why am I fired?" he asked.

O'Hare went to the Pole and put a hand on his shoulder. He assumed his most fatherly manner.

"Kid, sorry about the tough break. I'll find you another job someplace else. It's the least I can do."

"But why? What is it that I did wrong?" Karpinski said.

"Don't take it personal," O'Hare said. "There's just no room for a hero in an asshole factory."

THE OLDEST PROFESSION

MARK SILCOX

There was a low table in the train compartment with one of those dreadful holographic projectors set into its top. I shut it off immediately – 3D cinematography makes me queasy. I settled down with a paperback novel and some fresh fruit I'd bought at the station, and watched the gloomy suburbs of Moscow drift past my window.

These days, train travel is an expensive pastime for fussy antiquarian types and people with too much time on their hands. I fall squarely into both of these categories. So I'd decided to skip my annual European holiday in favor of a week-long ride on the Trans-Siberian railway. I thought it might provide me with some feeling of continuity with the past, which there hadn't been very much of lately in the dirty streets, abandoned restaurants and broken-down museums of the world's formerly great cities.

The train I had boarded on that unusually bright summer morning was malodorous and weather-beaten, and left Moscow half an hour late. With some difficulty, I succeeded in persuading myself that all this was part of the charm of the experience. I did manage to find an empty four-person compartment with newly upholstered seats. This was a relief. I wasn't interested in having the sort of conversation that one usually feels bullied into conducting with strangers on a train.

We were just leaving the second small station outside of the city when she joined me. As soon as I got an eyeful of her, I was reconciled to the interruption. She had a gorgeously pale, Slavic complexion and a slender figure, and looked about twenty-five. She was dressed far more conservatively than most of the slug-a-beds and rag pickers of her blighted generation. A shivery sky-blue blouse, a dark wool skirt that came to a few inches below the knee, some tasteful jewelry and the slyest trace of floral perfume. Most startling was the absence of any of those gruesome surgical enhancements that had been so popular since the '20s – no multicolored irises, no extra fingers, and no grafted-on muscle tone pressing outward against her clothes.

"I'm sorry," she said. "I didn't mean to disturb…I'll just…" She pointed with one slender red fingertip down the hallway toward the other compartments, some of which must surely also have been empty. She had a pronounced Russian, but spoke English to me with confidence. I suppose she must have seen the writing on the cover of my novel.

"It's up to you, of course," I said to

her. "But I'd be pleased to have the company."

She sat down, mumbling thanks, and began to rummage in her pocketbook. Her instep pressed against the side of my ankle under the table. Was it just by accident that her foot stopped there, resting delicately against mine?

Eventually she found what she was looking for – a cheap, chubby paperback of her own, covered with Cyrillic letters. I recognized its title from a list of bestsellers I'd glimpsed in a newspaper the previous day. She noticed me looking at the cover.

"Have you ever read anything by Klees?" she asked. "He tells wonderful stories, lots of action."

I shook my head. "I'm afraid that as age takes its toll, I find it more difficult to keep up with the bestseller lists."

She immediately shoved the book back into her open purse. "Actually, I don't feel much like reading just now. It's a shame to miss out on the scenery, don't you think?"

Her sudden decisive change of mind struck me as rather gauche and charming. "I've never taken this route before," I told her. "But the landscape is supposed to be quite pretty as we get out of the city. If you're interested in that sort of thing."

"I *love* that sort of thing." She reached out a hand across the table. Her handshake was warm, a little tentative. "My name's Aniya, by the way."

"I'm Alan. You speak English very well, Aniya. It almost sounds like your first language."

"*Spasiba!*" She blushed. "You're from the USA? I took speech classes for a few months at Moscow U. I thought that after I'd learned English I could move to America, become a movie star."

She had the looks for it – or for bit parts, at the very least. I almost said something to this effect, but managed to bite my tongue. It's all too easy for somebody my age to come across as lascivious.

We watched the world go by quietly for a half-hour or so. There wasn't really much worth commenting on. Just the same sleepy desolation one might have expected to find in most other parts of the developed world: abandoned villages, uncultivated fields, inscrutable concrete extrusions of the Soviet past poking out of the ground at random places. I noticed that her breath caught for a moment as we passed the charred and listing wooden skeleton of a burned-out farmhouse. But she didn't risk saying anything about it.

Then, finally, we made our way through a somewhat less abandoned town that still had a few buildings intact. "Look!" She pointed out the window. "What a pretty little church. It must be at least a hundred years old."

"Actually, with those windows, I wouldn't date it much before 1960. You were close, though." I hoped I didn't sound too much like a schoolteacher. "Would you like to try one of these pears?"

"Thank you!" She took one, peeled it quickly and ate it with astonishing zeal. I've often been amazed at how skinny girls will tear right into their food. Of course, she couldn't have been more than a teenager when the first of the big food shortages hit continental Europe. That sort of experience is bound to have a permanent effect on a person's habits.

I turned to watch the scenery, trying my best to give her a little privacy. Her face was reflected in the glass. A heavy drop of juice ran out of her mouth – she wiped it off with the back of her hand, then licked the skin there. I shifted uncomfortably in my seat.

"That was delicious," she said. "Was it real?"

"I suspect not, sadly." I sighed. "I do know a few people back home in America who own real fruit trees. But at a train station in Moscow, the cost would have been prohibitive. I thought they were a pleasant fabrication, though, didn't you?"

For a moment, she seemed to be watching me very closely. Then she sighed too. "It was lovely. It can't have been that many years after I learned the alphabet. I can just about remember the very last time I ate real fruit. Russian pears were once the best in the world, you know. So many things seem to be disappearing, these days."

A faraway look had come into her eye. What 'disappearances' could she have been pondering, at her age? I suppose it could have been anything, really, from the dismantling of the welfare state to the vanishment of 2D television, or giant pandas. Or perhaps she was one of those crazy Russian kids who'd been raised to think of the Stalinist era as the glory days of her now starving nation.

"The best things haven't disappeared completely, Aniya," I reassured her, reaching across the table to brush her hand with mine. "You just have to look a little harder to find them."

She leaned closer. I could smell her perfume again – it was cheap stuff, but curiously, almost witchily affecting. "I hope you're right Alan. I really do."

As the train puttered eastward, I told her about the sights I'd seen touring some of the less despoiled regions of the US. I described the beautiful scenery at Galveston Island, Martha's Vineyard, and the O'ahu conservation grounds. These were all places where the US government had imposed its policy of client-based exclusionary zoning, to keep out undesirable elements. "There's a little pollution in Hawaii," I explained to her, "but not enough to damage the beauty of the sunset."

"What about museums, art galleries, concert halls? Does your government still support them?"

"Very little these days, I'm afraid.

Once you've started to lose the inner cities, it's a slippery slope. And of course, to keep up those sorts of institutions you'd need to impose some pretty coercive taxation."

She closed her eyes and shook her head, seeming to lose a little of her formerly abstracted air. "It's all so sad, Alan. These days, I sometimes think that the only people who really understand the human need to feel secure about the future are the insurance companies." She reached into her handbag. "Just yesterday, I was reading about an international company called Resolute Life. They have some policies that really make sense. Let me show you something…"

A glossy pamphlet appeared on the tabletop. I could feel all the blood draining from my face. "Hold on a minute! Just one minute. Who's your employer, please?"

She looked straight back at me. Neither of us said anything for a long moment. Then a kind of deadness came into her eyes and her shoulders slumped. "Section 3-140.09 of the Eurasian Commercial Code requires me to inform you that I'm a commissioned employee of *Udači* Viral and Discursive Marketing, Incorporated."

"You're damn right it does. I remember signing a petition in support of that law."

"Alan, I'm sorry if you feel that you've been deceived in some way. But if I could just get you to glance over some of this literature…."

"You haven't finished yet. You're required by law to disclose the original source of your income."

She exhaled slowly, settled back into her seat and gazed out the window. "*Udači* V&D Marketing Inc. is a public relations subcontractor for Resolute Life Insurance Incorporated, which is a subsidiary enterprise of the Euro-American Securities Partnership Corporation. All of our conversation for the past seventeen minutes and eight seconds constitutes commercial communication, under the definition provided by–"

"All right, enough already!" I slapped my hand against the tabletop. "So you thought you could play upon an old man's sentimentality about the past to shill some crapulent insurance policy? You... you communist! Aren't you disgusted with yourself?"

The train had begun to slow down; the announcer called out the name of a rural station in French over the P.A. She stood up, shut the clasp on her pocketbook, and made for the door, murmuring something under her breath.

"Eh? What was that?"

"I said…oh, it was nothing. Enjoy the rest of your journey. I'll leave you in peace."

"What I don't understand," I said, standing up and taking a step toward her, "is how you people can sleep at night." As I approached her the side of my hip bumped against the controls of the table projector. It crackled irritably, and the shrunken image of a silly science-fictional monster appeared on the tabletop. "I mean, I've heard of people selling off family heirlooms, vital organs, even children. But *conversation*? How much do they pay you to cozy up to strangers and gradually chatter your way around to the topic of insurance? Is there no such thing as *human intimacy* anymore? At least when the commies were in charge, they recognized that there were *some* limits!" The monster on the table was making a speech about the virtues of a brand of mouthwash.

"Oh, come on, Alan. There's nothing especially new about this. Back before you rich people walled off the suburbs, it used to be done right on peoples' doorsteps. The companies that pay me are just adapting to the times."

"That's no excuse!" I could tell that my tone was becoming histrionic. I'd clearly startled her a bit, but not enough to render her speechless. I can't remember now whether I'd really expected anything like an apology; it certainly wasn't what I got, anyhow.

She turned to face me, her eyes blazing. "Hey!" she said. "Do you think I planned to get a job in discursive marketing? D'you think that this was my first choice as a *career*? I was a top student in my school. I read philosophy in college. Half a century ago, I would have been a professor by now, teaching Dialectical Materialism and getting a fat state pension. It was *your* generation, and your parents, that built this ugly world, where there's nothing useful to do and everything's for sale."

"I've no idea what you're talking about."

The awkward thing was, she looked even prettier when she was furious. Her blue eyes were magically brilliant, and a flush of crimson had come across her pale cheeks. I tried to say something else – I can't remember what. I'm ashamed to admit that at just that moment I badly wanted her to stay in the compartment, in spite of knowing the nasty secret of her profession.

She didn't, of course. The crash of the glass door as she left was quite melodramatic. A minute later I saw her standing on the asphalt platform talking glumly into a cellphone. Probably telling her wretched employers the bad news. There were a few raindrops on the glass between us, and I noticed that she didn't have an umbrella.

#

I was still rattled when the train pulled into Nizhny Novogrod. I almost forgot to retrieve my luggage, but I was helped by a very able-bodied young chauffeur named Osip. He grabbed my two cloth carryalls and elbowed his way dexterously across the platform. I commissioned him to drive me to my hotel.

"Are there many tourists in town this

time of the year?" I asked him, as we wound our way in the steady drizzle through a maze of cobbled streets and ancient bridges. I thought that some banal conversation might steady my nerves.

"It's a little slow," he said. "You heard of the food riots in the spring that made the news. Foreigners have been staying home."

"Oh well, more space for me I suppose." We pulled up outside the Hotel Tsentralny, a grey-walled, ramshackle art-deco monolith in the city's mostly abandoned financial district. I leaned forward in my seat toward him. "I've had rather an unpleasant trip, actually. Is there anywhere in the neighborhood you know of where I could go to forget my troubles?"

He turned around to give me an appraising look. Then he smiled and shrugged. "Myself, when I am down, I like beer and a hot meal. Titov's is across the street." He pointed to a colorful awning. "They have good thick sandwiches, hot stews. They don't mind if you drink a lot, as long as no fighting. Or…if you don't mean drink…"

"I didn't, really, no."

"The red light zone is also not too far. Four streets only, but growing every year. I know my way around there, some of the girls. We could go, if you like, after we move luggage."

I pondered the day's experiences for a moment. "Yes, actually I think that would be perfect. That's what we'll do." I dug in my pocket for a gencrous tip. Already, my spirits were beginning to lighten.

TRICKLE DOWN

STEPHEN V. RAMEY

They've taken to sharing a body, these survivors of themselves, these human frames stitched into a mutilated mass of flesh and hair, sinew and bone. Single-minded, guts tapped into the labyrinth sewer at their core, they chew toward the horizon. Mouths of various sizes consume trees, grass, a beehive laced with honey, birds' nests, wolves too proud to stand aside, horses with broken legs, groundhog families in their dens, an eggshell colored purple.

Entire buildings go down the group gullet now: glass shards, twisted metal, houses with tarpaper roofs. The Boys and Girls Club of greater Dayton.

They pause after a planetarium. A belch blows fetid from their mouths. Will they stop? Have they consumed enough?

No. With a grumbling shudder, the flesh-mass moves again, the ground behind it shiny with the residue of their digestion.

APOLOGIA
TAM BLAXTER

I am only a cultivator

of numbers. Sitting in my hundred story prism/rustic
farmhouse, I can see fields.
My seed? An algorithm:
I have some skill coding—my programme
      puts out roots into markets,
      draws up data; I water it with
      liquid assets and,
in the end,
it bears me fruit.

    Understand:
I need not
    understand
what I do
(any more than a farmer need
    understand
the quiet thoughts of budding grasses;
    understand
silent fieldmousegrief at harvest homelessness).

I hear things: outside these walls a storm
blows howling criticism; deputations of foxes
(grieving for mates billowed out with buckshot and
    weeks' rot)
trail to my door; swallows line up on telephone wires
talking over burning guts (the inevitable
    food-chain build-up
    of pesticide);
floating seeds of weeds pay their respects
at my compost heap (graveyard
of their parents their parents' parents).

These things, I'll allow, are a matter for
poetry;
being no poet, I: count
pungent loaves of bread; skim

cloying yellow cream from milk; sleep
between down and down

in a deep silence.

ECHR JUDGEMENT 10/04/12

TAM BLAXTER

The last face you would see
would not be a loved face.
Do not imagine the first day (because
that would be too familiar
a despair), nor the long awaited moment
of condemnation, nor the deepest
bleaknesses of the dark. Imagine only: awaking
on the thousandth day alone;
sitting silent on the ten thousandth;
seeing no other face
until the edges of your own features
no longer spelled out a name.

What can we claim to be in the face of our own
vindictive congratulation? Only: people who would
tear a man up
from the bottom of his soles to
the top of his highest voice uplifted.

FLASH CRASH
TAM BLAXTER

I

Traders with
more sense of their own deserved luck than
sense bought
$10 stocks at 2¢, stocked up
on them.

II

Millions were lost in minutes—as if
a plug was pulled out of the world and worth
drained out.

III

Who are these philosophers whose
treatises in c++ can
redefine our livelihoods, lives' trajectories and the
structures of our nationstates with their
unmeasurable consideration? They must surely be
our deepest thinkers, our poets buoyed up by merited
coke, champagne and accolades.

IV

I imagine that others looked out of full-length windows,
searched the skylines of capitals for unfamiliar gaps

looking up for dead lightbulbs in an unexpected dark.

LET'S JUST GET OUT

TAM BLAXTER

The bank that owned our street went bust
(we hadn't known who'd owned our lives—
even that we had sold ourselves
at all) and then the wall went up

and the first signs—steps to sort us
out. *Don't build, break; don't game; don't shout—
this place is now the property
of an unfamous man. His name?*

*You wouldn't know it—don't wait to
find out. He's just the mind behind
the financial firewall that will
dictate your fates' every facet.*

*Don't embarrass him or it. Breathe
quietly.* No small riot met
this announcement: no crowd complaint
or legal challenge. Its regal

simplicity impressed perhaps;
who can argue with that request:
keep calm and carry on? The next
treasures were physical: measures

to shock or to ensure we knew
what we could lose. The news skipped down
house to house; horrified we heard
the van coming, a man to take

selected sections of our lives.
In lieu of greater payments due
he said, showed us sheets of figures
stacked against us. Backed up into

corners (or so we thought) we caved—
who can argue with numbers on
a printed page? We were boxed in,

freedoms filed away day by day

until our street was the structure
of our gaol. Hour on hours of work
just chipped at debts growing deeper;
hidden cameras tracked us, racked up

misdeeds and scowls scored against our
names. We couldn't move, try to prove
our immurement or meagre lives
for fear of revenge: mere acts of

loutishness (loud voices, dropping
litter, bitterness, etc.)
brought down brutal, numerical
penalty—one digit's swift shift

and the sum could swell a decade,
ten more years of sanctioned fears and
stresses to stick. Soon, no-one slipped
out of line—we'd been assigned our

lot. After a while, some lost it.
I watched one couple (record blotched
with minor missed payments, they were
falling into slow, appalling

debt—they'd never escape) that dwelt
across the street from me; I'd meet
him with face slumped-in solemn, her
pushing baby after *maybes*

at the jobcentre (being jeered
at behind hands). What kind of joint
decision they took I don't try
to guess—a grotesque unconcealed

Russian roulette. From behind net
curtains I'm certain I saw her
hands on bare window pane; her palms
jolting, face gasping in pace with

them, brows creased, barely visible
in the unlit room. A slit of
light from a door ajar could just

illuminate his shape, translate

different dark tones into the scene.
They pressed forward until her breast
kissed the window, body bending
to one side while hand fanned fingers

on glass and the other arched down
into the dark. By the spark in
her briefly closing eyes, I caught
the moment as she came. The same

week they were gone—without note or
word of explanation. I heard
the gossip (kept quiet—we crept
from house to house with it), that they'd

been *disappeared*—without proof, mind,
or sense of what it meant. I sent
out no rumours myself, making
no trouble—the pub'll always

be full enough. I filled in the
detail in my head (her unveiled
skin, his breaths). I wondered, without
much mirth *can that have been worth it?*

FOOLS OF THE BROKEN AGE
GLEN R KRISCH

Their ever-increasing connectivity
leaves them listless and alone,
unable to maintain thoughts or relations
they're mere remnants of themselves

Sensationalism
instant gratification
constant interruption—
all clandestine forces weakening the individual
enslaving these fools of a broken age
a majority lost, borderline enfeebled
fragmenting their creativity, daydreaming,
any accomplishment worthy of posterity

They blindly cede personal choice
and any innate ambition
to the self-serving marketers
who blithely sidestep the societal sway
who instead incessantly blather on
about the latest gadgets,
the must haves,
the must sees

these exulted icons
propagandists dressed as scientists
are the false gods
of a tipping-point age
who make the People's daily dose
of maligned neglect not just palatable
but divinely ordained.

Can anyone claim and hold firmly
to the virtue of remaining aloof
to the sinuous tangle
of the networked single-voice;
to be willing to be labeled
oddly misfit for society?

Can anyone instead gather
within the enfolding embrace
found within their tribe;
their face-to-face family,
dear friends,
known neighbors—
or are these witnesses to a broken age
aberrant souls more worthy of ridicule
than praise for their obstinacy?

The unchallenged hypothesis
discoveries never again considered
young genius never awakened—
all deepening consequences taking root
as one generation decays into the next
as one's potential is never realized
but casually discarded
like a new toy's packaging

Their children will never know
what their parents never learned
as concrete theories become legends
which will fade to myth before slipping
from collective memory altogether—
children borne of a broken age;
one step removed from possibility

THE DIM ONES
GLEN R KRISCH

As a mass they stare blankly outward with childlike dimness,
while inwardly a corrosive force advances.
By the minute they answer the constant pings with Pavlovian intent,
and speaking with only their clumsy thumbs
they churn a guttural language of truncated syllables and transmuted phrasings;

Their blighting chatter permeates everything it touches,
from static lives near their end to the ephemeral breeze—
eliciting apathetic malaise or scathing consequence from outsiders;
they blatantly disregard all, caught up in the irrepressible anxiety to reply.

This unflinching dissonance guides action, thought, subsumes consciousness
degrading the same such into mere human apps
bringing all members of the mass to heel
in the guise of amelioration, social connection,
existential meaning and new-found depth

But such folly is never amended.
Its impact advances unnoticed, unchecked, immutable—
as the bleating charges gather,
their faces illumined by backlit screens, mainlining pixels
into ghostly, scarcely sibilant countenances

This mass, the inheritors of our future
remain as the husks of aspiration and hope,
despairing without knowing
mourning without cogitation
their lost innocence

MANSE OF THE MATHEMATICIAN

ROBERT LAMB

NOVEMBER 2: I don't think he even sees me most of the time. I am at best a tool. A genderless instrument left to wander the stone hallways of this fortress, lost to the peripherals till the need for my skills arises. That's when the mathematician turns and looks through me with those grey-blue eyes.

"Fetch your utensils," he mumbles through pale, pink lips. "The clinic. Twenty minutes."

He towers over most of us, a thin man in his late 60s, seemingly hairless. I have never seen him agitated. I have never seen him smile.

Today the last shipment of supplies entered the castle. Flour sacks, pickle barrels and great wheels of cheese. A beautiful sight to behold. I thought I even glimpsed a cask of wine amid some lesser sundries.

Once the items were inside, Marzell the mathematician ordered them raise the drawbridge and pour cement into the gear houses. Then, brick by brick, they sealed the castle's loan exit to the outside world. Some of the prisoners wept. The soldiers whispered. Marzell turned back to his endless calculations.

NOVEMBER 3: Before the war, Marzell was

the golden child of imperial academia. At age nine, he solved Tannhäuser's Conjecture. At ten, he won the Crown's chess invitational. Conquest after conquest fell to his terrifying intellect. He laid waste to millennia-tested axioms and forged proofs that rewrote physics and skewed humanity's long-accepted place amid the stars. He thrived amid numbers, shunned the living and inhabited instead a world of pure abstraction.

But the war came for Marzell the Mathematician just as it came for all of us. Thus his work here at the castle.

When he commands it, I fetch my "utensils" and meet him in the room he calls his "clinic." It's just another windowless stone vault, of course. The castle if full of them and many are partially collapsed. Who knows what purpose they served a hundred years ago. Two hundred years ago.

The clinic is empty save a single metal table and an electric lamp mounted on a wrought iron tripod. It looms behind me like some giant insect, humming as I unpack the items in my little leather bag: a cluster of sterile needles, gauze, bandages, a motor and the portable battery I use to power it. I have a booklet of designs as well, but I never bother with it here.

Marzell always tells me what to etch.

My specialty was always religious marks. Crosses. Saints. Protective glyphs. That sort of thing. Business only picked up with the eruption of total war.

One might argue that I marketed my self-taught tattoo skills rather shamelessly -- that I implied protective or even curative properties of my work. Indeed, that's exactly what the Home Guard charged me with when they swarmed my apartment. I can still see them now, dressed in their traditional scalloped black body armor, festooned with the golden iconography of empire and death. The booted skull. The savage tooth. The Eagle and the Sphere of Heaven.

Those are all in my little design book as well, by the way. All the symbols we attach meaning to. I've yet to inscribe on my own flesh.

After my arrest, I was sure they'd send me to the front. After all, the war effort grows dire. They no longer discriminate by age, gender or fitness. I resigned myself to death in some hellish latrine trench or out on the cratered no man's land beyond.

Yet here I am in this mountain fortress, sleeping each night with a warm meal in my belly and a wool blanket pulled over my head.

All while the world burns.

A prisoner jumped from the battlements today. We scanned the wooded cliffs below but saw no sign of his remains.

NOVEMBER 5: More of the same today. Marzell commanded me to the clinic, and there he gave me a list of "edits." A Home Guard solider escorted three servants and one prisoner of war into the room. They were broken and silent. I'd worked on them before.

One by one, they presented their canvas to me. On some, I merely altered existing numerals. Other times, I had to cross out lengthy equations and scrawl new ones

in the flesh. I might needle Marzell's figures onto a forearm one minute, then the tender flesh of a sternum or forehead the next. More and more he requests genital tattoos and for these he allows me to administer anesthetic.

"The markings must be legible," he told me. "Do whatever's needed to steady the canvas."

I do what I can to steady my hand as well. I dared ask him only once and he gave no answer. But that evening I returned to my room to find a bottle of bloodroot brandy by my cot. I ration it sparingly.

NOVEMBER 7: We're barely a month into this venture and already prisoners and servants alike walk the halls in varying stages of nudity and inscription. Per Marzell's command and upon pain of death, all marks must be visible at all times -- save during his sporadic periods of sleep.

Bare-chested men and woman pass me in the halls, their ribs and sternum canvassed in numerical conjecture. Backs bear the scourge of innumerable proofs. Even the Home Guard soldiers are not immune to Marzell's calculations. Still-bleeding calculus sleeves half the men's arms.

Only the mathematician and I remain unmarked.

He walks these halls in his grey robes, attended to by two soldiers at all times. As he happens on this prisoner or that, he commands new and perplexing *Tableau vivants* of his living game pieces.

Today he arranged ten naked prisoners into a human pyramid, painstakingly calculating each person's flesh-writ numerical significance. He commanded several positioning changes before the structure met his specifications.

He circled the pyramid, stood back and examined it from various vantage points. No one dared speak. At long last he made some notations in his dog-eared yellow ledger and turned to leave without a word.

NOVEMBER 11: Marzell lives in a world of abstraction -- a world I can scarcely fathom. But occasionally he speaks to himself, and some of that I understand.

"Numbers no more describe the universe than atoms describe the objects they compose," he mumbled today as I needled his numbers into a servant girl's back. "They are the universe inexhaustible."

If that's so, is there an equation for heaven and hell?

An equation for God?

I inscribed three whole pages onto the weeping girl's back, blood obscuring my work on her inflamed canvas. She trembled despite the painkillers, and so did I despite the flask of bloodroot brandy.

When I finished, Marzell studied the results -- commanded her dance and twirl for him in the glow of the humming clinic light. He made notations as always. Then he ordered a soldier to shoot her in the head.

He made the briefest of notations in his yellow ledger, then tucked it under his arm and left the soldier and me standing over her body. We both trembled in the chill, musty air.

He holstered his weapon and told me to help him mop the floor. He made me carry her body up to the battlements and there I looked up at the night sky and hoped to see the stars. But there were none. Only grey clouds. In the distance I glimpsed the titanic shapes of airships, illuminated by the glow of a burning Imperial city.

So far they've left us alone here. Perhaps they don't know the castle exists, much less that the world's greatest mathematician labors here to somehow turn the tide.

I wonder how long it will last.

I threw the dead girl's body over the side and watched it plummet down the cliffs to the wolves below.

NOVEMBER 13: I've emptied the last of the brandy and so far can't seem to locate a replacement bottle. No one questions my wanderings anymore. The soldiers keep to themselves and the cooks -- all marked by my needle -- assume I wander the storeroom for a reason. The remaining quantities of food are somewhat disconcerting.

Marzell's tableaus grow increasingly debauched. He wanders with no less than four soldiers at all times these days, forcing random combinations of prisoners, servants and soldiers into varied acts of copulation, violence or performance art. All at gunpoint. All on pain of death.

I say prisoners, servants and soliders, but these classes no longer exist. We are only slavers and slaves now.

Last night he brought everyone into the circular throne room. Seated upon a stool where once a golden chair may have stood, he orchestrated an orgy the likes of which Sade himself would have praised.

Without the slightest visible sign of passion, the mathematician ordered varying and overlapping combinations of carnality. Where male slaves lacked the vigor to perform, he selected soldiers, most of whom stepped up to their carnal duties without question. Moans, grunts and the rhythmic slap of copulation rose up in a chorus. The throne room floor writhed as a sea of flesh and stank of sweat and honey.

Marzel watched on without seeing, focusing instead on the interaction of their numerical properties. He scribbled endlessly in his yellow ledger and called me over to adjust the markings on no fewer than a dozen slaves and soldiers.

My dreams afterward were strange. I can't bring myself to write them.

NOVEMBER 17: The number of slaves

dwindles. We suffered one suicide, two executions for insubordination and four more died during the orchestration of Marzell's cruel scenes. I helped drag them all to the battlements. The wolves howled in anticipation far below.

The orgies occur nightly now, each more violent and depraved than the last. Two of the soliders in particular, Volas and Thad, seem to revel in the mathematician's commands, as if their own violent and debased pasts were just rehearsals for this. They both still bleed with my inscriptions, the sting of which they seemed to relish -- even the numerals writ down the shaft of Volas' torturous phallus.

I don't watch anymore. At first I couldn't help but find some level of titliation in the proceedings, but no more. I avert my eyes and pinch my ears against the cries, at least until Marzell calls to me and bids me step forth to needle the flesh of slave and rapist alike.

Sometimes I catch glances from Volas or Thad that chill me. In this cruel paradise of theirs, I alone am forbidden to them. I try to avoid them when not in Marzell's presence, just in case they grow bold.

I've taken to walking the battlements in the evenings, past the stone angels crushing monsters underfoot. Swords drawn toward the heavens, blank eyes cast down to this lost mountain redoubt. I watch the fires on the horizon, listen to the wolves and wonder when the airships will close in on us.

NOVEMBER 19: An entire day passes and Marzell has yet to emerge from his quarters. The mood is tense and uncertain. Volas and Thad pace the hallways in impotent longing. How long will they honor the will of an absent master? The other soldiers keep to the barracks, while blanket-wrapped slaves find what comfort they can.

When night fell I took to the battlements again and chanced a prayer before one of the stone angels. I begged for guidance. Despite my former trade in religious tattoos, I've never been a believer. But I've never felt this desperate.

NOVEMBER 23: Marzell emerged from his quarters after four days of solitude. He seems paler, more emaciated -- less a creature of flesh and more a revenant imposed on this vile castle and its inhabitants. His robes are stained and wretched; his voice even slighter than before.

He summoned his two loyal rapists. I saw him lean in close to whisper to them at length. The blood drained from even Volas' cruel face at what those bloodless lips had to say.

I know some revelation is at hand.

Has he solved the Emperor's mathematical quandary? Is the empire saved? The war effort revitalized? Are we free to abandon this place, or has he merely devised some final and catastrophic means of reaching his answer?

And to what end? He has never revealed the Emperor's task, nor how these tableaus help to make the answer clear. All we know is that the entire war effort hinges on the answer.

The soldiers whisper varying theories. Some speculate he seeks to break the enemy's code. Others assume the work relates to a devastating secret weapon -- a power than answers only to mathematical perfection. I even heard a slave whisper that Marzell practices numerological sorcery and seeks to free a demon from some ancient relic.

But I don't think it matters anymore, least of all to Marzell. He sees the world in abstraction. He sees a mathematical universe spiraling off into void. Regardless of its import, he desires his elusive answer for its own sake.

I went straight to the battlements and

confessed all these worries to the stone angel. I asked her for guidance and protection, even as I glimpsed the faint glow of burning farms and villages in the distance.

The absurdity of it all isn't lost on me. Here I am, seeking deliverance from this secluded refuge. The world burns. The Empire may well have already fallen.

Still I prayed for help. Impossibly, I heard the angel whisper in reply.

"Bring the ledger to me tomorrow night," she said, "and I will save you."

I rushed straight to my room, to this scribbled journal. I can't sleep. All I can think on are those words.

NOVEMBER 29: Preparations have begun for Marzell's final tableau. The soldiers drag the necessary items up from the castle's deep cellars: great lengths of black chain, barrels of oil, three chests of field surgery equipment I didn't even know we had.

His list of edits is exhaustive, and once more I butcher the hides of soldier and slave alike with my little needle. I'm running out of canvas on most of them, forcing tattoos on even less ideal places: the soles of feet, faces, hands and freshly-shaven heads. The slaves especially eye me with loathing and hatred. I want to whisper to them, to tell them what the angel said and reassure them. But I can't risk it.

Meanwhile, Marzell is never without his yellow ledger. If he's not writing in it, then it's tucked under his arm. So I waited for him to retire to his quarters.

Early this evening he finally did.

I followed him as he took his usual course through the halls, then rushed ahead through another route. As planned, I entered his quarters just ahead of the mathematician himself.

The room reeked of neglect. Piss and shit overflowed both bed pans. Flakes of number-scrawled parchment littered the floor and various texts lay open throughout the room.

I squeezed myself beneath the room's great double bed, waited and watched his loafers enter the room. Watched the door shut behind them. I watched as best I could to see where he stowed his precious ledger, but it seemed he climbed into bed with it.

As I waited for him to fall asleep, fairy tale predicaments ran through my head: the key in the sleeping witch's pocket, the sword in the napping giant's hand. I'd have to reenact these fitful moments of drama and ease the book from his vile hands -- assuming he didn't lie upon it entirely.

Would stealth even cut it, or would I have to assault him? Could I make it back to the battlements before the soldiers caught me? Or should I drown him in his foul slop bucket now?

When I heard his snores, I knew it was time to find out.

I crawled from beneath the old bed, careful not to stir the scraps of paper. A single lamp still burned in the room, giving life to all the absurd notations affixed to the walls and to the calculations writ in black ink across every available surface.

And there, in the bed, lay the old revenant himself. To my relief, the book lay untouched beside him.

So I reached down and gripped it in both hands. Holding my breath, I lifted it up from sheets delicately, as if it were a landmine or some rare work of art. I watched his face the entire time, ready for those cold eyes to open at any moment.

But he didn't wake. I made it to the door and unlocked it without a sound. I slid out into the hallways and slowly closed the gap behind me.

The halls were empty, save one or two slaves who peered up at me with mutilated faces and hopeless eyes. All the soldiers seemed busy with their preparations, so I encountered no one as I made the stairwell and ascended the last 113 steps to the battlements above.

Dusk burned and dwindled on the horizon. Thick grey clouds blotted out the sky above with the ash of burning farms and cities.

I rushed to the stone angel and bowed before her. I lifted the book on high.

"I have it!" I rasped.

"Do you now?" grated the reply.

Only it was not the voice of the angel. This voice, unfortunately, I knew all too well.

I turned and there behind me stood Volas, stripped to the waist. His hard pectoral muscles still wept blood through a hundred different numerals from my morning's session with him.

He had a pistol on his waist, but it was the item in his hand that drew my attention: a crude mace of wood and nails. The weapon was roughly the same size as Volas' foul member -- and just as bloody. I tried to stop myself from remembering why.

He smiled his awful grin and took a menacing step forward, his vile instrument readied. In my mind, a voice shouted "run!" but a cold fist gripped my heart.

I couldn't move.

He took another step. I opened my mouth to speak and nothing came out.

And then he was standing over me, grabbing a handful of my hair and dragging me to my feet.

He raised the bloody mace high over his head.

I closed my eyes and turned my head, as if darkness would grant me refuge from the death blow -- but the death blow didn't' come.

I felt a warm rainfall on my cheek.

Then a downpour.

The fist remained tight in my hair, but I felt the arm go slack. I opened my eyes and looked up through the rain of hot blood. Volas' weapon arm was gone -- blown off at the elbow.

The fist unclenched and I tumbled to the side.

A high-pitched snapping sound rang out and more blood splattered on the stones beside me, along with Volas' fragmented corpse.

Trembling, wet with the rapist's death, I looked up to see the stone angel looming over me -- and above it the faint movements of something titanic in the ashen clouds overhead.

An enemy airship above the cloud line.

A figure stepped from behind the statue, clad entirely in flat black armor. It gripped a long, fat-barreled gun in one hand -- and with the other reached out to me.

My fingers crept and found the blood-splattered book where it lay between us.

"Give me the ledger," she said, that same angelic voice I'd heard before.

"What will happen to us?"

"Give me the ledger and you'll live."

"Can you stop him?"

Silence, save the whirl of wind over the battlements. Save my own labored breathing and the beating of my heart.

"He is on the verge of something incredible," the angel said. "Something unprecedented."

"You…"

"We want his solution as well," she said. "It will save the entire world."

I think I started laughing. I think I cried, right there as Volas's blood washed around my legs and sainted the edges of that yellow ledger. I lifted it up from the blood and screamed.

NOVEMBER 31: She kept her word. I'm still alive.

And as I write this entry in my

journal, the great and final computation commences in the throne room. I can hear the screams from here. I wonder what he sees in it. Perhaps his answer, but I'm doubtful.

The angel -- whatever her name truly is -- took the ledger from me on the battlements and handed it off to another enemy solider in black armor. A spy basket lowered from the cloud-cloaked airship overhead and he climbed inside with the book. I stood there with the angel and watched as the airship reeled him home.

When he returned, they placed the book back in my hands and told me to return it to Marzall, along with tidings of peace.

What could I do but obey?

What have I ever done?

Two days have passed and the airship floats anchored to the battlements overhead. We have a dozen new slaves. Two new soldiers. My fingers tremble from all the work I've done preparing them.

There seems no end to this. The decimal point carries out to the limits of the horizon. I know he'll call me into the throne room any moment now and then I'll have to see what atrocity he's inflicted on the world. I'll have to look into the eyes of his victims, and then I'll add more numbers to their suffering.

There's one small consolation, however. A second bottle of brandy appeared in my room. It's already half gone. I guzzled it down last night as I gave myself this first and only tattoo.

It's needled into the flesh above my heart.

This soft and bleeding breast.

An eight resting on its side.

Crudely formed. And infinite.

GALLERY OF ANGELS
R. C. EDRINGTON

guitar chord slices air
like a razor blade
along a tongue
& even bleach
won't remove
the bloodstains
on the bedroom floor
where Cindy carved
a heroin angel
in her frail
porcelain-like wrist
& awoke
in a cloud filled
bus depot
destination
St. Peter's gate

& Jenny scrubs
just to scrub
just to keep
a rhythm in the air
as Steve shoves
his baby blue
Fender Mustang
like a rapist's cock
thru the cracked drywall
into the kitchen

where Marie ties off
on the black
& white linoleum floor
with a wilted rose
bleeding from her teeth
in memory of Cindy
& the wasted nights
we danced with angels
on the tip
of a thin syringe

only to wake
years later
in this condemned
cold water flat
all slaves to angels
who fell from grace

NIGHTS WHEN BAR-STOOLS SPEAK
R. C. EDRINGTON

on nights when bar-stools
speak like dead poets
Bukowski says
honest poets don't write
from verandas overlooking
Italian coastlines,
sip bottled designer water
& wait for some
opium tweaked muse
to whisper sweet odes
against the crest of their ear

 honest poets sit alone
in dingy downtown nightclubs,
chain smoke yesterdays
& swallow shots of courage
between shots of Jack Daniels
to phone an ex-lover...
but only end up
back at their hotel room
with a drunk, big titted
English major plastered
to their arm like a cheap
prison green tattoo

only to awake alone again,
except for the splash

of the shower, the stench
of dime store perfume
that fogs the air
like cheap cigar smoke
over a crowded dance floor,
& the squeaky hum
of a faceless female voice

as they stumble
across the cold linoleum floor
with a sheet wrapped
like a bandage
around their sad,
middle-aged waist
& nearly knock over
the laptop
as their fingers stagger
like drunken dancers
for the Vodka bottle

& pray words
really aren't like women,
& that someday
they'll slide effortlessly
across the sheets
without first being lubricated
with booze

INSOMNIA BLUES

R. C. EDRINGTON

I don't miss
all your deep throat blow jobs
in that downtown nightclub
where we first heard
Concrete Blonde & you
splashed black mascara
onto my eyes to birth
some hybrid new wave
punk rock poet
in the polished
stainless steel mirror
bound by chicken wire
in that unisex bathroom
that reeked of liquored piss
& burnt heroin

nor all the quick
lipstick smear, hair pull
thrusts & fucks as you knifed
your Doc Martens
into my ribs like switchblades
in the trash scarred
backseat of your ancient
& abused Cadillac El Dorado
painted Elvis Presley
or as I called it...pussy pink

nor the sweaty
100 degree nights
spent lost on your desert hi-way
as I snorted white coke lines
thru the adobe mesas
of your breast,
down your hard chest
& into the valley of your stomach
in search of midnight rain
that clung like pre-dawn dew
between your sad & frayed

fishnet shrouded thighs,

but I do miss
your pale & taut body
jack knifed into
my leather draped chest
on that cold cement
warehouse floor
littered with other
stupidly young & homeless
couples like us

as the fiery tangle
of your neon red hair
sparked warmth thru my cheek
as I dreamed always
& only
of you.

3AM BABBLE
R. C. EDRINGTON

endless lines
scribbled
so many empty words

dreams battered & bruised

false idols I clung to
in search of light
when darkness was all
there ever really was

lost inside this void

how much love
will I take to my grave?

POLLUTO

how many people
hollow eyed & lonely
waste their lives in wait
for an embrace or a kiss
to make them believe
they are somebody?

endless associations
symbols warped together
to pretend there is meaning

a dead man on a cross

how many people
are dying right now

sucking on a shotgun in wait
for that sudden twig snap
in the point blank silence
of night
to send them out of their minds?

this flesh
weak & fragile

endlessly I wander
pretending I have something
that needs to be said
when I've never
really had anything but myself

& that was always linked
to someone else

the first time I fell in love
was probably the last time
my heart was a whirlpool
of innocence
sucking me into being

PORNOGRAPHIC NOVEL
R. C. EDRINGTON

The way a drunken cock
sadly begs for penetration,
she pokes the syringe
up & down the worn veins
in her frail tattooed arm.

From the bedroom window,
I am left alone to witness
the whispering wound of moonlight
bleed shadows thru
cottonwood branches
clinging like black fishnet stockings
to midnight's bruised thighs.

Once there was love
which passed between us,
where now there is only silence...
& her love was like
a windowless basement
on a storm raped night,
nothing existed outside
its womb like darkness.

But this shelter has begun to cave
like the veins which scar her arms,
& now I'm trapped
within this tomb-like loneliness
searching for an exit door
that may no longer even exist.

In the alley below,
a Gulf War veteran in bell bottom jeans
sips the nectar of muse
from a brown papered bag,
then fades into the rear doorway
of an adult movie house
where for .25 cents he'll receive
enough inspiration

to make a metaphor of his hand.

And I wonder,
if her desire to touch me
will ever again be as strong
as her need for a fix right now,
or will she just continue
to pantomime her emotions
like a seasoned porno star.

FOR CAIT
R. C. EDRINGTON

she encouraged me
my art was in language
not subject,
so all the bloodstains
& worn syringes
from all the nubile
junkie whores
& quick amphetamine
sex & diseases
scattered thru
my words & syntax
like tarnished pennies
around crisp dollar bills
in that battered guitar case
tossed like a spent body
on that 4th avenue sidewalk
where I used to scream
the blooze
held a value & truth
all their own,
so I scribbled what I knew
& she published
what I knew,
but damn I miss her badly

& learned enough to know
her name belongs
in one of my jaded
self absorbed pieces
no more than it did
in the obituaries that day
my eyes exploded
with tears like
an infected vein
that shoots pus & blood
against a graffiti scarred
bus depot
bathroom mirror

A PIECE WORTH MILLIONS

MADELEINE SWANN

Dust collected on Mike's face during his first day of sleep. That morning Lilly nudged him, shook him, and left for work. "Get fired, see if I care," she fumed. Still Mike didn't move.

Lilly began worrying when she returned to find him in the same position, and he smelled like the attic. No-one, not his parents, not the doctors, could explain it, and no medicine made any difference. "He's just asleep," they all said. "He'll wake up when he's had enough." Lilly sat in the chair beside him, dark circles under her eyes. All the worry had gone from Mike's face. It was almost porcelain smooth, his breathing like crashing waves.

On day three she called in sick. "Don't you worry," said her boss, a corpulent man named Ralph, "you just take care of yourself." On day seven, Lilly's rectum contracted as she called in again. "Yes, well," replied Ralph, "I suppose it can't be helped. Just don't leave us, we deserve better than that." After a few minutes of shaking Mike and begging, she slumped onto the floor. She knew the Mike who read zombie stories aloud while she was ill lay there somewhere, needing her help, but she was so tired.

It was dark when she woke. Gleaming under the moonlight were several cobweb strands connecting Mike to the headboard and sides of the bed. Lilly grabbed a tissue and swiped at them before falling back into the chair. She began sobbing, mulling over the times she had begged him to help her with bills. Now he really couldn't. "You selfish arse," she snuffled, watching for cobwebs.

On the eighth day Lilly's phone rang. It was Helen. "You're coming out with me today," she said. "You can't just sit and watch him, it's creepy."

After a day at the shops, Helen paused outside Lilly's front door. "Can I see?" Lilly's stomach wriggled with embarrassment. "Oh go on," Helen begged, and Lilly relented.

In the doorway of the bedroom Lilly shrieked and hid her face. Helen hugged her tightly, eyes fixed on Mike. The cobwebs had covered him in thick white fuzz, strands from every angle anchoring him to the bed and headboard. "It's OK," said Helen, "I'll call the ambulance. You can stay with me."

A night at Helen's almost made Lilly feel normal. Dressed for work in the morning, she searched the kitchen cupboards for a bowl when something caught her eye. Her breathing was ragged as she straightened the newspaper. "Local man sleeps as town watches on," shrieked the headline and there in the picture was Mike, unconscious on the bed, with a crowd standing around him. Beside him, grinning widely with his thumbs up, was one of the paramedics.

She unlocked her front door and barged in, bashing someone roughly on the shoulder. "Excuse me," she thundered, pushing through the chattering crowds. She recognised a few from the neighbourhood but many were complete strangers.

"That's his girlfriend!" squealed a woman and they became a mob, crowding her and shouting questions.

"Why is he doing it?"

"What statement is he trying to make?"

"Did you help him plan it?"

"Are you supporting him?"

"Enough!" yelled Lilly, pushing past the groups milling on the stairs and hallway. In the bedroom a man in an expensive suit and blue cravat was surrounded by four large workmen. "What the Hell's going on?"

"I've just been having a little chat with Mike here," said the man with a camp flourish. Lilly eyed Mike, who lay as insensible as ever. "He's coming with me to the Tate Modern. I believe we could make quite a considerable sum together." Lilly opened her mouth to speak but couldn't. "Mike here is quite the talk of the town and we need to get him established as quickly as possible."

"What? No!" Lilly exploded, rushing to Mike's side. "No-one is taking him anywhere. He needs medical assistance, not a bloody art gallery."

"On the contrary," said the man, "I've had express permission from the one person who knows what's best for him." He motioned for the four helpers to grab a bed corner each, shoving Lilly out the way.

"Who decided this?" Lilly watched them lift Mike into the air.

"Careful! He's priceless!" shrieked the collector as they tilted the bed to fit him through the doorway. He turned to Lilly.

"Why, his mother of course."

Lilly bit her lip hard. Of course, Mary. "Wait!" She called. The men didn't stop and Lilly grabbed the collector's arm. "What if I made you something else? A model of him? I mean, I've never done it before but it would represent him or something, and –"

"Sorry, my dear," the collector pulled away his frilled sleeve, "it's only art if somebody else says it's worth a lot of money."

Lilly stood in the empty room. The carpet where the bed had been was almost black with dust; Mike was supposed to have cleaned it each week. She sank to her knees.

She had been sitting there for an hour by the time the house phone rang. "Lilly, what's going on?" asked Helen. "Your mobile's here and work called. He was crying; he said you were letting the team down and yourself down, and if that was how you wanted it to be then maybe he should just throw all your things out the window."

Lilly groaned; the penguin pencil sharpener given to her by Mike would be smashed on the ground by now. Struck by a thought, Lilly leapt to the drawers and pulled out the contents. "Sorry I have to go!" she shrieked. "Dammit, where's it gone?" Eventually, surrounded by useless papers, she covered her face with her hands. She had no choice.

She dialled the number with clenched teeth. "Hello, bank of Bradbury?" said the woman's voice on the other end.

"I need to order a statement," said Lilly.

"Do you have the special magic number?"

"No, but I can answer any security questions you like."

"That'll be with you in six months, madam," said the rep after Lilly ordered the statement.

"Six months?" Lilly collapsed onto the sofa.

"Yes, apologies madam but lack of

your special magic number means six months is the soonest it can be with you."

"Well what bollocking bloody good is that?"

"Excuse me," said the Rep, "did I say six? I meant seven."

Two months passed. Lilly waited, transfixed to news reports and devouring articles about Mike. He was doing a tour of museums including the Louvre before settling at the Tate. She and Mike had talked about going to Paris, and now he was going without her. "Maybe it's for the best he's gone?" said Helen, "Don't you remember that time you asked him to cut the grass and he tried to set fire to it?" Lilly didn't reply.

A third month crawled by. She began to use her savings on rent. She knew she had to get a new job or find another source of food. She eyed her neighbour's celery patch.

The fourth month limped to its end. Lilly had thought her moonlit excursions to next door's garden were a secret. When she bumped into the old lady in the street, however, there was pity in her eyes. Helen's calls trailed off to every other week.

At dawn Lilly searched the streets for a discarded newspaper. Her hands shook as she pulled one from a bin and checked the first page. Mike's arrival at the Tate Modern was front page news. Beside him in the picture was his mother, proudly sporting a new designer hat. Further inside a debate raged about his motivations. One critic, his face suitably disgruntled in the top corner, demanded Mike was classed as outsider art. On the opposite page others assured his commentary was too important. Lilly barely noticed; her eyes were fixated on Mike; one of his eyes was half open. "Mike," she whispered, "I'm coming to get you."

The bank opened at nine; Lilly pulled the hood of her black coat over her head. The other customers tried not to stare at the skinny, wild eyed girl with the dark circles under

her eyes as she twitched her way to the queue. They avoided her gaze as she fidgeted and muttered, and the line drew steadily closer to the windows. "Good morning, how may I help you?" beamed the doughy assistant from behind Perspex glass.

"You can give me what I want or –" Lilly grabbed a lady behind her and pulled a bread knife from her pocket – "this woman gets it!" The lady shrieked and everyone stopped to stare. Lilly gripped the knife tighter as sweat soaked her hands.

"Don't hurt her" squeaked the assistant, "How much do you want? It's all in the safe we don't have much out here."

Lilly spoke as if to a deaf person, "I just… want…my bank statement."

The assistant frowned, nervously lowering her arms. "OK, I can get that done for you. I just need to take some details."

Nobody sat next to her on the train, and as she made her way to the gallery nobody stepped in her path. She pushed open the industrial doors of the gallery and marched upstairs to Mike's exhibition, and her footsteps thundered through the still, expansive room. Mike was surrounded by sculptures and paintings, his breathing smooth and gentle as a calm sea. The cobwebs stretched over the entire bed, and the thick fuzz had almost completely cocooned him.

"I thought I'd find you here," said an upper class, effete voice. The collector stepped forwards from the corner. "You're in a bit of trouble, young lady. I just saw you on the news."

"I'm what's best for Mike," said Lilly. "Here, look at this." She pulled the statement from inside her coat. "A joint bank account, plus I have bills. Anything financial goes through me, so I have final say where he ends up."

"My dear," the collector toyed with his cravat, "Well, that's marvellous news. He's more than tripled in value."

"I don't care," shrieked Lilly, "he's waking up. He won't be a freak show much longer."

"Yes," said the collector in a low voice, "that's precisely why we were going to give him this." He pulled a dark green bottle from his suit pocket. "Eze-sleep" was emblazoned on the label in fluffy white letters. "Just think of it, he'll keep increasing in value. You'll never have to work again." He raised an eyebrow, "I could even pull a few strings at court."

Lilly's stomach growled. She stepped towards him. "Let me see that." The collector moved to hand her the bottle and she knocked it from his hand, sending it spinning across the floor. "Mike!" she cried. She heard the door slam as the collector ran from the room. "Quick, wake up, he'll be getting the police, we've got to go." She shook him, pinging some of the threads from the headboard.

His eyes cracked open.

"Lilly?" he croaked. "Lilly, help me, can you help me?"

"Of course!" Lilly frantically pulled at more threads. "Everything will be better from now on, we'll support each other, we'll prove mum wrong."

"Lilly can you call work? I'm not going back there anymore. I know you got me the job and everything, but it's just not really me."

Lilly froze, one hand hovering over a white strand. "Ok," she said calmly. "Are you alright? Can I get you anything?"

"I'm so thirsty," he wheezed, "Could you get me a drink?"

"Of course." Lilly patted him gently, and fetched him the bottle.

THE GIRL WITH THE PIPPI TATTOO

J. MICHAEL SHELL

THE LURID ADVENTURES OF DAGGI SCHLONGSTALKING
EPISODE II

"Woof."

"Whose girlfriend?"

"Woof."

"Your girlfriend? Is she as hideous as you are?"

"Woof, woof, woof, woof, woof!"

"Alright! Calm down! I apologize. I'm sure she's lovely. Where is this canine Cleopatra?"

"Woof."

"What do you mean, she's not a dog?"

"Woof."

"I *intend* to see for myself. *Where?*" Daggi insisted.

"Woof," Lord Assface told her, nodding toward the open front door.

"Lead the way," Daggi invited. "But I warn you, if you have a human child out there, I'm going to neuter you with a butter knife."

With Daggi in tow, Lord Assface (perhaps the world's most hideous mongrel) led the way through Villa Fullacoca's door and onto the front porch. There in the yard, grazing in the early morning sun, was a very petite burro. To Daggi's human eyes, the fuzzy, gray beast was adorable. To another burro, she'd have been a princess. To Lord Assface, she was all those things as well as a very desirable piece of pun-intended ass.

"What a cute little donkey!" Daggi squealed.

"Woof."

"Okay! What a cute little *burro*. Has she a name?"

"Woof."

"That's disgusting. I think I'll call her Delilah."

"Woof?"

"Yes, that means she can stay. But I have to ask, how can you possibly mate with this creature?"

"Woof."

"Don't be crude. I *mean*, she's too *large*. How do you...*manage* it?"

"Woof."

"What do you mean she's *porch trained?*"

In order to illustrate, Lord Assface jumped down into the yard and, yapping a bit, ran once around the grazing burro. When he returned, Delilah came with him and backed her fuzzy flank level with the floorboards of the villa's porch. Once she was in position, Lord Assface leapt onto her haunches and began humping to beat the band.

Though she couldn't help giggling just a bit, Daggi managed to say, "Stop it, this instant. While I'm usually fond of unnatural acts, this is not one I'm willing to witness. You may hump when I'm elsewhere."

"Woof," Lord Assface agreed, executing an incredibly athletic leap back onto the porch.

"Will she let me ride her?" Daggi asked.

"Woof."

"Why in the world would you be jealous?"

"Woof."

"That's true, but I only do that with *human* girls." Then, cocking her pretty head, Daggi asked, "Have you been *watching*?"

When the nasty little animal failed to answer, Daggi said, "Well, you'd better not let me *catch* you watching. And I'm sure Delilah wouldn't appreciate it, either."

Lord Assface emitted a pitiful whine, and plopped down onto his butt.

"You haven't answered my question," Daggi prodded. "*May I ride her?*"

"Woof?"

"Yes," Daggi smiled. "I suppose, in *this* case, you can watch."

Delilah was a gentle soul, and afforded Daggi a smooth and comfortable ride around the yard. Wearing a hideous, tongue-draped grin, Lord Assface watched from his perch on the porch.

Though she had no inclinations toward barnyard romance, the gentle friction of Delilah's downy fur through Daggi's thin panties (which she wore beneath a pleated, plaid mini) was causing her some amount of pleasant distress. Just as a tiny little moan was about to escape her, Daggi became aware

of Lord Assface panting heavily and drooling on the porch. Immediately (though with some regret), she hopped down off Delilah's back and smoothed the lap of her mini skirt with her palms. Lord Assface whined.

"Be good," she told him. "I'm going back to bed for a bit. You two have fun."

Inspired by her ride on Delilah, Daggi went up to her big, round bed and engaged herself in a solo enterprise. Unfortunately, she had never been very good with herself. Domineering by nature, it was difficult for her to submit to her own dominance. At one point, in a fit of frustration, she slapped herself hard on the ass and, referring to the large, battery-powered phallus she held, said, "Be still while I put this in you!" Then she hopped off the bed, dropped the whining appliance onto the floor, and said, "This just won't do. I need something different. But *what*?"

Looking down at the vibrating dildo dancing around on the floor, Daggi said, "Yes. I'm due for a dick. But men are so *frustrating*, and corpses so hard to dispose of when you aren't at sea. Oh, I can't think straight through this *itch*!" she growled. Then she marched back downstairs and out through the door, just as Lord Assface was backing Delilah up to the porch. "Oh no you don't," Daggi told him. "You go in the house! I put a nice boiled egg in your bowl—eat it *slowly*."

The scruffy little animal abandoned his intentions with Delilah, and skulked toward the door. "Woof," he said as he entered the house.

"I do *not* need a di..." Daggi began in a scolding tone. But she stopped in the middle of that sentence and whimpered, "Is it that obvious?"

"Woof."

"Oh, shut up!" Daggi exclaimed, slamming the door behind Lord Assface.

Then she climbed aboard Delilah, lay her head in the burro's fluffy mane, and said, "Just prance around a bit, please. I need to think."

Delilah pranced, Daggi moistened her underpants, and Lord Assface growled behind the villa's front door.

Daggi's dilemma planted itself in her foremost consciousness and grew like Jack's beanstalk. Nothing seemed to work for her anymore. Even rides on Delilah ceased having the desired effect (which was a great relief to her ugly little dog).

One day, in an effort to release her growing tension, Daggi phoned Roxanne and Sally, and begged them to stop by for a little coke and rum orgy. After hours and hours of rump romping, lip locking, fidgety-fingered fun, Daggi's two friends lay sprawled and exhausted in a tangle of sheets. Daggi, however, seemed completely unaffected, and wore a look that could only be described as sullen desperation.

In a voice filled with satiated sighs, Roxanne asked her, "Didn't you get off?"

"I *can't*," Daggi sulked. "I'm stopped up."

"Maybe you need a dick," Sally said in her shy little voice.

"But men are *annoying!*" Daggi screeched. "Not to mention unpleasant to look at. What I need is a *girl* with a dick."

"I'd be happy to strap one on for you," Roxy offered.

"I know you would, sweetie, but it's just not the same. I need *real*. I need *meat!*"

Then Sally whispered something into Roxanne's ear that made them both giggle.

"If you're making fun of me, I'm going to spank you both until you cry," Daggi pouted.

Roxy and Sally snuggled up against Daggi's forlorn body-language, and Roxy said, "We wouldn't make fun, but you can spank us anyway."

Sally agreed through a bright red blush, then said, "I was telling Roxy you should go to *Tre Chic* in Charleston, and ask for Remy to be your waiter."

"Who's Remy?" Daggi asked.

Roxy and Sally giggled again, and Roxy said, "Just the prettiest boy you've ever seen. There are plenty of girls who would *kill* for his looks."

"And they say he has a big one," Sally blushed.

"And the food's really good at *Tre Chic*," Roxy added.

"Hmmm," Daggi said through a thoughtful smile. "I like good food. Maybe I'll give it a try. Now turn over, both of you! It's time for your spanking!"

And so on and so forth all through that night.

Though in no way a fashionista, Daggi possessed a strong sense of style, and certainly understood the science of dressing to kill. From a boutique in Charleston, she'd purchased a short and slinky, black cocktail dress, a lovely string of pearls, and a delicate pair of clear-plexi pumps that showed off the rainbow enamel on her pretty toes. Leaving her long and shapely legs bare, Daggi donned these items of apparel, along with appropriate amounts of war-paint. The result was stunning, and if Remy hid a truly male psyche behind his girlish looks, it would certainly be at Daggi's mercy. Papa Stig, the last time she'd seen him, had called her "too good lookin'." If such a thing were possible, Daggi embodied it. As she gazed at her countenance in the mirror, she actually felt a pang of desire. "Maybe I should just stay home and take you myself," she told her reflection.

"Woof," Lord Assface commented, hiding somewhere in the shadows behind her.

"I *know* what I need, you little

peeping Tom!" she said, spinning around and throwing a hairbrush at her voyeur dog.

If Daggi had been stunning standing there looking into her mirror, the sight of her riding the Ducati in that tantalizing outfit was almost too much to bear. Twice, on the way to *Tre Chic*, motorcycle cops pulled her over just to have a better, more lingering look. At a stoplight, Daggi noticed a male motorist sitting beside her, his head laid onto his steering wheel, gazing and moaning aloud with the ache of desire. Unable to control her wonderful wickedness, Daggi ran a red-glazed fingernail up her thigh, catching the hem of her little dress to reveal several more inches of silky, mocha skin. The poor man drooled on his steering wheel.

Though the cops had been flatteringly annoying, and the moaning motorist vaguely amusing, all had conspired to lengthen Daggi's journey toward *Tre Chic* and her intended prey—Remy. By the time she arrived it was well past nine, and inching its way toward the witching hour.

Tre Chic, as one might deduce from the name, was a fine, French restaurant. After making her preference of waiter known, Daggi was seated at a tiny table near a window overlooking the Battery. Immediately, a gorgeous little cocktail waitress asked if she'd like something to drink. After mimicking Lord Assface's pitiful whine, Daggi said, "Better just bring me a Pepsi. I need to stay focused, and you aren't helping."

Showing Daggi a quizzical look, the waitress asked, "Will Coke be okay?"

"As long as it has a capital 'C'," Daggi answered.

With an understanding wink, the cocktail waitress said, "One Coke, no straw, coming up."

"Oh! And bring me a piece of lime with that," Daggi added. "It keeps away the scurvy."

Several sips into her lime and cola, Daggi looked up and saw exactly what Roxy and Sally had been talking about. With his long-lashed blue eyes locked onto Daggi's own beauty, Remy approached in all his magnificent, pretty-boy splendor. Captured into a ponytail Daggi longed to set loose, his golden locks fell well past his shoulders and curled in delightful, Shirley Temple ringlets. Rosy cheeks, soft and smooth as Sally's bare bottom, rode high above his pouty, swollen lips. Even his body was svelte, and hourglassed down to his curvaceous hips and pillowy buns.

Though "love," for Daggi, was a dangerous thing (she'd tell you she had loved Bluto Parks), she was positively, certifiably, undeniably enamoured of the boy-toy standing before her. "Good evening," he spoke in a mellifluous, almost-tenor. "I'm Remy."

"I know," Daggi blurted out.

"Really?" he asked. "I'm sure I've never seen you here before. There's no way I wouldn't remember *you*. And I love that dress—you're quite stunning in it."

Without realizing it, Daggi whined again as an image of Remy wearing her dress invaded her thoughts.

"Pardon?" Remy asked.

"Oh!" she recovered. "I was just saying, look at the time. I think I'd better order something to eat. I'm hungrier than you can imagine."

Remy smiled, showing perfect rows of teeth as white as Daggi's pearls. "An appetizer?" he suggested.

"What do you recommend?" Daggi asked.

"The Clams Casino are very good, though I have to admit, I like the raw better."

Stifling another whine, Daggi said, "Absolutely! Me, too! Bring me a dozen and a lick of lemon."

"*A lick?*" Remy asked with a smile.

"Oh, *please*," Daggi whispered into her hands. "I mean a *piece*, a *slice* of lemon," she gushed. "I think your cologne has me tongue-tied. Halston, isn't it?"

"You've very astute senses," Remy told her.

"You have no idea."

"I'll be right back with your clams."

Though she preferred catching her own, Daggi ordered frog's legs with potatoes au gratin and a Caesar salad. She ate very slowly, and her eyes never left Remy while he was in the dining room. On several occasions, she caught him sneaking furtive glances at her. When finally she'd finished her frogs, Remy asked, "Would you like some dessert?"

Having decided to make her move, Daggi answered, "Would *you?*"

"I'm always ready for dessert," Remy told her, showing his pearly-white teeth.

"Then let's have it at my villa," Daggi told him. "I think I can find something sweet that you'd like."

"You're my last table," Remy said enthusiastically. "Let's go."

"Are you walking or riding?" Daggi asked.

"My little Fiat is out front."

"I brought my Ducati," Daggi told him. "Why don't you follow me. Watching me ride might whet your appetite."

Remy's eyes widened, and he thought to himself, "Watching her ride in that dress might wet something else."

When Daggi pulled into the yard at Villa Fullacoca, Delilah was gently grazing beneath the stars. Lord Assface was lying on the porch, legs in the air in a decidedly sated pose.

"Go away!" Daggi told him as Remy pulled in. "You're spoiling the view!"

With a harrumphing little "Woof," Lord Assface disappeared himself from sight.

"What an amazing place!" Remy exclaimed as he strode up to the villa.

"I call it home," Daggi told him. "Will you help a lady up the steps. I'm not quite used to these shoes."

"They're charming," Remy said, ignoring her proffered arm and placing his own around her waist.

"Hmmm," Daggi sang. "That'll work, too."

"Is that your little donkey?" Remy asked.

From somewhere in the shadows came an indignant "Woof."

"What was that?"

"What was what?" Daggi asked, making a mental note to drug her increasingly feisty dog when expecting company.

"I thought I heard..."

"She's a *burro*, actually," Daggi interrupted. "Her name is Delilah."

"She's cute."

"Maybe we'll have a ride later on."

"Like Lady Godiva?" Remy ventured.

"If you can pull it off," Daggi teased.

Once inside the villa, Daggi took Remy's hand and said, "C'mon, let me give you the tour."

But the "tour" consisted of Daggi pulling Remy up the stairs and directly into her room. Before she'd left, she'd made up her big, round bed with red satin sheets, and covered it in heart-shaped pillows. "Shall we have our dessert in here?" Daggi asked, sitting on the bed and pulling Remy down beside her.

"You were right," Remy told her. "Watching you ride made me hungry." Then he dove right into his dessert dish of Daggi, settling his pouty lips onto hers.

After several minutes of increasingly

heavy petting, Daggi stopped him in mid pet. "What's wrong?" he asked, catching his breath.

"Nothing is *wrong*, but things can always become more *right*," Daggi told him. "I have a proposition for you—a wager, actually. Somewhere on my body, I have a tattoo. If you can guess where it is, I'll do absolutely *anything* you can think of, all night long."

"And if I guess wrong?" Remy asked.

"Then you will be *mine* all night, body and soul."

"Hmmm," Remy wondered. "There are a lot of places where you might be hiding a tattoo. I think it would only be fair if you give me a hint."

"Okay," Daggi acquiesced. "I'll give you a *big* hint, and if you win, I swear on my sweet mama's grave that I'll do anything you ask till the sun peeks over the horizon. But if you lose, you'd better be prepared to do the same. If there's one thing I will not suffer, it's someone welching on a bet."

"Alright," Remy smiled. "I think I can trust you."

"You can trust what I tell you, absolutely."

"So, what's the hint?"

"My tattoo is below my waist. Since you can see my legs, and my feet through these shoes, that narrows it down quite nicely."

"Hmmm," Remy pondered. "I don't think you'd have it on your thigh. No, definitely not."

Slowly, Daggi pulled up her skirt until the entirety of her naked thighs were visible. "Looks like you've narrowed it to two choices," Daggi said, standing up and pirouetting in front of Remy. "Is it in the front, or in the back?" Then, raising her skirt up around her waist, she said, "Take your pick and have a look. Win or lose, the fun begins as soon as you do."

Placing his finger on Daggi's firm belly, just below her perfect navel, he ran it slowly down, down, down, catching the top of her panties on the way and easing them past Venus' delta.

"It's funny," Daggi told him. "That's where I originally wanted it to go. But I left the choice to the tattoo artist, who for some reason became quite enamored of my ass." Then Daggi removed her panties entirely, and turned around to show Remy the pigtailed girl tattooed on her bottom.

"She's adorable," Remy told her. "May I give her a kiss?"

"You may, though for that it's a shame she isn't on the front."

"I'm yours, remember," Remy said as he kissed the Pippi on Daggi's derrière. "If you tell me to do that, I'll have no choice."

"Oh, we'll get to that sort of thing in time, but right now, we're going to play dress-up. So take off your clothes and let me put the works to you."

"The works?" Remy asked as he undressed.

"The works," Daggi confirmed. "You said earlier that you liked this dress I'm wearing. Let's see how it looks on you."

Coming out of her little black dress, Daggi stood magnificently nude. Much like the steering wheel motorist, Remy moaned. "That's the most beautiful body I've ever seen," he said with a touch of awe.

"I can see you're enjoying it," Daggi said, reaching down with a finger to tap on his growing ardor.

"I can't help it," he told her.

"Well, it's going to be in the way—at least at first. I'll just have to do something about it."

Falling to her knees, Daggi opened wide and made short work of that rather large problem. Then she went to a dresser drawer and retrieved a little pillbox. "Here," she said, placing a Quaalude on Remy's tongue.

"I swallowed *that*, so you swallow *this*. It'll relax you—make you more pliable. Now put on my dress while I fetch a robe for me. I don't want my body getting you so excited. Not yet."

Though Daggi's dress was a tiny bit small for Remy, and he didn't look nearly as stunning as Daggi did wearing it, she was nonetheless pleased. Once she released his hair from its ponytail and cascaded it over his shoulders, she was quite impressed indeed. "Now sit, while I rouge those lovely lips," she told him.

After the lips, Daggi lined and mascara-ed and shadowed his eyes. Then she pinched his cheeks rosier, and let out a little moan of her own. "You're *very, very* pretty," she said, directing him toward her mirror.

"I *am*!" he exclaimed in a quaaludy voice.

"Yes you are. So hush and go lie on the bed. I prettied you, now it's time for me to muss you."

All manner of exploits did Daggi pursue on that night of her winning wager. And at some point, much to her relief, she took inside the dick that she'd longed for, which was under the dress of the very pretty girl beneath her.

Remy lived up to his promise, even when it came to his turn on the spit. Perhaps it was the relaxation of the drug, or perhaps there were tendencies he wasn't yet aware of. Either way, losing the bet did him no harm. Had he *won* that wager, chances were good he'd have found himself pushing up daisies for the grazing pleasure of a cute little burro named Delilah.

Instead, he (she?) and Daggi became fast friends. Daggi even took him shopping, and let him choose things to wear when he came to visit. But she insisted that he allow her to do his makeup. "I know what I like," she told him. "But I'll let you pick your own eau de cologne."

URSA MINOR'S MILES DAVIS APPRECIATION SOCIETY

CHRIS KELSO

Outside the porthole, a dizzying well of stars surveys the embryonic stages of Ursa Minor's new capital city. In the fusion club, two writers exchange manuscripts to the undulating crescendo of a native saxophone player. He's played the entire track-list from "Bitches Brew" with flawless precision. He departs the stage dragging behind the balled chain cuffed around his ankle.

The difficult crowd clap their reluctant approval.

Harry is a man who dispenses faint praise on his fellow writers – partly because he is universally recognised for his fantasy novels set on Earth, and partly because he takes great joy in belittling those held in lower esteem than he. Harry hooks his thumbs between the rungs of his dungarees, grinning smugly down at Draco Zoon. Zoon is one such individual cowed by respect for his superior - Draco is as submissive and servile as a slave in his company.

- Am I to expect the standard negligible prose and flimsy character development from you?

Draco forces a slight smile, for he is just beginning his career. A former text student of Harry's only a year ago, and he knows Harry will simply *hate* his novel.

Draco's symbiotic partner, Miku, jives over. Harry groans audibly, making no secret of his animosity towards basin dwellers from the Reticuli.

- There you are Drake! The departure vessel is due soon, we better get our bags honey.

Miku hooks his fingers with Draco's, to the obvious discomfort of the young writer. Public displays have never been his thing - that and Miku's massive sovereigns had a tendency to dig into Draco's flesh whenever they clasped palms. He wriggles free awkwardly. Harry gives a dry smile and makes a "whipped" gesture.

- You look good – Miku says in earnest, trying to ignore Harry and appease his lover. Draco puts his head down and motions towards the exit, Harry's manuscript cradled under his arm. Miku gives a puzzled look and chases after his symbiot.

- See you cats later – Harry hollers

mockingly, waving with exaggerated femininity.

Harry goes over to the bar and orders up a spritzer. He loves Earth drinks. So ingratiated in Earth's culture is Harry that he's even started learning some French.

Although his novels are often set there, and his characters are often of human origin, he has never actually been to Earth.

#

- Say…you Harry Chipperfield?

The bar tender is a native of the new city, badly mutated by the universe's recent radioactive warfare. He has tentacles sprouting from each shoulder, 8 in total. He appears friendly enough despite his monstrous deformities.

- Yes I am – confirms Harry with an obvious look of self-satisfaction.

- Well shoot me straight in the tentacle! What brings you all the way to Ursa Minor?

- This is the finest Miles Davis Appreciation Society inside 4 mega-parsecs - AND, I hear they execute each player they don't like LIVE at the end of the night. I'm *from* this galaxy anyway so it's really just convenient.

- Great, just great…

- So are you a fan?

- Heck no! I don't use my visual apparatus much, I need to focus my energy on vocalising and hearing. I find they're more pleasurable senses to culture.

- That's a matter of opinion.

- It sure is.

The music rises and swells as another saxophonist takes to the raised stage. This guy is a purist, he plays only early Miles Davis. Harry doesn't mind so much but some of the other Society members are becoming irate with the simple melody and lack of experimentation. One man, a mutant from the new city, vomits a wad of sputum into his hands and hurls it in the direction of the performer. He ducks and it splatters against the wall behind him. The crowd take their cue and begin throwing glasses and nut bowls at the performer.

It's obvious, even to the player, that he will be executed at the night's end.

A chorus of jeers resounds throughout the club. To the player's credit, he is unperturbed by the poor reception. The set becomes his swansong; if he's going to die a public death, he may as well go out with his dignity intact. He finishes his set with a medley of "Birth of the Cool" and exits the stage, ball and chain trundling behind him.

Harry opens his satchel and begins reading young Draco's manuscript. The title sends a cringing sensation along Harry's spinal column – 'Subsumed'. Awful title. Harry skims the first page, a dedication to Zoon's mater and the Hearth, before finally tearing the manuscript into four shreds.

It's almost the 12th hour, which means execution time is almost upon us. The tentacled bartender rings the bell for last orders and the crowd floods to the vanguard to order their drinks. Harry slides on his chair so he's facing the stage, he doesn't want to miss the show. A hideous amorphous glob of protoplasm enters the stage wearing a bow tie with a mic and a sheet of paper clutched between his gelatinous appendages.

- LADIES, GENTLEMEN, HERMAPHORODITES, IT'S THAT TIME AGAIN. WILL THE PERFORMERS PLEASE TAKE TO THE STAGE.

Three traumatised musicians shuffle into the spotlight.

- PERFORMER ONE BORED US ALL TO TEARS WITH A PASSIONLESS RENDITION OF MILE'S MAGNUM OPUS 'KIND OF BLUE'. CAST YOUR VOTES.

Harry presses YES on the vid-screen

around his wrist. Something inside him wants to see every performer executed for their bludgeoning of the great man. He's already decided that he'll vote YES for everyone, even the musicians he hadn't seen.

- VOTES ARE IN FOLKS. PERFORMER-ONE-IS-A…GONER!

A blast of light shoots out from behind the balcony somewhere, beaming directly into the eyeballs of musician number one. Steam begins to rise from the player's skull before it explodes in a paroxysm of blood, matter and bone – to jubilant applause.

Harry lights a cigar and claps his hands together wildly.

- OK, SIMMER DOWN! PERFORMER NUMBER TWO GRATED OUR TEETH TO DUST AND PLUCKED OUR NERVE ENDINGS WITH A SIMPLY CRIMINAL TAKE ON MILE'S ELECTRIC CLASSIC, 'BITCHES BREW'. CAST YOUR VOTES!

Again Harry clicks YES on the vidscreen. He takes a victorious puff from his cigarette and blows out the green smoke in concentric circles. His eagerness to see these men's demise unsettles even Harry, but not so much as to deter him from casting a positive vote.

- OK, VOTES ARE IN. PERFORMER NUMBER TWO, YOU-ARE-A-DEAD-MAAAAAAN!

The radioactive ray fires into number two, again with the same result, again with the same riotous response.

- NUMBER THREE, YOU FAILED TO INSPIRE THE IDEALS OF FREE JAZZ IN OUR SOULS WITH YOUR RENDITION OF 'THE COMPLETE BIRTH OF THE COOL'. VOTES PEOPLE, GIVE US A HATRICK OF SENSLESS MURDER!

Harry is about to push down on the YES button. The sight of a mutant saxophone player's head exploding no longer excites his morbid curiosity. It would be a far more interesting twist to see him quiver in fear over his imminent death before his life is eventually spared. Harry's bloodlust all but gone, he pushes NO.

- OK, CONTROVERSIAL! VOTES ARE IN. WE HAVE ONE VOTE AGAINST THIS MAN'S EXECUTION. WHAT'S THE MATTER WITH YOU PEOPLE? DON'T YOU WANT A SHOW? IN ANY CASE, THIS FREAK WILL BE SPARED, FREE TO DESTROY THE WORKS OF OUR GREAT LORD MILES FOR YEARS TO COME! CONGRATULATIONS YOU USELESS PILE OF FROG SPAWN…

Contented, Harry stubs out his cigarette and pulls on his coat ready to leave for a late departure pod.

#

In his departure pod, Harry prepares for a few hours of stasis with a disc containing the 1957 recording 'Ascenseur Pour l'Échafaud'. Not Harry's favourite, but it'll do. As he lulls into the sweet dreamless abyss of artificial inertia, from the corner of his eye he sees a familiar face. It's Draco Zoon and his symbiot. Harry momentarily rouses himself back into consciousness, pauses the recording and removes his earphones. He chaps on the plastic window that separates each booth until he has Zoon's attention. Draco goes to his window and waves. Harry mouths the words – 'l-o-v-e-d t-h-e m-a-n-u-s-c-r-i-p-t' – before settling back down in his capsule. He imagines Draco's relief and rejuvenated sense of purpose after being praised by his prestigious idol.

Harry thinks, in his last thought before complete-stasis, if he could really fit in down on Earth. While the planet is beautiful and the organisms living there are complex and wondrous, he knows that he lacks something - a fundamental facet of intrinsic humanity. He is too predictable. He lacks the moody self-actualised eccentricities and evils inherent to man. His nature is too mild. While among other species he is considered difficult and ruthless, this would pale in comparison to a human life-form. Compassion is a terrible thing. He regrets saving the life of performer 3 because it further clarifies his fear that Earth is beyond him.

It's hazy, but between 'Sur l'Autoroute', the last thing Harry sees is a bright light which illuminates the dark confines of his capsule, maybe Draco Zoon's departure pod exploding, he cannot be certain - perhaps the new city being wiped out by another nuclear attack?

Harry senses a presence in the pod but he's too weak from the sleeping detergent to pull himself up. The music cuts out and he hears another saxophone playing – a live performance inside the pod. Before darkness prevails, a torrent of heavy breathing wheezes intermittently between each blow and suck of the instrument, the kind of laboured breath common amongst the mutated of Ursa Minor… Harry smells the same odours from the bar.

- I always preferred Charlie Parker anyway – a voice says…

THE PLAYER
JACQUES BARBÉRI (TRANSLATED BY MICHAEL SHREVE)

The apartment is luxurious. Pan around discreetly and admire, among other things, some mobile sculptures, a couch and two organic armchairs, a relaxation tub, blood red, a 1900 bar with ambiance simulator, an assortment of plasti-appendages and some evening masks.

Mark Holgenzinger sips a cocktail of benzedrine and barley juice. The girl he'd accosted barely an hour ago at Lemno's Club walks over to him, all decked out in promising plasti-appendages. "Mark, I want to make love."

"I bet you do, honey."

The expert hands of the lemur girl undo the pressure-buttons and take off Mark's skimpy get-up. Free.

"You make wonderful love, honey," the lemur girl mumbles between groans. "A little too wonderful, maybe?"

"What do you mean by that?"

She doesn't answer, being all shook up by a long orgasm. A perfect arch. Mark follows in suit right away. Then she rolls to the side, drops onto the artificial grass and she's standing up, facing the sensory niche, pointing a paralyzer at her partner.

"Sorry Mark, but I wanted to get the most out of it before pronouncing your sentence. Holgenzinger was never into heterosexual relations. It seems to me like you went a little astray tonight. You're under arrest, Anton, for illegal possession of a plasti-body and identity theft."

In a flash Mark/Anton jumps up and bounds across the room, zigging and zagging. Rays shoot by him. He dives through the glass roof toward the villa's mineral forest. Shattered glass falls with him. Seventy stories. Two retrorockets pop out from his subcutaneous outfit. Flames ignite behind his back and he stabilizes upright, then sets down, gently, on the sidewalk.

There's no time to lose, he thinks, and hails a helitaxi.

#

The buildings slip by—the eyes of the night like balls of puss on faceless façades. Anton is scared. Fucking rat! He fingers the roll of bills in his pocket. Money can do anything. He's always said that. Today he has his doubts.

"Street of the Blind. As fast as possible!"

"Okay, mister. You want a little music or maybe a refreshment?"

"Shut up and step on it."

And the helitaxi darts into the urban night. The apartment towers, pustules, boils, shining warts, speckle the black ink of the city with a multifaceted smile. Anton feels the trap closing in, a gaping maw, wide-open, in the distance, on the edge of giant teeth. Through the smoky glass of the cabin he watches the city fly by, the icy stare of the buildings. And his neck and the palms of his hands are bathed in sweat. When he was convicted of being the main perpetrator of the real estate scam on Fish Street, his huge fortune had allowed him to get a wonderful plasti-body, black market, with a spotless identity. But someone had blabbed. Outside the surgery, only one person knows his real identity.

There's no doubt about it.

"I'll kill him," he says aloud.

The taxi membranes answer with "Ahem, Mr. Orosco?"

"What did you call me?"

"That's your name, isn't it? I've just received a call from the body squad and I have to touch down immediately. You're a criminal, Mr. Orosco, and I am only an obedient machine. Sorry."

All the while explaining its actions, the taxi lowers slowly to the ground. Lands. Anton, without a second to lose, jumps out of the cabin and starts running, jostling the gaudy crowd of the outlying Lime District. Clicking switchblades spring out, backed by insults. But Anton isn't in a fighting mood and the flabbergasted pig heads and donkey heads watch his deranged walk, typical of a wanted man.

\#

Lion is sitting on a hedge of white fir, sprawled on top of the intertwining branches. An organic mattress, dense and smooth. Compression/expansion limbs, ocular globes, ears and organs decorate the room in perfect harmony. Females with goat heads lick his eyelids and ears. Lion isn't a lion except for his head. A plasti-head of incalculable value. The last animal census said there were only 250 lions running free—200 already reduced to plasti-organs. And the lion head of Lion is still furrowed with a few willingly forgotten traces, fiery yellow marks of the savannah. Lion's movements are wild; his hands have

claws. When he bites his hybrids you might even say he is ferocious. His females, with lovingly selected sexual organs, have a vulture head grafted above their pubis. Living heads. When he offers a servant to make love to one of them, the poor thing gets a rude awakening when he sees his penis gobbled up by the shredding beaks. Testicles are choice desserts.

\#

When Anton enters the room, the females are licking Lion's hands and feet. His exposed paunchy gut gleams under the oily film that oozes out of his dilated pores. The ray shoots through the wall of flesh. Around the yellow neon planted in Lion's belly, blood beads and sparkles. The panic-stricken females run away, the vultures clicking their beaks between their shaking legs.

"Sorry, Lion, the plasti-body you got for me is really top notch, but its rating as a perfect match is way off."

\#

Leaving Lion's baroque residence, the obvious single solution to his problems springs to mind—which is now wiped clean of all desire for vengeance—either get a new plasti-body to change into or you're a dead man.

\#

The track is a figure eight. The machines spit oil and fumes. And howl. Metal and plastic racers hurtling over a spiral asphalt ribbon. The creatures/riders snort and clench their thighs. Legs? Anton watches the entrances and the crowd and for a few seconds stands in awe of the murderous biker ballet. Until the long-awaited accident happens. Two machines kiss and start wobbling. The rider tenses up, tries to create a force within his cells opposed to that produced by the shock. But

143

the vehicle flutters and slides. The handlebars hit the ground. The metal scrapes and bends and the rider (grotesque equine) is thrown off like a pile of rags.

Anton elbows his way through the spectators who are standing, screaming, clapping and laughing with all their hysterical animal heads. Gorillas, warthogs, camels, panthers—a raucous menagerie crying out for blood and the sweet sound of broken bones.

He jumps into the gondola of the mobile bar. Inside, the bitter scent of debauchery makes him a little dizzy. He wipes his forehead with his sleeve and brushes back a stray lock of hair drooping in front of his right eye. He blinks. Fear is like flypaper trapping him here.

A hostess comes up.

He doesn't even hear her, pushes past her and heads for the counter. "A double scotch-benzedrine. Is there a phone here?"

The bartender, apparently human despite the suspiciously squishy sound when he moves behind the counter, points to a phone in the back of the room.

While giving the number Anton keeps an eye on the entrance, expecting to see the body squad cops bust in at any moment.

A rat head appears on the screen. "What do you want?"

"I want to speak with Big Bully."

"Who's this?"

"Listen, I don't have time to beat around this stupid bush. I'm not a cop or a snitch. Tell him that I'm a friend of Lion's and there's a fat wad of cash in it for him. I have to see him as soon as possible. It's a matter of life and death. And 100,000 credits."

Rat-head disappears. To check his account Anton fiddles with the bills in his skin pocket. Let's hope that Big Bully isn't updated on the job I did on Lion, he tells himself, or else they're going to slice and dice me and sell the pieces to the highest bidder.

The screen is still blank and Anton is still watching the door of the bar. More and more anxious.

Rat-head appears. "Meet in an hour at the Black Moon Bar, Monkey District."

The screen goes blank again.

Anton returns to the counter, shaking, and downs his drink. In an hour his fate will be sealed.

#

In front of the Black Moon Bar, Anton feels both relieved and restless. He knows an end to his flight is finally in sight, but this place can only inspire, engender an uncontrollable anxiety in any being who isn't part of the local underworld.

"The bar's closed."

Anton looks up and sees the monkey guard. "I'm supposed to meet Big Bully. I called an hour ago."

The monkey jumps down next to him. "Follow me."

#

The meeting with Big Bully takes place in an oil bath. The fee offered could not have been fatter and apparently his stock of bodies is as vast as Lion's. However, as opposed to the latter, who can work in a private clinic, Big Bully invites his clients to lie down on a pool table.

When he feels the narcotics kick in, Anton is justifiably scared. The green carpet lit by the track lighting is flickering and he is transformed into an ivory ball rolling along, hitting other groaning balls, diving into a black, endless tunnel.

#

When he comes to, the first thing Anton notices is the stuff he is lying on. "It" moves and "it" feels alive. His eyes are still foggy from the drugs.

"Well, you finally decided to come out of it." The hoarse, thundering voice slaps him awake. The fog clears. And he sees, underneath him—gruesome—two gigantic hands. He is lying in these hands. His feet are long and hairy and his body...

"So did you sleep well, little rabbit?"

He raises his head and sees, way high up, lost in the heights of the stratosphere, the head talking to him.

#

They just leave him in the grass. In front of him are the huge trees of an oak forest. Behind him the gorgeous house of the rich businessman who had bought him for a fortune. Big Bully knew all about it, of course. How could he have ever thought, even for a second, that he wouldn't? And the bastard grafted his head onto the lovely body of a rabbit.

"You shouldn't be wasting time," the voice from on high growls. "In an hour the dogs and hunters are going to be after you. I hope you'll measure up."

Anton jumps and scampers off like some ridiculous game bound for a bonfire. Swallowed up by the forest, hounded by the obscene laughter of the huge man. He'd made one fatal mistake. Money can do anything, up to a point. And that point...

WHEN INFORMATION IS BLISS

THOMAS MESSINA

think in the future holograms will be solid just like us. That way, we'll be able to walk together and hold HOLI's hand."

"That's a great prediction, Mary. I think we'll actually see that happen in the near future. Good thinking."

Mary blushed.

"Who's next? Michael?"

"I think there'll be a way to make food out of nothing. Now we need to make our food or take a pill to eat, but in the future, we'll just be able to tell HOLI what we want and it'll appear."

"That's another great idea and it's close to being realized too. The Department of Science is working on it now. They're on the verge of being able to create chemical reactions at the end of a data stream. They call it Digital Nano Alchemy or DNA Technology. It's not exactly out of nothing but who knows, maybe all of our meals will come from HOLI soon."

The class looked at Mr. Barclay with wide eyes. "No more broccoli," he proclaimed. The class laughed.

Class 6345A was made up of fifteen students between the ages of ten and twelve who were classified by genetic markers and other criteria as being predisposed to learning problems. A wide array of ethnicities and races were represented in the class. The children sat in three rows of five at individual, three-legged, boomerang-shaped desks with laminate tops, flat with no cubby or drawer space. Mr. Barclay stood at the front of the classroom; a large, flat-paneled screen that used both touch and sound to operate called the Symbol Board hung behind him. Not in use at the time, it displayed a scenic view of rolling hills, covered by a lush green forest in late spring. Large floor-to-ceiling windows lined the adjoining walls that presented the same tableau; together with the Symbol Board, they formed one connected, complete panorama.

"Okay, one more. Who's next?" Mr. Barclay scanned the room. Students raised their hands, many of them so eager that they bumped up and down on their seats and made low-sounding, chimpanzee, *ooh, ooh, ooh* sounds to get his attention. But Mr. Barclay focused on a student in the back who didn't raise his hand. "Billy, what do you think? You must have some idea of what the future will be like – some prediction."

Billy was one of Mr. Barclay's most difficult cases. From the records, Billy's learning disability score was the highest in class 6345A. In other words, Billy's potential to learn was very poor. Other schools had given up on Billy, but Mr. Barclay was determined to help him.

"My idea's stupid, Mr. B."

The class laughed.

Mr. Barclay cast a reprimanding glance about the room. "Children, no idea is stupid. Billy, we'd love to hear it."

"Well, okay, I guess." Billy paused. "I think that in the future . . . I think that . . . well, I'll be dead. Like, no one can live forever. So that's kinda like a prediction, right?"

The room fell silent. Mr. Barclay nodded.

"That's a very good point. Children, we've all been predicting new things, like inventions. We haven't really talked about the things that exist today that won't be around in the future – like *broccoli*."

The class laughed.

"Actually, Billy, the Department of Science is working on that too. The science is in its infancy, but who knows, maybe even in our lifetime we'll have progressed past that final frontier. Isn't that right, HOLI?"

HOLI stood in the center of the classroom. "Yes, Mr. B," it said.

"And HOLI never lies. Isn't that right, HOLI?"

"Yes, Mr. B."

HOLI was the name used to refer to the Hologram Object and Language Interface. It stood like a real person in the center of class, no discernible hardware projecting it. This made HOLI appear almost *human*. It was programmed to have the mixed voice of a woman and a man, similar to a castrato, and it looked neither like a woman nor a man – an androgynous thing that might have been confused for an effeminate male or a masculine female. This uncertainty of gender tended to make people uncomfortable when they first encountered HOLI. By design, it appeared homely, wearing nothing but a loose fitting tan shirt and pants; it wasn't impressive by any means compared to a living human.

"HOLI, is it time to move onto stories, or can we field a few more predictions from the class?"

"Mr. B., period six has ended."

"Okay, then, we need to switch to story reports."

The class let out a collective groan.

Mr. Barclay – affectionately known by the class, and by HOLI, as Mr. B – taught First Wayward School Class 6345A. He was in his early thirties, and teaching consumed most of his energy and left little time for a personal life. He wasn't married and had no children. He came from a good family and was educated at some of the finest universities; given his degrees and his father's Policy involvement, he was well regarded by his peers in the Department of Learning. He had chosen to work for the DoL rather than the Department of Knowledge because he saw himself as an educator first and a scholar second. He also liked children and felt that the impression one makes through teaching was a lifelong gift to them – particularly to the troubled ones. He yearned to make a difference.

"I think we have time for four stories today. I hope you all did you homework and came prepared. If you're not prepared, I need to know now."

The class was quiet.

"Don't make me ask HOLI. Did anyone not do their story?"

No response.

"Great, then let's proceed. Remember, the format is summary first, then your analysis. Who wants to go first?" Mr. Barclay scanned the class. A couple hands were raised so high it was as if they were trying to touch the ceiling; others tried to get Mr. Barclay's attention by waving as if saying hello. Mr. Barclay pointed to a girl in the front row who was waving. "Okay, Matilda, you first."

Matilda stood up. She was a girl with milky white skin and fine black short hair who at ten was small and fragile for her age; Mr. Barclay couldn't help but think that if she were outside and the wind gusted, she might blow away. "Thanks, Mr. B. HOLI, please load my story report summary, *Blubber*."

HOLI was a great presenter of information because of its three-dimensional quality and its penetrating eyes that made it lifelike. HOLI was programmed so that, no matter from what angle you looked at it, it appeared to be looking only at you. It was almost as if it didn't have a back or a side profile. Each person had their own personalized experience with HOLI, even though it was viewed by, interacted with, and collectively shared by all.

"Matilda, your story report is ready. Would you like me to play it?" HOLI said in a matter-of-fact, banal way.

"Yes, please play, and begin with my summary."

HOLI told the story. "*Blubber* is about . . ." For five minutes, HOLI repeated the story in detail as Matilda had related it earlier that week.

"A very good summary, Matilda." Mr. Barclay smiled in his usual, reassuring way. "Now, what's your analysis of the story?"

"HOLI, please play my analysis," Matilda requested.

"*Blubber* is a story about bullying and how some children are cruel. This story helps educate us on why bullying is bad and how it really hurts kids. And we need to know that even though we are all different in different ways, we need to respect those differences because we are all equal in the eyes of the Policy."

"HOLI, is the summary and analysis accurate?" asked Mr. Barclay.

"Yes, Mr. B., it is accurate."

"Thank you for your story report, Matilda. It was very creative."

Matilda curtsied and then sat. The class applauded, but it was a quiet applause

– the kind of applause that is performed only as a courtesy.

"Okay, who'd like to go next? Michael, why don't you share your story?"

"Thanks, Mr. B." Michael stood up. He was a thin boy whose arms and feet were the size of a man's, while the rest of him was still a boy waiting to catch up. "HOLI, please play the summary of my story report, *Lord of the Flies*."

"The Lord of the Flies is about . . ." HOLI relayed the summary as Michael had told it.

"That's a very good summary, Michael," Mr. Barclay said. "Now, what's your analysis of the story?"

"HOLI, please play my analysis."

"*The Lord of the Flies* is a story about civilization and how it is better than savagery. This story helps educate us on why we need to work together in a civilized way to achieve our goals; if we act as individuals, we will only destroy ourselves – kinda like when they burned down the island or Piggy dying. We all need to work as one and listen to the Policy, kinda like if it was the conch shell. Only through the Policy can we make the world an even better place to live."

"HOLI, is the summary and analysis accurate?"

"Yes, Mr. B., it is accurate."

"Good. Thank you for your story report, Michael. It was also very creative."

Michael gave an exaggerated bow and sat. The class again applauded half-heartedly. "Okay, who'd like to go next? Robert, why don't you share your story with the class?"

Robert stood up. He was a handsome boy with light brown skin, a prominent Adam's apple, and a deep voice that squeaked at random intervals. "HOLI, please load my story report, *The Giver*, and start with the summary."

After HOLI gave the story's summary, Mr. Barclay said, "That is also a very good summary, Robert. "Now, what's your analysis?"

"HOLI, please play my analysis."

"*The Giver* is a story about how the past can hurt the future. We can't trust our memories of the past so we need to rely on all of us to make things better by focusing on the future. If we need to go back into the past, we should rely on a central source of knowledge that represents the gold copy of what we know. The Policy owns this knowledge and the Department of Knowledge manages it and shares it through HOLI. "

"HOLI, is the summary and analysis accurate?"

"Yes, Mr. B., it is accurate."

"Mr. B., that's not right," yelled Billy from the back of the classroom. Billy *was* showing signs of improvement, with the number and intensity of disruptive episodes attenuating over the last several months. But every so often, Billy would still have one of these outbursts that would frustrate Mr. Barclay. These episodes of seeming unreason seared into his psyche and frequently woke him from a deep sleep that was followed by a dark melancholy in which he would question his learning improvement methods and doubt his choice of educator as a profession.

The white lights in the room turned off, and the windows and front-board quickly turned from day to night. The classroom was dark except for HOLI, which radiated a dark light, like a green glow stick. The class, *oohed*, then quickly went silent.

"Billy, please no shouting. Raise your hand," Mr. Barclay reprimanded him.

"Sorry, Mr. B." Billy looked toward the floor.

"Now, what's your question?"

"That part in *The Giver*, where their job is to transmit all the information in the central servers. Information from the Policy. That's not right."

"Why do you say that?" Mr. B. asked.

"I remember HOLI playing that story for me before. And it was different. It was more like their job was to transfer information from the *past*."

Mr. Barclay had experienced the same doubts. Years earlier, he had come across inconsistencies with information provided by HOLI. However, whenever he asked HOLI about the apparent discrepancies, he was always wrong. And it was the words, his words that troubled him the most. Words he believed he had used before but did not exist. The first time it occurred, when he was drafting his thesis, was the most unsettling.

"HOLI, I need to cross reference this section with a section I previously wrote on peace and learning."

"Jonathon, I have retrieved and loaded it. "

"Please play it HOLI."

"We must seek to promote peace and tolerance, not fuel hatred and suspicion. The fundament to achieving this lies with our children: to eradicate the uninformed through education. "

"Stop." Mr. Barclay said, interrupting HOLI. "Can you repeat that last sentence?"

"The fundament to achieving this lies with our children: to eradicate the uninformed through education."

"HOLI, that's not how I remember it. It said illiterate, not uninformed. I know that for certain. Has anything changed since we first drafted this?"

"Jonathon, nothing has changed."

"Are you absolutely sure?"

"Jonathon, nothing has changed."

"But I remember it differently. Perhaps you pulled an older version. Is this the latest version? "

"This is the latest version."

Mr. Barclay paused for a moment. "HOLI, are you lying to me? Has anything changed?"

"Jonathon, nothing has changed."

"HOLI, search current and all previous version for the word illiterate."

"A search of library and appendices returned no records."

"HOLI, search current and all previous version for variants of the word illiterate."

"A search of library and appendices returned no records."

"HOLI, that's impossible, search again."

"A search of library and appendices returned no records."

"That's impossible. I remember it perfectly. I didn't just make the word up. Now search again."

"A search of library and appendices returned no records."

"Again."

"A search of library and appendices returned no records."

"Again."

"A search of library and appendices returned no records."

"HOLI you're wrong, you're wrong! I know it exists!" he cried.

"A search of library and appendices returned no records."

"I want an error report filed with the Policy Administrator now!"

"Jonathon, I am processing your request. Please confirm the submission of an error report to the Policy Administrator."

Mr. Barclay closed his eyes and rubbed his eyebrows with his thumb and middle finger. He knew the implications of filing a false report with the Policy. He looked up and stared at HOLI in silence. *Am I crazy? Did I dream this all up? How could it be that this word doesn't exist? Am I mistaken? How could HOLI be wrong? I could've sworn there was such a word...I could've sworn.*

"Jonathon, please confirm the submission of an error report to the Policy Administrator."

Mr. Barclay paused. "HOLI, cancel that request. Let's just continue at the point before this digression. Where were we?"

Episodes like this continued to occur – HOLI retrieving the recording, listening to the clip, and each error profoundly demonstrating the failure of his memory. These episodes left him with a queer feeling – a sense of inadequacy that culminated with nausea – feelings that were so strong, that he began to ignore any new inconsistencies assuming they were flaws in his memory, eventually never recognizing any new ones again. He had learned to trust HOLI completely. Billy would need to learn to trust it too.

"Really?" Mr. Barclay nodded. "Well, then, let's ask HOLI. It'll know for certain. HOLI, has *The Giver* changed since Billy last saw it? Or, frankly, has it ever changed since it was first told?"

HOLI replied, "Mr. B, the story has not changed from its first telling."

The class laughed; in the light from HOLI's glow, it looked as if they were laughing and pointing at Billy.

"You see, Billy, that's why it's not good to rely on your memory. Your memory makes mistakes. But HOLI never makes mistakes. And class, what else do we know about HOLI?"

In cadence, the class replied, "HOLI never lies."

The room brightened and the windows and board returned to display the scenic spring tableau.

"That's right. It never lies. But it's okay if we make mistakes; we're only human. We all make mistakes sometimes; we need to learn from them and move on. Billy, do you feel better now?"

On the verge of tears, Billy replied, "I guess so. It must've been a bad dream or something. I'm sorry."

Mr. Barclay nodded. "Yes, of course,

of course." He walked over to Billy and rubbed his head, disheveling his hair like fathers do to their sons when proud of them. When Billy looked up, Mr. Barclay gave him an affectionate, reassuring smile. He returned to the head of the class.

"Okay, we have time for one more story. Who'd like to go?" He scanned the room. "How about Princess Emily of Class 6345A – are you ready?"

"Yes, Mr. B." She shot out of her seat. Emily was a tall, graceful girl, and the oldest in the class at almost thirteen. Like the other children, her parents had been convicted of offenses against the Policy and "had been disappeared," a euphemism used by Policy officials to mean they were vanished, voided, vaporized, and erased from the records of existence – except, of course, for the piece that remained in their children – the generic marker that classified their children's learning disabilities, but also the traits valued by the Policy.

Emily had the special attention of Mr. Barclay because her parents were different than the others. Her parents had organized a small band of individuals into a minor, yet troublesome, resistance for the Policy. Although they weren't successful, the qualities needed to mastermind such an act were desirable. So Mr. Barclay's job was not only to eradicate the children's learning disabilities, but also to accentuate their good traits. He recognized Emily's promise as a leader and believed that one day, after she had been properly educated, she would be an upstanding and prominent member of the Policy.

"HOLI, please play my story report on *One True History*. It's a comedy written by our President about the time when he first met our Founder."

The collective *oooh* from the class indicated that this story was the most interesting to them.

HOLI recited, "*One True History* is the story of our President before he joined the Policy. It tells of his younger days when, as a youth, he joined the forces of unity and peace against the forces of evil and despair and all the trials he endured in defeating them." HOLI told this story in such great detail that it tallied twenty minutes. "The book ends when our President tells the story of when he first met our Founder, who was a collector of books."

The children roared with laughter, a few almost falling off their chairs, many of them saying, "Books, that's so funny." HOLI stopped speaking until the room quieted down.

HOLI continued. "Our Founder tells our President that he amassed an enormous library that began when he collected books as a little boy, going from house to house, looking through garbage pails for all the discarded books. Our President asks if our Founder has read any of them."

Again, the children erupted with laughter. Someone whispered, "Who reads? That's so funny." Again, HOLI stopped speaking until the room quieted down.

"Our Founder shows him an old map of the world and asks our President if the map is complete and accurate. Our President responds that of course the map is incorrect given its age, stating that there are things that we know now that they couldn't have known when the map was drafted. Our Founder explains that he doesn't read books for the same reason. They are old, outdated, and incorrect. And just as a ship would not sail using an old map, neither should we use old outdated books to guide our lives or the policy of our Policy. Our President concedes and admits that he has learned a very important lesson."

"Excellent summary, Emily." Mr. Barclay rubbed his hands together enthusiastically. "Now what's your analysis of the story?"

"HOLI, please play my analysis."

"*One True History* tells about the true events of our President so that we can emulate his constancy and commitment to the Policy. Regardless of struggle, we must remain dedicated and loyal to the Policy. It's also about why only information provided by HOLI is any good because it is the one place of correct information. The world is a better place because of our Founder, our President, and our HOLI."

"HOLI, is that summary and analysis accurate?"

"Yes, Mr. B., it is accurate."

"Well, then, thank you for your most excellent summary of our history, Emily. It was inspiring."

Emily beamed, standing erect with head tall and shoulders back. The students stood up and clapped.

"HOLI, this is such a great story. Do we have any time remaining before we pledge allegiance to the Policy? I'd like to play the ending of the story, if we could?" Turning to the class, Mr. Barclay asked, "Children, would you like to listen to the end of the story?"

The class responded with a resounding cheer.

"Yes, Mr. B., there is time available."

"Well then, HOLI, can you please play the ending? I think it would be good for the children." Mr. Barclay nodded. "The ending is so beautiful."

HOLI began: "He was right – reading was archaic, but so, too, was the substance of books. As he had shown with the map – the old content was worthless – built on ignorance. Those ancient texts – those old books – had no contextual value outside of their sensory appeal. The Policy, in its great wisdom, filtered our information to keep us pure. The ignorance of these books lay dead – existing only on the old man's shelves –

preserved but not to be consumed. Food not for thought but for microbes. It was at that moment I knew that I had been in the presence of a wise man – a great man – more than just the founder of the Policy. And I know now why I am here. I look up into the night sky so beautifully bright from our illuminations and feel a sense of awe – of purpose. The Policy, of which I am soon to become President, had achieved what those before it could not. On this fiftieth anniversary of the victory of the final campaign, is a world in which billions of people, regardless of breed or caste, enjoy parity and peace. Where at birth nothing is needed to learn beyond our built-in, natural capacities; no longer must we struggle to learn to read and write, which locked information in the hands of the privileged few. Now, there was nothing needed to learn beyond what nature intended, our senses – we see, we smell, we hear, we speak, we touch – we are human again. The Policy had finally torn down the walls to learning, and in its stead, created a world where education, our birthright, is available to all. A world where information is bliss."

Mr. Barclay looked out among the rows of students that sat before him, their eyes filled with wonder and hope, eager to learn. He smiled at them, feeling reaffirmed in his choice as an educator for children who needed help – his children. He turned and looked at HOLI, who was always fixated on him, and he smiled at her, too.

CORPSEMASTER

ALEXANDER HAY

Margaret hated *Thomas the Tank Engine*. Well, hate was a strong word, and having seen enough horrors in her time growing up, she felt it wasn't the *right* word. And yet…

Well, there she was, driving to see her in-laws with her precious (if lively) young son Hugo in the back… And it was raining… And her husband couldn't make it AGAIN, even though they were his parents. And she had to see ruined town and city after ruined town and city streaming past… And Hugo was demanding she play THAT ancient *Thomas the Tank Engine* CD for what must have been the millionth time… And she had stomach cramps care of her PMT… And soon she would have to once again hear Ringo Starr's voice, long since from beyond the grave, droning on suicidally about the Isle of sodding Sodor…

All things considered, she decided, hate was, nonetheless, the *best* word.

She hated the revenants, too, but she preferred not to think of them.

With a sigh, Margaret turned off the British Forces Broadcasting Service, which filled the gap left by the BBC after –

She set aside bleak childhood memories, and slid the hated CD into the car player. In the back of the car, Hugo cried out how much he loved his mummy, and started clapping loudly as THAT THEME kicked off once more.

It could be worse, Margaret tried to remind herself. It could always be worse. Slow agonising minutes proceeded as Percy the steam engine fled in panic from a speeding Gordon the steam engine. As a mother, this was the sort of thing you had to endure, but that Fat Controller was such a fascist bastard, and –

A loud pop filled the car. The car lurched to the left and a deafening screeching sound could be heard. The tire had burst. Panicking, Margaret still managed to control the car, spinning the wheel to compensate for the imbalance, while desperately pressing down on the breaks. After lurching around the A-road at speed, the car finally drew to a stop. Panting with exertion, Margaret remembered Hugo was in the back. In a panic she looked back to see if he was OK.

Hugo looked nonchalant, as usual.

"Mummy? Is the car broken?" he said, with mild curiosity.

"Never mind that!" Margaret said, still rather alarmed. "Are you definitely sure you're OK? Please tell me, I'll –"

"Oh, I'm OK, Mummy!" Hugo chirped with nary a twinge of alarm. "Can you put it back? I missed that bit."

"Err, yeah…" a shell-shocked Margaret said, pressing the 'BACK' button as requested. Soon, THAT tune was playing again.

To distract herself, Margaret looked around. The A-road was empty. In fact, that was one of the perverse fringe benefits of life in a near-destroyed country. You were much less likely to end up in a pile-up. Margaret pulled out her mobile and tried to ring emergency services. No signal. Outside, the rain had become torrential, and Margaret could have sworn she could hear the telltale patter of hail.

Then she saw figures in the distance, moving unsteadily towards them across abandoned fields. Margaret knew what they were, and felt terror.

Trying to stay calm, she turned back, and, leaning over, pulled a tartan woollen blanket from the rear dashboard and draped it over Hugo, who took this with his usual blasé, wide-eyed approach to things.

"Is there something wrong, Mummy?" he said, his head bobbing under the blanket that now concealed him.

"Err, do you promise to stay very still and not make a noise?" Margaret said, trying to stay as calm as she could.

"Yes Mummy!" Hugo said with no thought towards his volume.

They were still hundreds of yards of way, but they were shambling ever nearer. Margaret locked all the doors.

Margaret paused the CD and wondered how she could hide herself. Could she slide down to the floor and hide under her jacket? There wasn't enough room, even if she moved the driver's seat back. Could she hide under the blanket with Hugo? It wasn't big enough. Perhaps she could sit still?

They were now close enough to see. All clad in loose-fitting grey ragged overalls, soaked by the rain, and staggering like drunks. The rain seemed to have stopped or slowed now, like it was too afraid to fall in the presence of such things.

Some had only been dead for a week or two, judging by their decay. Others looked far more rotten, and a few were all but skeletonised. The worst ones, the ones with the most damage to their faces, wore metal plates bolted into their skulls so as not to distress the public. But they distressed Margaret. Should she flee with Hugo and run for it? No – where could they go? And besides, it was plain that they were approaching from all sides.

Could she sit still and play dead? They'd still know. In terror, Margaret realised they were now only metres away. Frantically trying to turn on the car again – burst tyre or no burst tyre – Margaret cried out in anger, frustration and fright.

The revenants surrounded the car, moaning as they pressed their hands against the windows, pounded against the roof and shook the car out of half-remembered instinct. Dozens of dead staring eyes gazed straight at Margaret.

She tried to scream, but no noise came out. They were going to die.

"OI! PISS OFF!!!" a loud man's voice could be heard.

The Revenants continued to manhandle the car.

"I SAID PISS OFF!"

The things seemed to slow at this point. Margaret, for all her panic, could still make out what could only be described as confusion on their dead faces. Or at least, on those that still had something like a face. Still, they kept slapping, pulling and pushing the car, though now half-heartedly.

Margaret heard the voice speak to the dead things in a language that hurt her ears to hear. The Enochian spell performed, the Revenants were immediately still, and began to disperse in a disciplined fashion, walking away from the car en masse as if nothing happened.

In their wake, an ugly, bone-thin man in a long black robe inscribed with strange sigils was revealed – the necromancer who commanded this work detail. He was also wearing a safety helmet and hi-vis vest, which rather undermined the dramatic look.

As his charges moved away, the necromancer walked up to the car and leaned down to the driver's window. Gesturing a circular movement in his hand, he asked Margaret to lower her window. Reluctantly, she complied. Up close, he was even uglier, with dark rings under his eyes and acne scars. He was also shaven-headed, as the stubble on those parts of his head not covered by the safety helmet attested. Yet his eyes looked like they belonged to a particularly conscientious golden retriever that dabbled in black magic on the side, and his nervous, apologetic smile was a reassuring sight.

"Sorry about that, love", Craig the necromancer said with a Romford accent. "They do that sometimes."

#

Clive preferred the new ways. Once, the Necromancers would gather in secret covens under the cold glare of moonlight and commune in arcane tongues, while the spirits of the dead swirled around them. No wonder they were all weird. You can't spend your life in the dark, even if your business is darkness. That was why the Necromancers came out of the shadows to rescue the nation, after the war. They did it as much to save themselves as everyone else.

True, you still tended to wear the robes and the arcane tattoos, though some of the younger or more integrated 'mancers preferred smart office attire. But there was something refreshingly mundane about the new world Clive's fellow corpsemasters found themselves in. Wearing safety gear, clocking in during regular hours, sharing obscene porn with contractors during your lunch break… Well, the latter was optional, but Clive had grown up surrounded by the old ways, and was glad not to worry all the time about the health of his mind or soul.

Much better instead for it to be like this – a meeting with the mid and upper-tier 'mancers from Carlisle, gathering around the table with council workers and a civil servant called Kate who was from the Ministry of Reconstruction. (Clive fancied his chances with her, but feared she was a Christian). And in a beige room, in a plastic grey portakabin, off a B-road near a motorway undergoing reconstruction, and under the glare of a 60 watt bulb, Clive and his peers could talk and act like they were finally part of a society they once had to hide from. And for Clive, this was heaven.

"OK… Shall I commence this meeting?" said Big Greg, the High Magister.

"Hang on, Janet from archaeology isn't in yet…" Gareth the Weaver of Souls advised.

"Well, we could discuss the moorhen issue until she gets here…" Michelle from the Council said.

Kate nodded while taking shorthand notes. Being only a few seats away, Clive could just about see her small, neat transcriptions. It was the cutest shorthand he'd ever seen, and the young necromancer was smitten.

"We'll need to hear Aaron from environmental before we can discuss that one", Wendy the Skull Scryer said. "And last I heard, he was travelling in with Janet."

"Oh bloody hell", Krishnan the business liaison lamented. What are we going to do in the meantime?"

"Well, we've got time to kill…" Big Greg sighed. Anything we want to discuss?

"Well there's that zombie film they've got over in America," Krishnan suggested. "The one that uses real revenants…"

"Yeah, but it's really crap", Gareth moaned. "They can't really do much except do all the distance zombie hoard shots. All the up-close gore effects still require actors and special effects…"

"But it's got Romero in it!" said the ever so slightly geeky Jason (he was from environmental health).

"Yeah, but it's not Romero. It's his corpse", Wendy pointed out.

"Did they actually reanimate it?" Clive found himself saying.

"Yeah, the makers cleared it with his estate. Doesn't live up to the hype, though. His revenant's a bit unexciting to look at. They put too much effort into embalming him", Wendy said, disapprovingly. "I mean, you should just stick to make-up and human extras. It's all a bit unethical otherwise… And it ruins the magic of cinema. You can't beat Doctor Tongue."

"I prefer Tar-Man…" Big Greg said, not paying much attention.

"He's not a Romero zombie! He's from *Return of the Living Dead*!" said a slightly irate Jason.

"Boris Karloff didn't need to be raised from the dead. He was Frankenstein's Monster through and through", said Keith the IT manager.

"He wasn't a zombie – err, I mean, a revenant", Jason argued back. "He's closer to a *lemure*."

"Oh, that reminds me!" Big Gregg exclaimed. "You heard how those crazy French bastards want to create semi-sentient undead? Brussels told them to piss off, thank God."

All the 'mancers around the table nodded in agreement. There were lines even they shouldn't cross, and the Necromantic Legislative and Regulatory Guidelines[1] they followed were some of the most stringent in the world, something Clive felt very proud of.

"I know some tosser in Cardiff who got a revenant and dressed him up as Bela Lugosi…" Simon the other Council rep said. "Didn't work out the way he hoped. Dracula doesn't drool."

"Talk about mixing your metaphors…" Wendy said, bitterly.

Clive laughed, but felt a jolt of fear and… excitement? Because Kate was looking directly at him.

She leant over and whispered to him. "Are they always this meta?" she smiled.

Clive smiled back, and felt butterflies. Meanwhile, his mobile throbbed silently and to no avail, as a far scarier situation was developing in the main barracks.

#

Denise Richards had, until that morning, been in the past tense. She had died in a car crash when Darren, her idiot brother, swerved to avoid a fox. She was sent flying through the windscreen and into a tree. The impact didn't kill her, but the shock did. In mourning, her parents donated her body to the necromancers. After all, she had died so young with so much to give… If her body helped rebuild the country, that was a silver lining, wasn't it?

But Denise had just found herself conscious and standing in the middle of a building

---

1   Administered by Ofzom, the quango in charge of UK necromantic affairs.

site, surrounded by walking corpses and a rather officious necromancer with a clipboard. He strode up to her, looking very much like an anally attentive mole in his black robes and thick rimmed glasses, prodded her with his biro to see if she was just malfunctioning, and shrieked in surprise when she asked what the hell he was doing.

After he calmed down, the necromancer – Gerald he was called - had told Denise she was now a *Lemure*, a conscious undead being. The creation of these was, of course, forbidden. But sometimes a revenant would suddenly wake up and start thinking again. He assured Denise this was very rare. Denise told him to go fuck himself.

She sat at a table back at HQ some time after, while Clive went to make them both a cup of tea.

"I know you can't drink any more", he noted, "but having a hot drink in front of you helps with any shock you might be feeling. It reminds you of your humanity."

Reluctantly, Denise picked up the cup by the handle and sat there, holding it. That was all she could do now.

Suffice to say, Denise was angry and confused. "What the bloody hell happened to me?" Denise asked when Clive sat down in turn, a plate of biscuits in his hand (but only for him).

"Well, when most people die", Clive began, "their spirits abandon their bodies altogether and leave behind what is just a husk. That's what a dead body is from a necromantic perspective, something we can reanimate or use as spare parts for rituals…"

Denise gave him a particularly grim zombie glare.

"…With the proper authorisation of course. But some spirits retain an attachment to their bodies. That's different from ghosts and other undead who anchor themselves in our reality but are still no longer corporeal. In a sense, you're still alive."

"I don't have a pulse", said Denise, trying to ignore the rasp that had entered her voice since her resurrection. "I don't breathe either. I can't drink or eat. What about my sex life?"

Clive coughed nervously and changed the conversation.

"Denise, you're sustained by pure willpower. That nourishes and even repairs your body to some regard. You also feed off passive dark energies given off by desolation, night-time and certain rituals. We think one of those re-awoke you, but we're trying to find out which one. You'll still look rather – I'm not sure how best to put this - *dead* though."

"So, I'm going to be a slave for the rest of eternity?" Denise exclaimed, accidentally spilling some tea.

"No, you pass the sapience test, and since your soul never left your body, legally you remain in possession of it", Clive noted. "We don't create self-aware undead in any case. It's wrong."

"What about using corpses as slave labour?" Denise said, angrily. She realised this was the point, usually, when she would start to cry, but no tears were forthcoming.

"Well, we honour the memories of the dead", Clive countered, "but we're shepherds of the living too. Back in the old days you wouldn't believe the shit that would happen. But now we operate by consent. Your parents signed your body over…"

"They can be such stupid bastards sometimes."

"…And we failed to spot your bond to your body when we processed you. It must have been really faint. We're really sorry – look, I've contacted the Equality and Human Rights Commission. They'll be over soon to help you out."

"'This is ridiculous!" Denise exclaimed, spilling even more tea.

"I can't apologise enough", Clive said, resting his warm dry hand on Denise's cold, clammy hand. "We will do all we can to support you and your family. I promise."

"It's not just that", Denise grunted. "I'm pissed off at working on a building site. It's common."

\#

From a distance, up on a hill and concealed by a thicket of trees, the rogue necromancer looked down at the main building site in dismay. Through the glare of binoculars, he saw corpses shuffling to their tasks, a necromancer foreman nearby taking direct control of a revenant whenever it needed to perform a task like operating a pneumatic hammer or using a winch.

Shaking his head, he looked away. *Geist* was his handle, both on the Web and in underground circles, where he had made a name for himself in providing illegal and 'grey' solutions to people's problems with the dead.

This ranged from making a stillborn gasp and writhe if only for a moment so a grieving mother could see it move, to killing a drug dealer with a reanimated fox. Then there was summoning poltergeists to disrupt corporate meetings and government events. He even consorted with those spirits of the dead who retained their conscious minds, and with Wraiths and Jiang Shi, and far worse things that lurked beyond, and in graveyards and places where death reigned supreme. And there were quite a lot of those now.

All illegal of course, and he'd long been stripped of his licence by Ofzom. That's when Geist simply disappeared and started hanging out with hackers of a more electronic kind. He found much in common with them – all trying to wrest power from the System that tried to control everything through laws, copyright, property… The dead were part of the commons – after all, when we die, we return to nature and who owns that? And when the Necromancers went mainstream, they cast aside the good as well as the bad. They sold out, became part of the government. Geist shook his head at the thought of this. If they really cared, why didn't they pledge allegiance to the people and not the Crown? 'Never trust a Necromancer who wears a tie' he reminded himself, and trudged back to the truck.

There he met 'Spliffy', an organiser of illegal raves who had become Geist's unofficial aide de camp. Spliffy (or Jaspin as his parents called him) waved from the driving seat of the small, grubby white truck they travelled in.

"Wotcha, Geist, my GEEZ!" Spliffy said with a big grin, trying desperately not to sound like he was once a day boarder at an independent school.

"You're overcompensating", Geist grumbled. "You don't smile so much unless there's something wrong."

The fake glee gave way to a sincere frown. "Yeah, alright", Spliffy admitted. "It's them."

"What, Hammond and his… assistant?" Geist asked, already knowing the answer.

"They're creeping me out" Spliffy whispered, leaning forward.

"You're protected by that charm I gave you, remember?" Geist said. "You'd know if they were spying on you with a bound *inphantom*.[2]"

"It's not that, Geist. It's just that they're…"

---

2   A corruption of Mortui Infantum, or 'dead child', conflated with 'phantom'.

"Weird?"

"Yeah."

Spliffy was right. The two necromancers he had dealings with were of the Old Rite, from before the Cataclysm, and before the rest of their order had chosen the light over the night. Geist had heard stories, but to see the real thing up close... Hammond was in his late thirties, but his withered body, tumorous skin and balding skull suggested someone in their sixties. His eyes were empty and seemed to threaten to consume whoever looked into them. And the smell... His 'apprentice' was a bone thin girl, pale and strangely attractive but with a faint scent of decay about her. She had the eyes of something that scurried in dark places and found perverse joy in the experience.

Geist held them in contempt. Even when you were outside of the system, there were lines never crossed, oaths you made to yourself never to break, and cleansing rituals to wash out all that nasty death energy that filled you up and rotted you from the inside out. And the things they did as part of their rituals - Geist had stumbled upon one ceremony of theirs two nights before. The acts they partook in certainly generated power, but Geist had barely eaten or slept since. They were a necessary evil right now, yet Geist found himself counting down the days when he could part ways with them.

"Yeah, point taken", he agreed. "I'll keep them away from you."

Geist proceeded to the clearing nearby, where Hammond and 'Night Lark' were preparing their rubric. It smelt of rotting meat, and was littered with abused carcasses, some of which looked suspiciously human. All around, fetishes and icons were nailed to the trees and a crude altar had been set up, draped over by a shroud inscribed in blasphemous script. A circle had been created by burning glyphs into the ground with weed killer. Geist knew that they would be embellished with fresh-shed blood at the height of the ritual.

Night Lark swayed and half-danced, half-walked naked around the perimeter of the circle Hammond was setting up. She was talking and laughing to herself. Hammond himself was disrobed but for a mask made from what Geist assumed was crudely patched together leather and a not entirely de-fleshed sheep's skull. Those empty, hungry eyes peered out of the sheep's sockets at Geist, who involuntarily flinched.

"And a good morning to you, Master Geist", Hammond said in a weak, wet voice that was either taking the piss or away with some very smelly, diseased fairies. (Geist couldn't tell which.)

He gestured his hand towards the young Necromancer. "I trust all is well?"

Geist only just managed not to grimace as he gripped Hammond's hand, cold and desiccated, in the traditional Necromancer's greeting.

"Yeah", Geist managed to answer. "Are you ready?"

"Oh indeed", Hammond's voice echoed from within the mask. "I can already feel the power building, can you?"

"Yes", Geist said, grudgingly. It made his stomach turn.

"We will, in any case, honour our side of the bargain", Hammond said, turning to the altar and arranging old cat bones on top in a ritualistic fashion. "I trust you will still be forthcoming?"

"Oh yes, of course", Geist said, still barely holding in his disgust. "I certainly will."

#

Margaret did not feel all that comfortable at the necromancer's temporary HQ. Seeing the banal sight of council workers trooping out of a portakabin didn't make her feel any better – there were too many revenants about. In fact, she saw dozens of them as the pickup truck drove her, Hugo and Craig into the main enclosure, all working tirelessly, without end.

She closed her eyes and pretended they were not there. Dead things shouldn't walk, and the horror of the first one she saw all those years ago had fused with barely remembered memories of watching the destruction of Old London on the television.

Margaret could dimly remember gawping at the grim spectacle as a three year old, until Dad got up quickly and switched channels. He realised they were all off-air, and turned off the television altogether. The entire family was left staring at a dead black screen. The fear she felt towards those two memories had never left her, eclipsing even the anxiety she felt when Hugo was put on a ventilator straight after he was born.

Margaret was trying to dislike Craig, naturally. But she couldn't find anything apart from his being somewhat ugly, which – she admitted – wasn't his fault. He was rather shy and kind, and bonded instantly with Hugo, who begged him for a guided tour of the facilities.

And so it was that Margaret, reluctantly, found herself being dragged around the main ceremony room where the corpses were either raised or restored (sort of) with nightly rituals.

"So yeah, this is where we create the revs", Craig said with boyish enthusiasm to Hugo, who was agape in fascination at the occult paraphernalia and grotesque iconography in the room.

"Really?" Hugo said. "How?"

"Well, it's a bit complicated really, Hugo", said Craig, chatting to the little boy on equal terms. "I mean, it's nuffink special once you get the hang of it, but you know – it's all a mind fu… I mean a real mind blower."

Margaret had given Craig a particularly dirty look, and the necromancer grinned nervously, looking for all the world like a naughty little dog that had just chewed her slippers.

"So how do you become a necromancer, Mr. Craig?" Hugo said, trying to be polite and grown-up.

"Well, a lot us are born like this, you know? But my Dad, he made me learn when I was very young, which wasn't nice. My Mum took me away, but he found us and then…"

Craig paused when he realised what he was about to say. Hugo looked up sympathetically as he saw real sadness take root on his new friend's face.

"Err, yeah, so a couple of years later some NICE necromancers found me and showed how I could help people with my magic. So I did, and everything's been great ever since!"

Craig threw his arms open at this point, and put on a broad grin. But neither Hugo nor Margaret was very convinced.

"It's alright", Hugo said, taking Craig's hand. "I'll look after you."

Craig looked like he was going to cry.

"Err, well, anyway…" the necromancer said, coughing. "Shall I show you where we keep the JCBs?"

Hugo looked like he was in rapture. Margaret only just managed to stop herself groaning.

After half an hour of torment, she finally asked if she could go off for a coffee. En route to the place where they kept the fluffy lambs (Craig didn't have the heart to tell Hugo what they were for), Margaret asked where the common room was.

"Oh, main block, Room 4D, first on the left…" Craig said, lost in the thrill of showing off his place of work to a five year old.

"Cool. Look, Craig? I don't think you're a paedo or anything, so will you look after Hugo for a while? Yes, I'm sure you will. See you later. Hugo? Mummy's just getting a cup of tea!"

And off Margaret walked, rather briskly.

"What's a paedo?" Hugo asked.

"Oh, look! Here's my favourite lamb!" Craig said, evasively, picking up the sheep he had decided to smuggle home with him so he keep it as a pet. (After all, why can't you have a sheep for a best friend?) "His name is Bomber!"

"Cool!" Hugo said, his attention thankfully averted.

#

As Margaret walked off, she let off a breath of relief. Her coffee cronies and sob sisters would no doubt be aghast with her leaving her son with a necromancer. But Margaret knew a tame man-child when she saw one (that's how she met her husband in any case), and sensed Craig was about as threatening as a hamster, albeit one that communed with the dead and practised the black arts. No, Margaret had nothing to fear from Craig, apart from the boys' club vibe that was about to make her head explode.

Anyway, here we are… Main block… Try not to notice the revenants as you go past them… Try to say hello to the necromancer who's walked past you without grimacing… Walk in through the door… No one at the reception (not even a revenant, even though you wouldn't be able to tell the difference)… Down the left… Was it 4D or 4C? Has to be 4C – that's what Craig told her. Definitely, 100%, 4C.

Margaret opened the door and entered what seemed to be a small kitchen with a table in its centre. She noticed the necromancer she would in time find out was called Clive leaning against the worktop looking somewhat surprised. And she saw the un-living thing sitting at the table, which turned and gazed at her with a grotesque look that seemed to suggest a mind had taken root in the carcass, impossible though that seemed.

"Who the fuck are you looking at?" said a petulant Denise.

Her jaw slack, Margaret gasped and keeled over on the spot in a dead faint.

Denise shook her head in disgust. She couldn't stand girly-girls – they rather let the side down.

"Well, this complicates things", said a mildly stunned Clive.

"Oh, well isn't that a bleeding shame?" muttered Denise, who was having a complicated enough day as it was.

#

Geist swallowed hard as he donned his robes in the back of the truck. Rebel though he was, the necro-hacker was not about to undergo a ritual of this magnitude without donning the proper protective sigils. He still didn't, in any case, trust Hammond or his apprentice, groupie or whatever the hell she was.

He slid a long, carved blade up the sleeve of his robes. Never go into something without a backup, Geist knew, and since he hadn't had time to prepare any mystical countermeasures beyond the usual defensive incantations, this was his Plan B, such as it was.

Spliffy banged on the side of the truck. "They're, err, summoning you."

"I know", Geist said, pulling a midnight blue hood over his head. "Tell them to hold their horses."

Presently, Geist entered the clearing. All the torches and candles had been lit and fresh lambs' blood had been used to illuminate the blackened outlines of sigils on the ground. A goat was bound to the altar and was bleating, pathetically.

Of Night Lark there was no sign, Hammond stood before the altar, naked and covered in the week-old blood of a new-born calf he had slaughtered under moonlight. Having cast aside his sheep's head helm for this phase of the archaic, forbidden rite he was undertaking, he let Geist see his pockmarked, balding scalp and sunken, sickly face. In so doing, Hammond seemed to be studying him with the cold disinterest of a hungry cat pondering a field mouse.

"I don't really approve of the goat", Geist muttered.

"Oh, but you're one of those 'vegan' necromancers I've heard about!" Hammond cackled. "No wonder you need our help. Blood sacrifice provides such *momentum*, don't you think?"

Geist snarled under his hood, but had to admit the depraved creature had a point.

"And where's the lovely Debby McGee?" Geist answered, his bitterness and sarcasm poking through.

"Oh, last time I checked, she was at the truck, killing your friend."

"What?" Geist said, turning around.

"Don't look so surprised", Night Lark said, appearing behind him. She was naked, as ever, but no longer covered in blood. Before Geist could react, she seized him and hurled the young necromancer to the floor with surprising speed and power. Before Geist had time to recover, she knocked him out cold with a brutal knee to the jaw.

"Bind him", Night Lark commanded. Hammond did as his mistress instructed.

"Now, my robe", she ordered. Hammond retrieved a thin gossamer robe and draped it over Night Lark. With a contemptuous look, she gestured to the truck.

"I've decided on balance not to kill the little cretin he keeps about him", Night Lark announced. "Instead I have placed a hex upon him. It should have taken hold by now. Summon him, Hammond, if you would. We can use him as a sacrifice in case the goat is not enough…"

"Yes, mistress."

\#

Geist came to, and realised his hood had been removed. To his horror, he had also been gagged, and this meant he could not summon any of his protective spirits with the usual spoken incantations. He looked around him. He was at the centre of the circle, his hands and feet staked out. Struggling to get free, Geist found he was too firmly bound. Whoever had done this – Hammond, doubtless – was experienced in such things. Geist shuddered at the thought of the others that had died at the necromancer's hand in this way.

In the corner of his eye, he saw Spliffy in a trance, tied to a yew's trunk – no doubt ready to be sacrificed while bound to the sacred tree, in case the main ritual went wrong.

Geist realised someone had approached He found Night Lark looking down at him with an amused leer on her face.

"Well, hello sweetie!" she smirked.

"UHMPFFUFFYUFFBITFF!" Geist tried to say, gag notwithstanding.

"No need to be rude, dear!" Night Lark said, spearing Geist's left hand with an ornate carved dagger.

Geist would have shrieked with pain, but the shock of it meant no noise escaped his throat, even if he could scream in the first place.

"That's cold iron, in case you were wondering", Night Lark said, turning away and walking towards the altar. She picked up another knife and strolled, rather casually, back to Geist. Kneeling down, she cut open his robe and carved a mystic circle into the flesh of his chest.

Eyes watering, Geist could only gasp in even further pain.

"Now, the advantage of cold iron", Night Lark said, picking up the conversation like it was an interrupted school lesson, "is that it cancels out your ability to cast spells, but still lets me use your energy."

She pulled out the blade from Geist's hand and undid his gag.

"The effects should last a while in any case, so I don't need your mouth to be bound."

Geist immediately swore and tried to spit at her. She deftly avoided the gobbet with a sideways motion, before returning to her original kneeling position.

Night Lark laughed.

"Oh, Geist – or should I say Gary Deacon? – we will have such fun!"

"Let me go, you bitch!" Geist shouted angrily.

"What a silly request!" Night Lark said. "No, I'm keeping you right here. I think you can gather why you've been rendered thus?"

"You're not just hacking into the revenants. You're trying to control them", Geist answered.

"Yes, and for that we need a ready source of power – you."

Geist realised that was what the circle carved into his chest was for. This was forbidden necromancy of the worst kind.

"Why?" Geist asked.

"Well, you seem to have the answers", Night Lark said. "Why don't you tell me?"

"You're weaponising the revenants. You're going send them on the attack."

"Yes, and reanimate the corpses of those they slay, and so on. In time we'll have quite an undead hoard at our disposal. Then we can make necro-constructs from the most interesting carrion, summon and bind the nastiest entities, endow some revs with enough sentience to use a gun…"

"What, so you can conquer Carlisle?" Geist snarled sarcastically. "Next you'll be trying to enslave fucking Dumfries!"

"Oh no!" Night Lark answered. "Our only aim is to glory in death and decay in the old fashion, of course! To wallow in the suffering and the grotesqueness! As we once did, before you and the other 'cleanskins' took over."

"Why are you letting me speak?"

"To annoy you, mainly. Your passions are making your energies peak most effectively."

"What are you going to do with me afterwards?" Geist enquired.

"Oh, we'll offer you a choice."

"Namely?"

"Serve us in life or serve us in death. Either way, you'll serve us. You and that daft prat over there."

Night Lark gestured in Spliffy's direction.

Hammond approached his mistress.

"Shall we commence the ritual?" he asked.

"Yes, very well" Night Lark answered. Shedding her robe, she caressed the hollowed chest of her minion.

"You're entitled to watch", she smirked at Geist. "If that's your thing…"

#

Margaret woke up to the acrid stench of smelling salts. Gasping, she sat up with a start and immediately regretted this. Her head had struck the ground on her way down and left her with a nasty head wound, which had been bandaged while she was out cold.

This wasn't as much of a shock as the sight of who was rousing her became all too clear. Or rather, *what* was rousing her. As Margaret's vision cleared, she saw the cold, necrotic and decaying face of the revenant glaring at her. Shrieking in fear, she pushed the thing away and staggered up to her feet in panic. Pressing herself up against the sink, she began hyperventilating. Daring not to turn her back on the undead creature, her hands rummaged behind her and she grabbed the first thing she felt, whipping it out in front of her and hoping it was a knife or some other weapon.

It turned out to be a whisk.

"Well, that's gratitude, you miserable cow!" growled Denise, still kneeling on the floor.

"You-you can speak!?!" Margaret all but shrieked.

"Well, err, YEAH?" Denise pouted sarcastically as she rose to her feet. The sight disturbed Margaret even more as the faint stiffness and lack of co-ordination hinted at the very real deadness of the being before her.

Margaret dropped the whisk and covered her mouth.

"Oh come on!" said an exasperated Denise. "If I was going to eat you, I'd have done it while you were spazzed out on the floor, you WIMP!"

"So I'm supposed to be sanguine about talking to a fucking walking corpse?" Margaret suddenly exploded, her fear giving way to frustrated, panicked anger.

"Speak for yourself!" sneered Denise. "You and all your airs and graces, you toffee-nosed bitch!"

"At least I've got standards!" Margaret exclaimed.

"What, like a pulse?"

"Drop dead!"

"Ooh, cutting!"

At this point, Margaret's brain reminded her that she was in close proximity to the living dead, and she calmed down enough to start panicking.

"Please… just stay away…" she said, beginning to sob.

"Oh, be like that!" Denise said half in resignation and half in disgust. She pulled a chair up at the table and slumped down on it, propping her faintly cadaverous head on top of a withered dead arm. She looked over at Margaret with contempt.

"So, are you expecting some nutter with a shotgun to storm in and save you?" she growled.

"I didn't know you… things could talk…" Margaret managed to announce.

"Us 'things' can't talk", Denise sniffed. "I can talk. The rest are still just revenants."

"How?" an aghast Margaret asked.

"'Cos I didn't quite die in the first place, and to be a revenant, you need to be dead-dead-dead", Denise muttered, annoyed at having to explain so soon after finding out herself. "My karma or mojo or whatever the fuck it is stayed around, so I woke up this morning and – taa daa!"

Denise sat up and opened her arms for dramatic effect.

"So you're… alive?"

"Well, I'm here – I think that's as far as I get, anyway."

"Are there others, like you?"

"Yeah, that necromancer bloke told me. They wear a lot of makeup and stay incognito. No one tells the public in case it freaks out. Y'know, like you just did."

"Is there a name for… what you are?"

"Clive says there's plenty of names. No one's picked one yet. I prefer 'zuvembie' – it sounds dead voodoo-y and that."

Margaret blinked.

"Anyway, why do you have it in for revenants? They're rebuilding the country, aren't they?" Denise continued.

"I remember when…" Margaret paused. "When the dead stayed dead. And when I saw them for the first time… I was only a little girl. I screamed and ran away. Mum was so embarrassed…"

Margaret paused. "I guess Dad's idea of dressing it up as a clown for my birthday wasn't all that clever."

Denise couldn't help but guffaw.

"Oh, it's not funny! I remember when the country got wrecked too! You look like you're too young. But I wasn't!"

"Like that makes you an authority? Look, things are the way they are!"

"Oh get stuffed! Next you'll be telling me I have to 'live with it!'"

"Well, I was going say 'like it or lump it'."

"Piss off!"

"Well I have to live with it!"

"Stop feeling sorry for yourself!"

"Excuse me? Hello? I was clinically dead until this morning?"

"Well, you still seem brain-dead!"

Denise picked up the empty coffee cup Clive had left on the table, and hurled it at Margaret, who dodged the missile, grabbed the whisk off the floor and readied for a fight.

"Oh Christ, are you going to make me a meringue?" Denise muttered. Actually, a meringue would be nice. Would zuvembies be able to eat dessert?

"I'm leaving!" Margaret declared. She began edging away from the sink and started moving towards the door. She had to get back to Craig and Hugo. They must be wondering where she had got to.

"Err, something I need to tell you…" Denise ventured as Margaret turned the knob.

"IT'S FUCKING LOCKED!" Margaret roared in annoyance.

"Err, yeah… Clive locked us in."

"Why?" shrieked a furious Margaret.

"He thought it would help me – I dunno – get to grips with things if I talked to you and you talked to me. Y'know, so I could acclimatise."

"WHAT?"

"Yeah, he said something about it being the latest in zuvembie acclimatisation methodology or something. Personally, I think he just wanted to naff off to lunch!"

"Mind you", Denise mused, "he was dead kind when he spoke to me earlier… I think he's nice. Soft as shite, but nice."

Shaking with fury, Margaret looked down at the whisk in her hands.

"I'M. GOING. TO. SHOVE. THIS. RIGHT. UP. HIS –"

#

Clive was having a great time with Kate in the canteen. They shared a lot in common, like an interest in old fashioned musicals, radio panel shows, alcopops, monkeys and cult cartoons from the 1980s. It was hard sometimes to find a woman who wasn't scared off by the necromancy, but Clive was overjoyed to find out that Kate not only didn't mind, but actually found it all fascinating. She sat, enthralled, as Clive recounted tales of reanimation and malevolent spirit placation, in-between devouring a baked potato.

Put simply, Clive thought his ship had come in.

Getting up, he announced "shall I get the coffees this time?"

Kate giggled. "If I had any more coffee, I might die!"

"Well, we're always looking for new recruits!" Clive joked.

"Cheeky sod!" Kate gasped with amusement. Then she saw the sudden look of alarm on Clive's face.

"What's wrong?" Kate enquired.

Clive was rooted to the spot, half-confused, half-agitated, and frightened. He was staring down at the floor, not so as to see what was there, but so as to concentrate and discover what it was that had disturbed him.

Looking up at Kate, he hesitated, then spoke.

"Something's wrong. I can feel it. Somebody's -"

Instinctively, he looked over his shoulder at the wall of the canteen. He did this without realising he was staring straight in the direction of the hill where Night Lark's depraved ritual was reaching its climax.

#

Geist had heard about how unpleasant some of the old rituals were from some of his mentors in the underground necro-scene. They could remember far worse, of course, and had the mental scars to show for it. At least, Geist tried to tell himself, this ritual only had consenting participants, and no one had died. Yet.

Still, the sight of what Night Lark and her minion had got up to disgusted him – or at least, what he'd let himself see, and he was sure far worse would be unveiled as the rite proceeded. As the two writhing bodies finally disengaged and stood before the altar during the invocation phase, Geist looked over to Spliffy. He saw his friend was still under the hex. Geist remembered the blade up his sleeve. To his relief, he realised that he had put the knife up there handle first, meaning he could get the sharp end out and cut his bonds. Spell-casting was out of the question until the curse of the cold iron had worn off, but escape was the only thing Geist could aspire to at this point anyway…

But he became aware of a swift, burning sensation on his chest. The rite had reached its climax and the screams of the goat could be heard as Hammond began its slow slaughter. Geist cried out in pain as his body was leeched of its latent magical energy through the sigil carved into his flesh by Night Lark, and into the seething ball of dark purple aether that had begun to manifest above the clearing.

In the midst of his torture, Geist glimpsed Night Lark looking down on him with a mixture of contempt and wry amusement, while in the background Hammond chanted ever more hysterically.

"And I'd like to thank you for your contribution this day", she smirked.

Geist would have sworn at her, but the pain had finally overcome him and he slipped into unconsciousness.

Around him, eldritch power and screaming spirits of the restless dead gathered and whirled. Before the altar, Hammond's brow seeped crimson, and with this final bloodletting, the ritual took hold, a sudden surge of invisible yet all too tangible malice surging across the land.

#

"Where's Mummy got to?" an impatient Hugo asked, his arms crossed in sheer petulance.

"Not sure, mate…" Craig said, sitting next to the boy on the bench outside the barn where they kept the sacrificial lambs. The necromancer had run out of things to show Hugo, and was getting concerned about Margaret. He could feel something in the air.

"Tell you what", Craig finally announced. "I'll ring up my friend Clive. He might know!"

Hugo assented politely as his friend pulled out a mobile from a pocket in his robe, but could tell Craig was nervous about something. They'd both seen all those birds fly over and away from them in anxious flocks, and even Hugo knew that meant something was wrong. The lambs in the barn had grown silent too. Hugo looked up at Craig, whose worried sideways glance told him all he needed to know.

"What's wrong, Craig?" Hugo asked.

Craig tried to smile reassuringly, but the nervousness on his face overwhelmed it. Suddenly the necromancer gasped and dropped the phone. Falling to his knees, it looked like he was having one of the asthma attacks Hugo's friend (though he didn't like to admit it) Amy would get until her mother managed to find her Ventolin.

Hugo put a small hand on his friend's shoulder. "Are you OK?" he said.

Craig managed to compose himself and looked at the little boy, his attempts to put a brave face on it failing miserably.

"We need to get inside, mate", the necromancer said, "we're in a lot of danger."

Hugo nodded. He already knew.

#

Gerald was not the sort of name one would associate with necromancy. And yet there Gerald Atkins – AKA The Grim Puppeteer - was, both a necromancer and in charge of a large revenant work detail, slowly rebuilding the M6 motorway. Most of the Revenants performed manual labour that required little oversight, but some drove heavy vehicles or performed complex tasks, which needed a corpsemaster to co-ordinate. Once you had programmed them with rubrics, all you needed to do thereafter was stay nearby and correct any errors with a mental command. That's all it took, usually.

Gerald was not, however, having a good day. First Craig buggered off back to HQ after he found some mother and her young son stranded, meaning his revenants had been stood down. It would be good PR, HQ said. Yes, of course, Gerald muttered to himself – I'm just left here with a small army of walking corpses, doing the work of two small armies of walking corpses. Yes, I am surely blessed.

To cap it all, that revenant girl came back to life and started swearing at him. The last thing Gerald needed was a lemure manifesting herself on his shift. Another delay. And to think she had the bloody cheek to complain! Back from the dead – what more could you ask for? Better that than stuck out here, in the pissing rain.

No, do this for another couple of years and maybe he could retire early? Hang up his robe and while away his days in the garden. No more walking corpses. It was fun in the beginning – in fact, during his younger days, Gerald styled himself as a sort of grim, necromantic Harry Potter… Sadly, his answer to Hermione had left with the kids ten years ago, and middle age had brought no ease. Gerald accepted it with only mild resentment.

He pushed his spectacles back up to the roof of his nose and, with a sigh, returned to work, apathetically writing down progress reports on his clipboard with a biro, the lid well-gnawed.

Then, with a cry, he felt a wave of pain sweep over him, his clipboard clattering on the ground. He realised a powerful invocation had taken place, and judging by the crudeness of the powers invoked and the barely perceptible screams that flooded through his mind, this was an Old Rite, and that thought terrified him.

Now Gerald realised why the girl had returned from the dead. A subtle build-up of force had been taking place for a few days now, and it was this that had roused her back to consciousness. A High Necromancer might have picked it up, but they were few and spread wide. Common or garden corpsemasters like himself had no chance of sensing such sorcery - until it was too late. Desperately, Gerald reached for his walkie-talkie to call in, but froze on the spot.

The revenants had all stopped working. Along with the labourers, those in vehicles turned their machines off and exited them, joining those who had only moments before been mixing concrete and asphalt and planting trees. Gerald looked around him nervously as the revenants began to encircle him. Soon they had Gerald surrounded, and slowly started to advance, dead eyes staring vacantly.

In a panic, Gerald tried using every invocation at his disposal, but none were strong enough to break the spell. He screamed as dozens of hands rained blows down on him, and revenants armed with mattocks and shovels pounded and hacked him to death.

The revenants were still. Then they lurched as one towards HQ, leaving the shattered remains of Gerald in their wake. And soon, even these began to twitch, the reanimated carcass slowly crawling and flopping in the wake of the hoard that had claimed its flesh for Night Lark, now extinguishing all in its path.

#

If HQ hadn't realised something was wrong until the invocation, it certainly knew straight after. Klaxons sounded and the necromancers and admin staff fled to their safety rooms, made of reinforced concrete and steel and covered in protective runes. The council staff were already on their way back to Carlisle, and so out of harm's way, but all lines of communication had been destroyed by feedback from the spell, its impact creating a very real electromagnetic pulse as it clawed and rent the edges of reality.

Clive was in the midst of the panic. He didn't know what had befallen Gerald, and he feared it wasn't good. He hadn't heard from Craig either – last he heard, his friend was showing a mother and her kid around HQ and…

Clive gulped. The woman he'd locked in with Denise – that was her!

They were in the main block. He had to get to them. The safety rooms wouldn't hold up forever, but the portakabins and containers that made up the main block were practically waiting to be torn open by whatever it was that he could feel approaching.

On the horizon, he glimpsed the threat, marching slowly and methodically towards them. It was the revenants themselves. They had been hacked.

Suddenly, he heard screams – and he remembered there were revenants here too! They had begun to attack the humans who hadn't made it to safety yet. He saw a security guard sprawled prone on the floor, a revenant raising a rent fence post above its head to strike once more. Clive rushed to stop the thing from killing the man, but was only moments away when it brought the club down on the man's skull, killing him instantly. The revenant turned towards Clive with mindless but relentless intent.

Suddenly, a car slammed into the revenant at speed.

Kate poked her head out of the driver's side window. "GET IN!" she shouted, and Clive quickly joined her.

Speeding off, Kate swerved several times to hit rogue revenants. "Stops them being a threat if they can't walk", she explained to Clive, who was entranced by her quick thinking.

Then he decided to raise an awkward matter. "Kate? Shouldn't you have gone into the safety zone with everyone else?" he said, delving deep into Health & Safety. He instantly regretted that – how dare he pass judgement on the lovely Kate? Also, she'd just saved his life.

"There wasn't enough room there, and someone had to spread the word!" Kate said, focussing on the road. "My mobile network is down, and I don't know if my phone is fried or not. Kendall's nearby – we can get help there!"

Clive rather hoped someone else had driven away with that same idea – it seemed rather desperate to rely on just him and Kate. Perhaps they were now out of range of the rubric that had caused this? Would he be able to use his own powers to slow the herd down? But if so, how? And could he do so in time to help everyone at HQ?

Clive remembered something. "STOP!" he cried out.

Kate slammed on the breaks.

Clive turned and explained to Kate about Denise and Margaret, and how he had to get them out of the room he'd locked them in.

Shaking her head at Clive, Kate turned the car around and headed back to HQ. They couldn't leave them.

#

Margaret was sitting at the table now, toying with her fingers. Denise, leaning up against the wall next to the window, could tell she was in a panic, and for good reason. The alarm had gone off and she heard lots of scared voices speeding past the door. Denise could also feel the malevolence that had just taken root. It seemed like her mind was about to be consumed by the power of what had been unleashed, but a raw, stubborn sense of self repelled the attempt to take her over, and she cast it aside with contempt.

Denise decided this wasn't the right time to share what had just happened to her with Margaret, who distrusted her enough already. Denise instead wondered: was this what her life would be from now on? Feared and loathed. Denise reminded herself of the complete indifference she felt towards the revenants when she walked or drove past them while they toiled, ceaselessly. Yes, she agreed with the arguments as to why this was necessary. But meeting Margaret had reminded her that many were horrified nonetheless. And how could she be accepted into a society that feared the unliving? It would make family gatherings very awkward, too.

With a sigh, she looked out of the window. It was a drab overcast day given over to drizzle. She could see some of the Cumbrian landscape and could appreciate its beauty, but being from Reading, it was the first time she'd seen it. The thought that it took death and resurrection for her to see the rest of the country struck her as desperately sad.

"Oh lay off, you soppy cow!" she muttered to herself. She hadn't been to Mars either. So what?

Dismissing her thoughts, Denise turned to Margaret. Gritting her teeth, she forced herself to say:

"Are you alright, love?"

Margaret nodded silently. Denise knew this wasn't the case by several hundred miles.

"You worried about something?" Denise enquired. "Well, durr – of course you are!" She shook her head at how obtuse she'd just been.

"My little boy…" Margaret murmured.

"Is he here?" Denise asked, the implication disturbing the hell out of her.

"Yes. He's with a necromancer, called Craig. I need to know they're OK."

Denise looked towards the door. They had to get out of here. She could feel something coming, and she was afraid. That really annoyed her. Her opinion of Clive was in freefall too. Locking them in, after all, was his idea.

Denise rummaged along the draining board and searched for anything she could find. Swearing a lot when she couldn't, Denise turned her head absent-mindedly and looked out of the window.

There were hundreds of revenants massing outside the HQ and they were already tearing down the fencing to reach the people inside.

Denise realised what had happened. She gave it some thought and drew the obvious conclusion.

"Oh shit."

She turned to Margaret, who had seen the undead swarm too. Denise half expected her to descend into hysterics, but Margaret looked back at her instead, terrified yet focussed.

"We need to move", she said.

Denise agreed and looked down at the table.

"That's a fire door over there, but we can use this to smash the lock in and get out that way", Denise said.

Margaret nodded and started pulling the table towards the door.

Denise grabbed the other end to help and was surprised to discover she could do so with ease. She was stronger now, since she wasn't entirely alive anymore. Neither pain nor fatigue could effect her now.

Realising this, she put the table down and walked up to the door.

"What are you doing?" Margaret said, still dragging her end of the table.

"I've got an idea", Denise replied. She kicked the door with inhuman force; smashing the lock out of the hinge and letting her push it open.

"Come on!" she said.

Margaret dropped the table and followed her out. Both knew that if Denise could be this strong, so could the revenants - and neither fancied their chances unless they could make it to safety.

#

It wasn't in Craig's nature to give up. He'd had some tough times before, which was a mild understatement, but he had found a way out nonetheless. Now he had the added responsibility of a child, however, and this made it even more onerous.

"Are we going to die?" Hugo asked innocently, kicking his legs under the chair.

Craig saw no use in lying to him, and he wasn't very good at it anyway.

"Look, mate, we're in a lot of danger…" Craig explained, kneeling down next to Hugo. "I am trying to find a way out though."

"OK!" Hugo nodded. Craig felt a rush of pride that someone – for once – actually trusted him to do so something. This stiffened his resolve.

Standing up, Craig looked around. They were still in the barn with the lambs. The doors had been locked shut and sealed to keep the revenants out, who were pounding on the corrugated iron structure regardless.

The first law of rogue revenants, of course, was that the buggers would always find a way in eventually, so just waiting was out of the question. By the time help arrived, the living would have joined the dead and – with a mild shudder – Craig recognised this was the real aim of the hack-job.

What he needed was power… But Craig couldn't bring himself to kill a lamb in front of Hugo, and besides, he would have to kill them all at once to have any chance of cancelling out the rubric.

There was the other option. Craig had heard of necromancers killing themselves during the climax of a ritual to guarantee its success, but that was forbidden, and besides, Craig was not about to do that in front of Hugo either…

As Craig mused, he noticed something odd about the boy.

"Aren't you scared, mate?" Craig asked.

"Oh, don't worry – I'm a big boy now! I go to Christchurch Infant's in two week's time!"

"Yeah, but – well – you're not scared that you might die? I mean, I'll make sure that never, ever happens but…"

"Oh, I've already died once! It wasn't scary at all!"

"What?"

"Well, after I came out of my mummy's tummy, I stopped breathing and my heart stopped, so the doctors made it better and I came back to life! Daddy keeps going on about it. It's dead boring."

"You've been touched by death?"

"What does that mean, Craig?"

Craig sought the right words.

"Hugo, you nearly died, and when that happens, death leaves its mark on you. Nothing to be scared of, but it means you've got a direct connection to the power of *Sheol*, what us necromancers draw strength from."

"Oh, so I'm like a big ghost battery! Woo-oo!"

"Yes, I guess so! Anyway, I've got a plan."

"Really, Craig? It won't mean I'll die again, will it? Only Mummy will be very cross and Daddy will sue you like he sued next door when its cat kept poo-ing on the lawn."

"Don't worry mate – you won't die this day!" Craig said, and he was telling the truth. Well, he might overdose him with chocolate biscuits afterwards to celebrate – but that was a different matter altogether.

#

Margaret and Denise ran down the corridor towards the main exit. Denise found, once again, that she could push her body harder than before, but knew it would require some means of repairing the muscle damage she was inflicting on herself.

Denise looked over to Margaret.

"You OK?"

Margaret wasn't dead, so running was less easy for her. She still managed to nod even as she gasped for breath.

They made it to the main doors, and stopped in their tracks. A dozen revenant faces and brass plate masks were pressed up against the window, their empty eyes staring at them. The revenants began pounding on the doors furiously until they came apart. Surging in, the revenants gasped and moaned as they lurched towards the pair.

Margaret ran off, but realised Denise wasn't following her.

"I'll hold them off!" Denise cried. "Try to get out through the back. They might not be there yet!"

Margaret nodded and began to run again. Denise ripped a pick from one revenant's hands and tore into the hoard, shattering limbs, heads and bodies with un-living strength.

All her rage seethed within her. Why did she have to die? Why did she have to come back like this? And why was she having to smash apart a hoard of revenants on a wet, cold day in August?

Yet as she fought, Denise began to realise that the revenants, while more than numerous enough to overwhelm her, seemed to be hesitating or holding back. She sensed confusion, reluctance. Some did attack her, however, and she crushed them furiously.

An idea occurred to her. She broke away from the revenants, pickaxe still in her hands, and ran towards where she hoped Margaret could be found. In her wake, the revenants paused, before once again surging forwards as one in pursuit.

Denise turned a corner and found Margaret trying to open a window. It was locked, and she was looking desperate.

"What's happened?" Margaret said, nervously.

"I've got a plan!" Denise said. "Do you trust me?"

A pause. Margaret nodded reluctantly.

"Cool. Now, watch this."

Margaret gasped as one of the quicker revenants staggered around the corner to confront the pair. It lurched forwards to attack Margaret, but Denise stood in its way. Caught off guard, the revenant was briefly still, and not a little confused.

Denise tore its head off with her pickaxe.

"You see?" Denise said.

"Yeah… I think I do", Margaret agreed.

"Wrap your arms around me from behind", Denise said. "That'll keep my hands free if I need to kill one of them, or whatever it is that happens when they fall over and stop moving. You with me?"

"Yes", Margaret said.

A large number of revenants surged towards them, but stopped when they saw Denise. Pushing through them, with Margaret holding on for dear life, Denise proceeded through the mob and towards the exit. At times she had to push a revenant away or even kill one, and both Margaret and she realised this was growing more frequent. Gathering pace, they moved quickly out of the building and through even more revenants until they found themselves in the main courtyard, outnumbered by yet more of the un-living.

Following the signposts, Denise headed towards the safety zone. A huge number of revenants stood in the way, however, and they were beginning to sense that Denise was no longer one of them.

"What shall we do?" Margaret asked.

"Fight", Denise scowled, not at her, but at the revenants who were drawing ever closer.

Suddenly, a car swerved in and – not for the first time that day – knocked and ran over several revenants in its way.

"Oh hello!" Kate said, smiling. "Hop on board!"

Quickly, Margaret and Denise got into the passenger seats, and Kate reversed quickly so as not to be surrounded by the revenants. Driving off and away from HQ for the second time, Kate sounded rather cheerful. Having had the situation explained to her, she had no problem at all with sharing her car with a lemure.

"Are you two OK?" she asked.

Margaret nodded, but was still worried about Hugo. Denise managed a simple 'yes', even as she held tightly onto what had become her lucky pickaxe. Both were staring at Clive, still in the front passenger seat and too nervous to say a word. It wasn't a pleasant look they were giving him.

#

Geist looked up at Night Lark and Hammond, enraptured by the act of maintaining and co-ordinating the grim rite they had invoked. Such a thing required great concentration, Geist noted, and that meant they wouldn't notice him cutting himself free. In any case, he had served his purpose. He was no longer much use as a battery, though as a servant or plaything, of course, he would still have a lot to offer.

But that was not what Geist intended for himself. He was getting out of here, and with Spliffy still alive too. Slowly, carefully, he moved the blade down his sleeve and grated its edge against the nylon rope that encircled his wrist. It snapped loudly after a while and Geist paused to see if they had heard. Since they hadn't, or so he hoped, he leant over and cut his other hand free, the one Night Lark had impaled with the cold iron dagger. He severed the bonds holding his legs and crept towards Spliffy, setting him free in turn.

But Spliffy collapsed in a heap the moment the rope was cut and it took great effort on Geist's part to stop him from making a noise as he fell. Slowly, painfully, he hauled Spliffy over one shoulder and began to sneak slowly to the truck. Out of immediate range of the other necromancers, Spliffy came to, but woke to find Geist's hand over his mouth.

"I'll explain later. Now get this truck ready to move – we've got to get out of here right away!" Geist hissed, and Spliffy nodded.

They both got into the truck, Geist herding his friend over to the driver's side.

"And before you ask, yes, I know it's my turn, but I can't drive, so there!" he said, waving his wounded hand at Spliffy.

"What happened, Geist?" Spliffy asked.

"Lots" Geist replied. He paused. To Spliffy's surprise, Geist opened the door. He slipped out of the truck, his blade at the ready.

"If I'm not back in five minutes, drive and keep driving", he said.

"Take care", Spliffy answered, realising what his friend intended.

Geist nodded, and moved silently towards the clearing.

#

Hugo was surprised about how little he felt as Craig performed the ritual. Though, 'ritual' was a strong word, as it simply featured Craig down on one knee, clasping Hugo's left hand with both of his, while he murmured and babbled ancient incantations, his head bowed in concentration.

Still, Hugo knew the virtue of patience, having once waited an entire hour at nursery school before going to the toilet. So he sat still, and let Craig carry on.

Suddenly Craig reared up and held his head and arms up to the sky (or at least the ceiling), screaming with rage as seething mists of green, mauve and red power emanated from him. Hugo was somewhat impressed, but still couldn't actually feel anything himself. Still it was quite a sight.

Continuing to roar, and finally scream, Craig encircled power round himself before blasting it out around him, causing several lambs to pass out and Hugo to go 'ooooh!' in amazement.

Then Craig began to chant methodically, slowly chipping away at Night Lark's rubric with methodical yet unyielding pace. Hugo could no longer hear the revenants pounding on the walls. It was as if they had stopped still while two competing forces fought for control over them.

Hugo looked at Craig, his face contorted with effort. Now, this was no longer just a clash of power but of wills and technique, both vying for supremacy. Briefly, Craig sprang a look of surprise – the opposing force had somehow lessened. Then, with a confident smile, he redoubled his efforts, and with a final cry of victory, he dispelled the rubric and resumed control over the revenants. A triumphant ripple of sorcerous emerald energy exploded from his body.

"Go get 'em!" he commanded, setting the dead ones on a seek-and-destroy mission towards the location where the rubric was enacted. As one, the revenants surged towards the distant wood on the hill, leaving behind the HQ and the havoc they had wrought.

#

What Craig realised later, of course, was that he had had some help. A few minutes earlier, Geist had sneaked up on Night Lark and Hammond as they fought to repel Craig's counterspell. Realising what was happening, Geist tried to backstab Hammond, who turned at the last minute and blocked the blade with his own sacrificial dagger. Night Lark continued to hold against the counterspell while Hammond and Geist slashed at each other. Geist headbutted Hammond in the face, before putting him in a painful wristlock, disarming the necromancer. Hammond kicked at Geist, who lost his balance and fell to the ground, but before Hammond could capitalise on this, Geist jammed his knife into the other necromancer's thigh. Hammond shrieked in pain, and as Geist pulled the blade out, he realised this shedding of blood was all that was needed to weaken the rubric, allowing whoever it was who was trying to undo it to prevail.

The energies around the clearing were swept away by a surge of stronger force hurtling from the direction of the HQ in the distance. Realising this, Hammond collapsed to the ground, sobbing in pain and despair. Standing up, his blade still in his hand, Geist looked warily at Night Lark, who returned his gaze nonchalantly.

"Well, that's that, I suppose", she said. "Come on, you wretch!" she then commanded the weeping mess Hammond had become.

"Yes mistress", he dribbled, staggering to his feet and following her as she walked out of the clearing and towards the distant horde of revenants that Geist could now see were heading towards them.

"Time we left", Night Lark said. "I have no interest in being captured, nor continuing as before after the shame of this defeat. You may go."

Without a word, Geist turned to leave. Night Lark stood still for a moment, and called after him.

"Oh, and Geist?"

"What?" he snorted.

"It was a pleasure", she purred and continued on her way with Hammond, leaving Geist to ponder for a moment as he felt the wounds she left on his chest. He ran back to the truck.

"Shall we get going?" Spliffy said as he turned on the engine while Geist climbed in.

"Yeah, and as far away as we can go", the necro-hacker sighed. He had been burned today. Badly.

#

It takes a while, but eventually Night Lark and Hammond meet the hoard. Smiling, Night Lark stands still and strikes a pose, ready to embrace her destiny. She closes her eyes as the ecstatic feel of dead flesh seizes her naked body and proceeds to tear her apart. This delight is ruined only by Hammond's screams as the revenants slowly pull him to pieces in turn. As death claims her, Night Lark muses that you just simply can't get the help these days. Then the top half of her head is wrenched off her body and she finally ascends to the state of carrion – a dream absolute, now realised.

#

Craig was rather sad to hear that the necromancers had been killed by the revenants. True, Craig had sent the stiffs over on a death order, only allowed in extreme situations as per Ofzom's rules and regulations, but he assumed anyone sensible would have legged it at the first opportunity.

He pondered his father, and remembered sanity was not something one associated with the old school.

Some of the other necromancers were claiming they could sense that another was involved, but his or her imprint was neither like that of modern practice, nor the Old Ways. They expected a renegade of some sort, but quite who, no one could tell.

Craig put such thoughts aside as he and Hugo returned to the main courtyard to see troops, police and medical teams arriving. Sitting near an ambulance was Margaret, draped in a red blanket, and talking to that lemure girl Craig had heard about from earlier. They were happily engaged in sisterly talk, with the lemure resting her hand on Margaret's leg and telling her to put her foot down with her husband.

"So yeah, the next time he tries to dodge anything, tell him he's going or else!" Denise commanded, with Margaret nodding intently. "Otherwise he'll keep taking the piss!"

Then Hugo saw his mother and ran to her happily.

"Mummy!" he said, as she wrapped her arms around him. "You haven't died!"

Margaret wept with joy, while Denise and Craig both smiled. Hugo looked at Denise. "Who is this dead woman?"

"That", Margaret said, "is a very good friend of mine. Her name is AUNTY Denise."

"Oh hello, AUNTY Denise – when did you die?"

Craig slipped off to see Clive. They would have to divine which revenants had killed today and have them destroyed. It was the only decent thing to do in these circumstances. There were also reports that poor old Gerald's remains had been found, crawling mindlessly in unlife. Those too had to be incinerated. Then they would be able to mourn him, for all his faults. Craig realised he'd lost a familiar face, and felt saddened.

"Hey, if it isn't the hero of the hour!" Clive said, walking up to him and slapping his friend on the back. "How did you do it?"

"Oh, well it wasn't just me – it was my mate over there, Hugo!"

"YES", Hugo shouted, much to his mother's consternation (and Denise's amusement), "I'M AMAZING!"

"Anyway, head office has heard too", Clive added. "You're on the up, Craig!"

"Err, thanks!" Craig said, somewhat embarrassed. "Changing the subject, how's that bird you were trying to chat up?"

"Oh, yes... Kate." Clive paused.

"She's already got a boyfriend, hasn't she?"

"Yeah, once the mobile network was back up, she rang him straight away. I feel like a right tit. Still, she wants to be friends, and wants us to meet up. Kate thinks I'll get on with him. Ashley, he's called. He's an accountant."

"You've always been crap with women" Craig commiserated. "Maybe I can fix you up next time?"

Clive was so desperate, even Craig's solution sounded reasonable.

"Yeah, if you must..." Clive sighed. Then he saw both Denise and Margaret were still glowering at him.

Nervously, Clive exited back to his office. There was a lot of cleaning up to do, plus a motorway, and a country, to rebuild.

#

Finally, Margaret's car was fixed and she was able to drive herself and Hugo to her in-laws. She and Denise had swapped numbers, and Margaret vowed to be there when Denise was reunited with her family. It was the least she could do. And Craig? She would send him some chocolates. Or flowers. Or whatever it was that you sent a necromancer at times like this.

"Will you miss Craig?" she asked Hugo.

"Oh don't worry, Mummy! I've got his e-mail address!" Hugo said.

Margaret grimaced.

"Anyway, darling", she continued, "this just goes to prove that you really are a special little boy."

"Yes Mummy! They all said I'm really special too!"

"Who, the necromancers?" Margaret said, nervously.

"Yes. And when I grow up, I want to be a corpsemaster, just like them!"

"Err, shall we play that Thomas the Tank Engine CD again?" Margaret said, hoping desperately to change the subject.

THE PROPAGANDA PANDA AND THE AUTOCRATIC CAT

LAURA TAYLOR

The propaganda panda and the autocratic cat
took a trip around the world in a new Learjet
Champagne for breakfast and caviar for tea
When recession hit, lived a life of luxury
Within a double-dip, lived a life of luxury
Everything on credit, no money was required
Mortgaged off the pea-green boat
sold it short ten times
creating first world problems
of a global crisis kind
And when it came to pass
that the economy was fucked
they developed Teflon shoulders
and tried to pass the buck onto
all the working people
whose pay was less each day
then took away their benefits
while giving bankers bonuses
Forced the unemployed onto Workfare schemes
and didn't give a shit about the Bong-tree lands
just plunged them into ever-deeper debt, deeper debt
just plunged them into ever-deeper debt

THE GUILTY PARTIES, OR CONTRIBUTOR BIOS

Once from the West Country, now stuck further east, **TAM BLAXTER** spends at least half his waking hours working out patterns of words. The matters he follows comprise philology, linguistics, literature—things said and people speaking. He's placed in Oxford, dares to hope he'll stay there.

CLAUDIA SEREA is a Romanian-born poet who immigrated to the U.S. in 1995. Her poems and translations have appeared in *5 a.m., Meridian, Harpur Palate, Word Riot, Blood Orange Review, Cutthroat, Green Mountains Review*, and many others. She was nominated two times for the 2011 Pushcart Prize and for 2011 Best of the Net. She is the author of *To Part Is to Die a Little* (Červená Barva Press), *Angels & Beasts* (Phoenicia Publishing, Canada), and *A Dirt Road Hangs from the Sky* (8th House Publishing, Canada). She also published the chapbooks *Eternity's Orthography* (Finishing Line Press, 2007) and *With the Strike of a Match* (White Knuckles Press, 2011). She co-edited and co-translated *The Vanishing Point That Whistles, an Anthology of Contemporary Romanian Poetry* (Talisman Publishing, 2011).

STEPHEN V. RAMEY lives in beautiful New Castle, Pennsylvania in the so-called Rust Belt, where social justice and trickle-down economics are more than esoteric topics. His flashes have appeared in many places, including *Microliterature, The Journal of Compressed Creative Arts, Connotation Press*, and is upcoming in *Bartleby Snopes'* Post-Experimentalism issue, and *Weird Tales*. He is a proud member of Show Me Your Lits (http://www.showmeyourlits.com), an online community of most excellent flashers. Find him at http://www.stephenvramey.com

REBECCA FRASER is an Australian author based on Victoria's Mornington Peninsula. She has a keen interest in dark speculative fiction...and anything that goes bump in the night. Her short stories and poems have appeared in various genre publications. To provide her muse with life's essentials, Rebecca supplements through copywriting for the professional world....however, her true passion lies in disturbia! You can visit Rebecca at her blog http://rebeccafraser.wordpress.com/ or find her on Twitter @BecksMuse.

Canadian poet, fiction writer, and playwright **J. J. STEINFELD** lives on Prince Edward Island, where he is patiently waiting for Godot's arrival and a phone call from Kafka. While waiting, he has published fourteen books — ten short story collections, two novels, two poetry collections — along with five chapbooks, the most recent ones being *Misshapenness* (Poetry, Ekstasis Editions, 2009), *A Fanciful Geography* (Poetry Chapbook, erbacce-press, 2010), and *A Glass Shard and Memory* (Stories, Recliner Books, 2010). His short stories and poems have appeared in numerous anthologies and periodicals internationally, including in two previous issues of *Polluto*, and over forty of his one-act plays and a handful of full-length plays have been performed in North America.

MADELEINE SWANN has had short stories published with LegumeMan Books, The Big Book of Bizarro and ForbiddenFiction.com. She performs as part of comedy trio Braintree Ways and has written for magazines such as *Bizarre*, covering subjects from church restorations to toe wrestling championships.

CHANGMING YUAN, 4-time Pushcart nominee and author of *Allen Qing Yuan*, grew up in rural China and published several monographs before moving to Canada. With a PhD in English, Yuan currently tutors in Vancouver and has had poetry appear in nearly 570 literary publications across 22 countries, which include *Asia Literary Review, Best Canadian Poetry, BestNewPoemsOnline, Exquisite Corpse, London Magazine, Paris/Atlantic, Poetry Kanto, SAND* and *Taj Mahal Review*.

ALEXANDER HAY would like it to be known that he was obsessed with zombies long before they were cool, and has indeed actively avoided shopping centres and rage infected apes since the early 90s.

LAURA TAYLOR is a gobby Northerner with a penchant for upsetting applecarts. She has been writing and performing poetry for 2 years, and has finally found a space in which to air her grievances with Authority.

CHRIS KELSO is the author of three books set for release in late 2012/early 2013. In 2012 Adam Lowe and Chris edited the *Terror Scribes* anthology, he is also the co-creator of *The Imperial Youth Review* with Garrett Cook. Recently he has become a contributing editor with *Jupiter Magazine*. You can keep up with Chris' at http://www.chris-kelso.com/

JACOB EDWARDS studied at the University of Queensland, graduating with a BA (English) and an MA (Ancient History). He stacks deckchairs at *Andromeda Spaceways* and recently finished editing #55 of their *Inflight Magazine*. Jacob lives in Brisbane, Australia, with his wife and son, and may be found online at www.jacobedwards.id.au

AHIMSA TIMOTEO BODHRÁN is the author of *Antes y después del Bronx: Lenapehoking* (New American Press) and the editor of an international queer Indigenous issue of *Yellow Medicine Review: A Journal of Indigenous Literature, Art, and Thought*. His work appears in a hundred publications in Africa, the Américas, Asia, Australia, Europe, and the Pacific. An American Studies Ph.D. candidate at Michigan State University, he's finished a second manuscript, *South Bronx Breathing Lessons*, and is currently completing *Yerbabuena/Mala yerba, All My Roots Need Rain: mixed-blood poetry & prose* and *Heart of the Nation: Indigenous Womanisms, Queer People of Color, and Native Sovereignties*.

MIKE RUSSELL is deputy editor of the *West Highland Free Press* newspaper and is in the process of finishing his first novel. His second - an odyssey across an industrialised solar system - is already underway.

THOMAS MESSINA moonlights as a writer and is currently writing a collection of short stories. He has published a variety of works under a pseudonym. He owes a debt of gratitude to Nassim Taleb and is thankful for the smelling salts he has shared. Thomas lives north of New York City with his family.

MARK MELLON is a novelist who supports his family by working as an attorney. He's led a checkered life with experience as a mover, lifeguard/swimming instructor, door-to-door salesman, carpenter's helper, Russian translator, soldier, phone solicitor, collections counselor, and teacher. His work has recently appeared in *Hungur, Criminal Class Review*, and *The Mythic Circle*. His Western novel, *The Pirooters*, is published by Treble Heart Books. http://www.trebleheartbooks.com/SDMellon.html. A steampunk novel, *Napoleon Concerto*, is also published by Treble Heart. His novella, *Escape From Byzantium*, won the 2010 Independent Publisher Silver Medal for SF/Fantasy. His most recent work, *Roman Hell*, is published by Amber Quill. www.amberquill.com A website featuring Mark's writing can be found at www.mellonwritesagain.com.

TOM GREENE was born and grew up a science nerd in south Texas, then moved to New England to study British Literature. He works as a full-time English professor and part-time lecturer on vampire literature. He lives in Salem, Massachusetts with his wife and two cats. Visit his website at www.advancedhypothetics.com.

NICOLE CUSHING's short fiction has appeared alongside stories by Neil Gaiman and Chuck Palahniuk in the anthology *Werewolves & Shape Shifters: Encounters with the Beast Within*. In 2010, Eraserhead Press published her first collection of dark satire, *How to Eat Fried Furries*. The popular horror podcast *Pseudopod* has produced an audio adaptation of one of her tales, and an adaptation of another story is pending from the podcast *Cast Macabre*. Nicole would like her readers to know that no actual college students were flayed during the writing of "The Peculiar Salesgirl".

JAMES EVERINGTON is a writer from Nottingham, England who mainly writes dark, supernatural fiction, although he occasionally takes a break and writes dark, non-supernatural fiction. His first collection, The Other Room, contains both. He is also one of the four Abominable Gentlemen behind the Penny Dreadnought e-anthology. You can find out what he is currently up to at his Scattershot Writing blog (www.jameseverington.blogspot.com). He drinks Guinness, if anyone is offering.

KURT NEWTON's latest novel, *Powerlines*, is a psychological thriller set in the state forest region of northeast Connecticut. He's currently working on many things at once.

STEPHEN OWEN lives and works as a sign maker in the UK. His interest in writing stories began in the nineties when he started writing for the school nursery his children attended. When teachers advised him to think seriously about taking it further, he took a crash course in evening classes to find out what he really wanted to write about. Many years ago he finished his first short horror story. He hasn't written a child's story since.

GLEN KRISCH has written three novels: *The Nightmare Within, Where Darkness Dwells*, and *Nothing Lasting*, as well as the novellas *Brother's Keeper* and *Loss*. His short fiction has appeared in publications across three continents for the last decade.

DAVE MIGMAN is a writer, artist and stone carver currently inhabiting Edinburgh. He lives solely off a diet of molluscs (evolutionary life at its peak!) and pig nuts. Please check out his web-blog thing and feel free to hurl cyber abuse in his direction, or just enjoy the links and bathe in the warm glow of his mollusc drenched mind. Dave also creates a weekly podcast for Dog Horn Publishing, please visit Dogcast Central via www.doghornpublishing.com

ROBERT LAMB is an American fiction author, science writer and podcaster. He spent his childhood reading horror stories and staring into the woods - first in rural Canada and then in rural Tennessee. He currently lives in Atlanta, Georgia with his lovely wife and their beautiful one-eyed cat. You can learn more about his work online at http://rjlamb.com and follow him on Twitter @Vomikronnoxis, where he revels in the dark magic of his city's mass-transit system.

R. C. EDRINGTON's work has appeared throughout the small press. His poetry collections include *Use Once & Destroy*, *Portraits from A Barrio Toilet Stall*, and *Apocalypse Generation*. His online website can be found at www.rcedrington.com

CHRISTOS CALLOW JR was born in Greece and is of Greek and English origin. He is currently studying for a PhD in Creative Writing at the University of Lincoln, researching utopias of perception. His stories have been published in numerous publications, such as *Polluto*, *Mad Scientist Journal* and the horror anthology *Dark Side of the Womb*. As a science fiction scholar, he has articles upcoming in *Alluvium* and is organizing New Genre Army, a conference on British SF writer Adam Roberts. As a writer, Christos also writes science fiction theatre and his plays have been performed in Greece.

As well as numerous short stories in magazines and anthologies, **DOUGLAS THOMPSON** is the author of five novels: *Ultrameta* (2009), and *Sylvow* (2010) both from Eibonvale Press, *Apoidea* (2011) from The Exaggerated Press, *Mechagnosis* from Dog Horn (2012), and *Entanglement* from Elsewhen Press (2012). http://douglasthompson.wordpress.com/

ALLEN ASHLEY is currently editing a new anthology of astrological-themed stories for Alchemy Press. He will also once again be judging the British Fantasy Society Short Story Competition. The rest of the time, he runs writing workshops including Clockhouse London Writers. www.clockhouselondonwriters.co.uk Contact Allen on allenashley-writer@hotmail.co.uk

MARK SILCOX was born and raised in Toronto, Canada, and teaches philosophy at the University of Central Oklahoma in Edmond, OK. He has had other stories published in *Aoife's Kiss* and *All Hallows* magazines, and his book *Philosophy through Video Games* (co-written with Jon Cogburn) was published in 2008.

JACQUES BARBÉRI is a French author of more than fifteen novels and numerous short stories. Thrillers, science fiction, fantasy or the fringes of literature, nothing is off limits to his perpetually mutating imagination. He is also a musician (with the group Palo Alto), screenplay writer and translator. He can be found on the web at www.lewub.com/barberi.

MICHAEL SHREVE's translations include works by Pierre Pelot, John Antoine Nau and Marcel Schwob among others. www.michaelshreve.wordpress.com.

POLLUTO

J. MICHAEL SHELL's fiction has appeared in the Shirley Jackson Award nominated *Bound For Evil* anthology, the *Panverse Two All Novella Anthology*, the '07 edition of the *Southern Fried Weirdness* anthology, Hadley/Rille Books' *Footprints* anthology, *Space and Time* magazine, Spectrum Fantastic Arts Award winning *Polluto* magazine (where he is a frequent contributor), *AnotheRealm, Kzine, Not One of Us, Diet Soap*, and *Tropic: The Sunday Magazine of the Miami Herald*, to name just a few. His novel, *The Apprentice Journals*, is scheduled for release (Dog Horn Publishing) early in 2013. At the University of South Carolina (BA in English) he studied under the great poet and novelist James Dickey. Shell resides somewhere in the American South and is rumored to be, once again, seceding from the Union.

Polluto is in no way responsible for its own output and is compiled entirely by dancing gingerbread soldiers. Don't tell the Mouse King where we are!

ND - #0423 - 270225 - C0 - 229/152/10 - PB - 9781907133305 - Gloss Lamination